Brian Aldiss was born in Norfolk in 1925. During the Second World War he served with the British Army in the Far East. He began his professional career as a bookseller in Oxford and then went on to become Literary Editor of the *Oxford Mail*. For many years Brian Aldiss was a film reviewer and a poet. The three outspoken and bestselling novels making up *The Horatio Stubbs Saga* (*The Hand-Reared Boy* (1970), *A Soldier Erect* (1971) and *A Rude Awakening* (1978)) brought his name to the attention of the general book-buying public, but in the science fiction world his reputation as an imaginative and innovative writer had long been established. *Non-Stop*, his first SF novel, was published in 1958, and among his many other books in this genre are *Hothouse* (published in 1962 and winner of the Hugo Award for the year's best novel), *The Dark Light Years* (1964), *Greybeard* (1964) and *Report on Probability A* (1968). In 1965, the title story of *The Saliva Tree*, written as a celebration of the centenary of H.G. Wells, won a Nebula Award. In 1968, Aldiss was voted the United Kingdom's most popular SF writer by the British Science Fiction Association. And in 1970 he was voted 'World's Best Contemporary Science Fiction Author'. Brian Aldiss has also edited a number of anthologies, a picture book on fantasy illustration (*Science Fiction Art* (1975)) and has written a history of science fiction, *Billion Year Spree* (1973). The first two volumes of the epic Helliconia trilogy, published to critical acclaim, are *Helliconia Spring* (1982) and *Helliconia Summer* (1983).

D0230707

By the same author

Fiction
The Brightfount Diaries
The Primal Urge
The Male Response

The Hand-Reared Boy
A Soldier Erect
A Rude Awakening

The Malacia Tapestry
Life in the West

Science Fiction
Non-Stop
Galaxies Like Grains of Sand
Equator
Hothouse
The Dark Light Years
Greybeard
Earthworks
The Saliva Tree
Cryptooic (An Age)
Barefoot in the Head
Enemies of the System
Moreau's Other Island
Helliconia Spring
Helliconia Summer

Fantasy
Report on Probability A
Frankenstein Unbound
Brothers of the Head
Pile (with Mike Wilks)

Stories
Space, Time and Nathaniel
Starswarm
The Best SF Stories of Brian Aldiss
Intangibles Inc., and Other Stories
The Moment of Eclipse

Comic Inferno
Last Orders
New Arrivals, Old Encounters

Nonfiction
Cities and Stones
The Shape of Further Things
Billion Year Spree
Hell's Cartographers (with Harry Harrison)
Science Fiction Art (Editor)
This World and Nearer Ones

Anthologies and Series (as Editor)
Best Fantasy Stories
Introducing Science Fiction
The Penguin Science Fiction Omnibus
Space Opera
Space Odysseys
Evil Earths
Galactic Empires 1 & 2
Perilous Planets

With Harry Harrison
Nebula Award Stories 2
Farewell Fantastic Venus!
The Year's Best Science Fiction (annually from 1968)
The Astounding-Analog Reader (2 volumes)
Decade 1940s
Decade 1950s
Decade 1960s
The SF Masters Series

BRIAN ALDISS

The Eighty-minute Hour

A Space Opera

TRIAD
PANTHER

Triad/Panther Books
Granada Publishing Ltd
8 Grafton Street, London W1X 3LA

Published by Triad/Panther Books 1985

Triad Paperbacks Ltd is an imprint of
Chatto, Bodley Head & Jonathan Cape Ltd and
Granada Publishing Ltd

First published in Great Britain by
Jonathan Cape Ltd 1974
Copyright © Brian W. Aldiss 1974

ISBN 0-586-06237-8

Printed and bound in Great Britain by
Collins, Glasgow

Set in Times

Four things one particularly notices after wars of any respectable size: preparations for the next one, confidence that armed conflict is finished for ever, starvation and feasting.

First, take a romantic setting.

In the stolid old castle of Slavonski Brod, on the night in which determinism forces me to open the story, feasting was the thing. Outside the grounds, over the walls, across the sea – all about – rumours of more terrible things were scudding like cloud. For a few hours, they had been shut out, fended away chiefly by dint of the personalities present at the roistering, by the languorous bravado and genial nature of Mike Surinat, whose castle it now was (his parents having died during the war); by the beauty and sweet perceptive nature of Becky Hornbeck, who now lived at the castle; by the cheeky dearness of Mike's small cousin, Choggles Chaplain; by the stolid capability of Mike's C-in-C, Per Gilleleje; by the hard work behind scenes of such loyal friends as Devlin Carnate; and of course by the glamour of the many guests, at the castle to celebrate Mike's simultaneous demobilization from the army and appointment to diplomatic rank in the councils of the Dissident Nations.

Among those guests, I need mention only three. First and foremost is the peerless, glamorous figure of Glamis Fevertrees, about to embark on a perilous mission for the DN. She is old enough to stand for me as at once sex-symbol and mother-figure. She dances with Per, and I wish I were able to glide across the great marble floor with her in my arms, out into the courtyard with its marble patterns, swirling among the pergolas and lanterns!

Mine are not the only eyes to fix on Glamis. A slight comedy goes among the other two most noted guests, the epicene genius of dream, Monty Zoomer, and his companion – who hastens to leave him – the stately and leather-skinned Sue Fox. Monty came with Sue and has eyes only for Glamis. Not that Sue cares – she is a woman who plainly hates sheep's eyes.

Sue and Monty, of course, are not on our side. Yes, you might put it that way. They are not on our side of the political fence. They stand for the USA–USSR merger, the so-called Cap–Comm Treaty; we are against it. But as yet – or during this evening of festival – Sue and Monty are being nice to the minions of the DN. Sue Fox can afford to be nice; she's on the World Executive Council.

So much for the cast. Move nearer and hear what three of the groups are saying on this beautiful evening.

First, let's go to the little pavilion perched at the end of the estate, on top of the wide stone wall, long ruined, now built up with a wooden ramp for this occasion. Go up the ramp! Observe that the pavilion has been repainted.

Inside, a little man in Hungarian gipsy costume plays a fiddle. He is a Hungarian gipsy. His melodies, gay but full of an irreparable loss, float out across the ground. Only three people are in the pavilion, and they are not listening.

This first group consists of Becky Hornbeck, Sue Fox, and Choggles. Becky, like Mike, is in her late twenties and still somewhat mystical. Sue is older and a good deal grimmer, though not in a grim mood tonight. My dear Choggles is – herself. But I will stop talking so that they can be heard.

Sue Fox said, 'As you say, the world is tightening up after the war. Dwight Castle and I were remarking the other day how work on the World Executive Council gets heavier week by week. And now the Computer Complex

6

intends to introduce the concept of the eighty-minute hour . . .'

She caught the expression on Becky's face.

'I'm sorry, Becky – I shouldn't be talking politics. Perhaps I only do it because – well, perhaps there is a little guilt there, especially when I find you and me on different sides of the fence, politically. Your mother and I were such great friends.'

Becky smiled. '*We* have always been great friends, Sue. We must not let politics alter that. I realize you hold your beliefs as honestly as we do ours.'

'Of course. The world must unite, must forge one single central government, and the Cap–Comm Treaty is a way of beginning . . . No, no, not a word more! I'm not propagandizing, merely justifying myself!'

They both laughed, and the gipsy began a passionate lament to death, roses, Smederevo, red wine, white hands, and the passing of time.

More relaxedly, Sue Fox said, 'They were telling me you found the Koh-i-Nor, Becky. How incredible!'

'It was incredible,' Becky agreed. 'But I expect incredible things. In fact, it was an old associate of my father's, a man called Youings, who found the jewel on a beach near Bordeaux, France, washed ashore. He posted it to me as a Christmas present, wrapped up in an old newspaper!'

Choggles, who had been sitting with them and gazing silently over the Pannonian Sea, said, 'The newspaper was called *The Trafalgar Square* – I've still got it, Becky. Let me keep it as a souvenir.'

'Of course you can.'

'You're going to keep the diamond?' Sue asked Becky.

'I regard it as a souvenir of England. It's in my suite. You must come and have a look at it.'

'What fantastic things do happen!'

'They aren't fantastic if you believe in determinism. Recent brain research has proved that free will does not exist—'

'Becky, I am not of the generation to believe in determinism. I refuse to believe, and facts will not sway me. I prefer your mysticism. Tell me more about the Koh-i-Nor. It was in British hands?'

'Yes, ever since the British conquered India in the nineteenth century. It was on display in the Tower of London for many years – before the war.'

'Hard luck about Britain . . . What are you going to do with it? What's it worth now?'

'I thought I'd keep it. When it was first heard of in history, one of the Moghuls – Humayan, I believe – that was in the early sixteenth century – claimed that it was valuable enough to feed the whole world for two-and-a-half days!'

Sue Fox smiled. 'Now the population has gone down a bit, it might do so again!'

'That stone – well, it's an emblem with no precise financial value – it has woven in and out of history like a needle through fabric. At one time, it spent six weeks in the waistcoat of a Victorian politician!'

A second group, a larger group (all male except for a pregnant Miss Dinah Sorbutt who sat unobtrusively in the background), sprawled over a dinner table, smoking cigars and every now and again summoning a fresh bottle of brandy or Perrier water. There were six of them – Mike Surinat himself; two of his staff, Carnate and Per Gilleleje; two guests, the Brazilian Geraldo Correa da Perquista Mangista, and a Japanese politician, Sanko Hakamara; and Becky's old frail father, George Wainscott Hornbeck, retired industrialist. They were talking politics. Oh – and Choggles was also there; she had already heard the history of the Koh-i-Nor, and moved on elsewhere to avoid hearing it again.

8

Da Perquista Mangista was laughing at something Mike had said. 'You are just a romantic, Mike. You should have worked as I have, for many a long year, in São Paulo, and then you would see how hard people really work!'

'I could say the same about Tokyo,' Hakamara said.

'I know, I know,' Mike said, laughing also. 'Europe is now more or less played out, and the Eastern seaboard of the United States the same. We have recently witnessed the establishment of a Pacific Community, with California, Japan, South Korea, China, all labouring away hammer-and-tongs. I've no real objection to work, except that it now means work-plus-deadly-monotony. With the establishment of a single world-state, work-plus-deadly-monotony is going to rule the roost, forced home by computerized arguments about "efficiency", such as CC is now using to ram in its Eighty-Minute Hour schedule. I'm for inefficiency, smaller nations, slack in the machine, chaos and all the other things for which I founded the IDI, my own personal club!'

Da Perquista Mangista said, draining off another large brandy, 'Mike, I love you, and I love the totally outdated concept of IDI . . . You are a gaudy figure and the be-leaguered Dissident Nations will surely need you as we get more beleaguered in the years ahead. But do not use that argument of yours in public – not for instance, at the Dissident Nations economic conference I'm organizing in Friendship City. Because the world on the whole believes in order and efficiency, even the nations of the DN.'

'Them especially,' Hakamara agreed. 'Japan, Jugoslavia and Brazil are cases in point. Recall the legend on the Brazilian flag – "Order and Progress". Our nations have become great through work.'

'If you'll allow an old man to express his point of view,' George Hornbeck said, 'I believe that work is mankind's worst vice and affliction, killing more people year after

9

year than all your drugs and automobiles combined. Even worse, it exhausts the planet as well as mankind. Of course, that's only my view. Order and Progress lead to war. But then – I was born in the First World War.'

Mike Surinat smiled warmly at the old man. Since the death of his own father, he had invited the Hornbecks, father and daughter (just as he had me), to live in Slavonski Brod Grad, and had come more and more to love them both. The old man's philosophy was particularly simpatico.

'Determinism saps our will not to work,' he said. 'The Cap–Comm merger merely gears everyone to work harder.'

Choggles piped up. 'It will make the world like a police state, won't it, Mike? Particularly with crooks like Attica Saigon Smix running the American end – he was involved with my father, and you know how awful Daddy was, introducing ZPG and everything.' She glanced at Dinah Sorbutt's greatly enlarged body. 'Sorry, Dinah, old horse, *almost* ZPG – the human race has got to keep going somehow, hasn't it?'

Dinah said, 'Choggles, *old horse*, your zippy comments are rather out of place in a political discussion. Why don't you buzz along, like a good girl?'

The Brazilian politician threw Dinah an admiring and grateful glance.

'Suits me!' Choggles said. 'Politics isn't as interesting as sex, is it?'

As she drifted off, Per Gilleleje laughed and said, 'Out of the mouths of babes and sucklings! She is correct, of course, about both Smix and her father, Auden. Auden Chaplain is dead now, but both he in scientific circles and Attica Saigon Smix in managerial circles showed genius. World-units have grown so large that we need genius, even when it is evil – that's to say, against humanity. And

10

it is this need for the anti-human which has led to the take-over of human affairs by the computer complex.'

'Unfortunately, CC represents a genuine human desire to repress its humanity,' Carnate said. 'How else can you explain the atrocities of World War III, and all those poor wretches shipped out to Mars?'

'My daughter among them,' sighed Hakamara.

Let 'atrocities' be the key-word that allows us to slip away to the third group.

This is a more romantic group, although it numbers three, and three is not conventionally a romantic number. The group is sitting in the room generally known as the Green Tower Room. Most things in the room, human beings excepted, are green; and, to match the room, the articles in it are also round wherever possible. Spinet, radio, holocube – even the holocube contradicts its own terms and is round – chairs, sofa, chaise-longue, all attempt rotundity; carpet, lampshades, footstools, occasional tables, precious vases – for them, conformation to circularity comes less oddly.

Monty Zoomer, the only one of the group of three to attempt even a perfunctory rotundity, was sitting on a pouffe. This pale young man, king of the pop world, whose holodreams had been shared with audiences all over the uncivilized world, wore velvet and directed a flow of velvet words at the second member of the trio. This was the slender, austere, still dazzling – though faded – figure of Glamis Fevertrees, a much-married American lady with a Persian style of beauty, a sallow smooth complexion, pale pink lips and dark and lucid brows and eyes. It was with reference to these attributes that Zoomer was now reading a verse from a circular copy of *Lalla Rookh* which he had seized from a side-table:

' "And others mix the Kohol's jetty dye
    To give that long, dark languish to the eye . . ." '

11

The third member of the trio, Choggles, who had just sneaked in, burst into laughter. 'You can't be serious, Monty! You ought to be reading that doggerel out to me – except I prefer Shelley – and anyhow I'm fair, not dark, a real little blonde—'

'Nauseating child!' Zoomer said.

'Child! I'm nearer your age than Glamis is! She's old enough to be your mother, Monty! You can't really think she fancies *you*! You're too fat to be any good as – help!'

She ran around the room and out the door, laughing and screaming, hotly pursued by spherical cushions and a round of abuse.

Zoomer slammed the door and turned back to Glamis, adjusting his hair and the pendant that swung against his breast.

'Glamis Fevertrees – now that that little pest has gone, let me declare my admiration! My heart yearns for you – it's lonely enough being a real creative artist, see, I got the gift from my father, so I suppose it was predetermined, but you have to work at it, and my life – well, there's a great big Glamis-shaped gap in it. I could design a whole holo-life for us together – you know the power I wield, now that I supply holodreams to anyone who wants them, keep the millions of oppressed happy through their comp-terminals. Well, it's the responsibility, to supply something clean, nursery-pure, but still entertaining, and—'

'You see, Monty,' Glamis said, interrupting rather desperately, 'you're very sweet, but I don't go much for sex, to be frank, despite all my marriages. I met a man called Jack once, on the very eve of my first marriage. Well, that's another story . . . As a result, I get hooked on men of action, not artists. Either they're too mixed up or – no, it's probably because I have no free will, which is what everyone seems to be saying nowadays. I have no free will to love you, Monty, please understand.'

She wondered if he would grab her and whether she would faintly enjoy that. After all, it would be a conquest for her, a defeat like that!

But she had his measure: a man of words, not of action. The words poured from him as sweat from a labouring man.

'And another thing, Glamis, that I ought to draw your attention to. The world's in a very troubled state, I think you'd agree. All those big nuclear bombs let off everywhere – mucking up space as well as this poor old Earth of ours – conditions could deteriorate. Easily deteriorate. People need a bolt-hole. Well, perhaps I could find such a bolt-hole. Just for the two of us. Now that I've won this enormous contract with CC, supplying everyone with holodreams, I've come in contact with Mr Attica Saigon Smix. He's a very very nice old man, not at all like the villain his enemies say he is – haven't I designed a nice little set-up for him and his missus! Wow! Now, *he's* got a bolt-hole nobody knows about, and maybe one day I can find out where it is, and then—'

She had been standing against one of the little round windows, knowing her slender lines showed up to best advantage there; but the spate of his eloquence caused her to sit on a little circular Marie Thérèse armchair. She took his hand.

'Monty, dear, that's another thing! You work for and with Attica Smix. He is married to Loomis, and Loomis is my sister. We are not at all good friends, not at all. Not by temperament, not by upbringing, not by political conviction. I know she and Attica think well of you. It would complicate things too much if you and I had any sort of a thing going between us. You're awfully sweet – no, don't protest, but I have to go away on a mission tomorrow – forget about me, Monty, stick to Loomis!'

13

He flung himself at her beautifully shod feet, reached up dramatically, clasped her hands in his.

'With Loomis it's just mother-fixation on my part, honest! You're younger than her, a little bit, anyway! I can't help these things! You said it yourself – determinism. All this recent work on the brain – the neurosciences have proved that we do what we must do, right? I can't help feeling like this about you, Glamis. The moment I saw you, I knew I was in the shadow of destiny!'

'Does destiny really cast a shadow?' she asked softly.

'Okay, it picked me out in its headlights, then. Look, Glamis, if you're going, you'll be back, won't you? Let me give you a memento of me, something to remind you of the pallid and lonely existence of that wayward and eccentric world-genius of the inner landscape, Monty Zoomer, okay?'

As he spoke, he was bending his neck, removing the pendant and chain from his neck. He rubbed it on his velvet shirt.

'Here, slip it on while it's still warm, Glamis! A keepsake from me to you!'

'It's beautiful!' She took it and examined it. She had already admired it from a distance.

It was of silver, heavy to hold, and some eight centimetres across. Across one side of it were depicted two male figures, one of them bearded, staring at each other or across each other's shoulders. The workmanship was rough but powerful.

'It really is beautiful!' Covetousness rose in her.

'Yes, it is a replica of an old Martian design, from a pendant that actually came from Mars. Attica bought it at a fabulous price and had copies made.'

'From Mars! But it depicts two humans!'

'Well, that was the story I heard. I'm no connoisseur. It's yours if you will accept it with my humble admiration.'

'But Attica Smix gave it to you – or was it Loomis? You can't give it to me.'

'Yes, yes, have it with love!'

'Let's exchange pendants, then. I have one I always wear, though it doesn't go with this dress. It's in my bag . . .' She put his pendant round her neck, and produced hers, a smaller one, with an image of two graceful people, male and female, engraved on it.

'Ooh, Glamis, they're naked!'

'Put it on – it's fair exchange. They're Daphnis and Chloe, from an ancient Greek engraving. It was given me by the man I mentioned earlier, Jack Dagenfort.'

'That's the guy that made that old film, *The Heart Block*! I'll always wear it, Glamis, and always think of you!'

He summoned an oleaginous tear for the great occasion.

2

Through the barren castle of Slot Surinat went the conspirators. They laughed as they went, for the castle was theirs. Battles had been fought, hardship overcome, blood shed, money spent and many a tear dropped in shuttered secret or down into an open grave – all for the moment when the War of Continuance would be won. Now few were left to mourn or cheer . . .

But there were other dimensions.

The ravaging weapons of war had revealed them, had so torn the fabric of the universe that now strange paths to Otherwheres and Otherwhens lay open to those who were knowledgeable – or courageous – enough to tread those paths of madness.

The first of those conspirators, walking so forthrightly now through the long corridors, was Julliann of the Sharkskin. A small man he, booted, belted, buckskinned, broadsworded, to the hilt, his face like an old brown canvas sail, his hair whirling like smoke about his head. And flame seemed to crackle in that smoke as he flung open his mouth in a harsh laugh.

'So Mad Mike Surinat is not here to meet us, my friends! So much the worse for him! He may rob us of a further triumph, but he yields us his castle!'

So saying, he clapped Harry the Hawk on his back. Harry laughed in response, and the goshawk riding hooded on his shoulder never fluttered.

'The Surinats are too decadent for these warlike times, Julliann,' Harry said. He was large and heavy. He held himself, physique and psyche, under tight control, like a bear on a greyhound's leash. As he moved, he flashed his torch from side to side, scanning every doorway as a matter of rote, in case they were surprised.

The third conspirator never spoke. He also was built tall and solid, but in his bulk was something animal and ungainly. Something animal lurked in his silence too. The lick of the torch revealed a mighty face with a small expression, tiny eyes set in dark sockets, a minor fortress of a nose and a great immobile mouth plastered across the lower half of the face. This was Gururn, fugitive from the Smix-Smith world, slayer of life, the secrets of his own life as mute as granite.

They moved now through a floor of the castle newly painted, its surfaces smothered in a prismatic white reflectant paint, so that everywhere the opened colours of the spectrum, newly released, leapt at them and assaulted their vision. To walk down a corridor was to be battered to death by the plumage of courting peacocks.

Growling, Gururn flung open the shutters of a tall

16

window and peered out. Only the perspectives of the façade of the castle met his gaze, near, distant, remote, winding over hill and valley, punctuated insanely by courtyard and tower and minaret – a vision by some crazed Gustave Moreau compiled of Henri Christophe's *Sans Souci*, Padua, Hambi, Polonnaruwa, Amber, Alcatraz, Blenheim and the terrifying repetitions of the Escorial and Ramesvaram. Its fretted surfaces were like a myriad dead moths, pinned recklessly one atop the other by a frenetic lepidopterist in his cups.

Slam! The shutters went shut again. The three conspirators moved among the ruinous glory of peacock light. Now there was no laughter between them.

They came to an elevator. The elevator lifted them ten storeys. So elaborately had the Surinats built, that none but they and their nearest allies could locate the jet-powered elevators that sped in one continuing movement from bottom to top of their warrening house.

They were walking through suite after suite of interconnecting rooms, each bigger than the previous one, until the ultimate room of the series encompassed all the others and they were forced to turn about and seek another way. Julliann's legs ached. Now the elaborate heterochromatic effects were lost. The three companions found themselves tramping a forlorn corner of this building men had once called The Ultimate Structure. The basic crain, that man-made stone which nothing could corrupt, stood naked; doors and casements had been but casually slotted into it. Nothing had been dressed. Every perspective had a perspective encased within it, like the receding oily pools of death within a basilisk's eye.

'I knew this castle as a lad,' said Julliann.

The others said nothing, merely marched.

'Spent my entire adolescence trying to find my way out of it,' said Julliann.

The others said nothing, continuing to march.

'Have I ever been free of it?' said Julliann.

The others said nothing, still marching forward.

But Julliann reeled sideways, clutching at his brow, gasping, and struck his temple against a crain pillar. He managed to stand, rocking, supporting himself with one hand, staring ahead in fear as if he gazed into one of those dimensions so lately and so unpleasantly revealed to man.

Then did Harry the Hawk and Gururn halt, and turn, and go uneasily towards him.

'What ails you, Julliann of the Sharkskin?'

He closed his eyes. When he reopened them, he looked less curiously.

'You see me clearly enough, don't you?'

'Clearly enough,' said Harry, and Gururn nodded.

'Come near and touch me, touch my clothes.'

Wondering, they did as he bid them.

'You feel me, don't you?'

'You know we do.' A nod.

'You can smell me, can't you?'

Two nods.

'For all that, I could be an hallucination. Or we three could be caught in some kind of illusion. Death in a basilisk's eye, sort of thing.'

Harry clouted him on the arm and set him moving again. In his harsh and rapid voice, he said, 'You recall when the fight was on between our friend Milwrack and the Whistling Hunchback? We stood up to our knees in that muck like mud which vanished even as the Hunchback fell? You recall that time?'

'I had forgotten. Now I recall. The sky ran with suns until it resembled a pin-table machine. What of it? It was far enough from this castle!'

'Would we were there, then,' mumbled Gururn.

18

'In that place and that hour, Julliann, you clutched your head and cried that life was an illusion, even as you did just now. And a further time. We sat and drank the poisons with the Spider King. You won't forget that in a hurry!'

'I had forgotten the Spider King . . . Did he not turn into a woman? Was there not also a Queen of All Questions? But the poisons I remember – two of them, taken by turns, to serve as an antidote to the other. It's long past. What of it?'

'In that hour, Julliann, when I swear my soul was snow-white with fear, you clutched your heart and vowed you were no more than a puppet in another's dream, even as you did just now.'

Julliann strode down the corridor, eyes on the floor.

'If I did . . .'

'Just this, my friend – that you have no business to let your mind feast itself on such fancies, for you are the realest man I know . . . And if the day ever comes when I am truly tested by the Powers Above, then I pray you will be by my side!'

Juliann looked sideways at his companion – mutely, but with his storm-dark eyes speaking volumes. Then his gaze slid away again, as will the gaze of men who are burdened with things of which they will not or cannot speak.

The passage down which they strode met another, a meaner one. They took it. A row of small shops stood here. The blank eyes of their shutters were presented to the world, like the eyelids of sleeping merchants. No man could guess what lay behind them.

After the last shop stood a swing door. Julliann pushed through. A stairway lay beyond; it had a window on it, but the window only showed further rooms and corridors, all desolate. They mounted the stairs.

19

The stairs rose straight, then reached a landing, then turned and went up again. There were more landings, more turns, more and more stairs.

At last, exhausted, they came to a landing where they were forced to stop. They leaned on the balustrade and breathed deep. The unrelenting windows showed the same unrelenting views.

Julliann was suffering great pain from both legs, though he forebore to show it.

Gururn lifted his great paw of a hand. They listened, knowing how sharp his hearing was. A sound of irregular crying came to them.

Turning his shaggy head, Gururn looked at Julliann in silent question.

Julliann nodded.

They moved silently forward, down a corridor carpeted in some kind of wickerwork. This time, Gururn led.

Without hesitation, he headed for an elaborately carved door. In his posture, in his tread, in his eagerness, was a bestial thing hitherto half-unexpressed. As he pushed open the door, Julliann peered under his mighty arm.

A woman sat at a small pattern-organ, which threw out a yellow and black helix unregarded, for her delicate hands were over her face.

She wore a dress, simple in its authority, which revealed the sweep of her shoulders and thus emphasized her vulnerability.

The slight sound of the door opening jerked her from her tearful reverie. Slowly, lowering her hands as she did so, she turned to face the intruders. Julliann, with a gasp, recognized her as Strawn Fidel, the betrothed of Fletcher Surinat.

As her eyes lit on Gururn, the latter moved into the room. With one sweep of a paw, he dragged the mouth-mask from the lower half of his face, revealing the unhuman jaw, the powerful yellow teeth, the blond hair growing in twists from his gums. Her first screams set him bounding forward at her with a cry of hungry expectation.

3

Space had a floor. It stretched below the hurtling sunship as the ship's transverters dragged the vessel from microspace to the ordinary dimensions of the X-World.

The floor looked like nothing more than a sheet of typing paper floating down towards the bottom of some translucent and undisturbed pool. But it grew. It grew as the *Micromegas* burst towards it; it came upwards, upwards from its translucent and ripple-innocent waters, upwards, spread far beyond the confines of any pool, until it threatened to dwarf the limitless spread of starlight above and round it.

The sunship was decelerating, tearing down through the resonating Gs in one grand orchestral crash as if ripping the rivets out of Nature itself.

Unstirring and unstirred, Attica Saigon Smix sat with his wife Loomis watching the mighty floor of space rise to meet them. They were comfortable in their embracing chairs before the visiscreen, with Captain Ladore standing immaculate behind them.

Loomis's unchanging beauty was, like her sister's, of a Persian kind, her face as smooth and beautiful as an Isfahan dome of cerulean china, her hair sable and coiling, uncurled, about her neck with an intent of its own. She had rested one hand on the wrist of her husband.

He – he whose least word to the computer pentagons of Earth was unrecognized law in every last household of its numberless warrens – he – boss of all bosses, last overlord of all commercial overlords – he – great communist-capitalist of the united capitalist-communist empire – he – Attica Saigon Smix of Smix-Smith Inc. – was a pale shadow of a man. The slight pulsations of his ivory skin revealed, not the normal circulation of a normal bloodstream, but the unfaltering beat of internal servo-mechanisms.

He turned his head and smiled at her, at she who was more precious to him than the unendingly complex financial para-systems over which he held sway. Ghastly though his smile might have seemed to others, it woke an answering smile of love from her.

'Nearly there, my love.'

'Nearly there!'

'You weren't bored by micro-space?'

'Not at all, Attica!'

'Nor I, with you beside me.'

He turned his thin skull half-way towards Captain La-dore. 'See to it that we disembark immediately we land. I have no desire that we be kept waiting.'

'Sir.' The captain turned, barked briefly into the inter-com by his side.

The orchestration had faded now into a depth beyond music or sound.

The great white floor, unshadowed by starlight, now stretched before them, magnificent, bleak, unbelievable, the logical extension of a zero-infinity nightmare topology, undiminished by distance, unfamiliarized by any proximity.

In a brief while, they touched down upon it, light as daylight on a snow-crowned peak. From the porcine bulk of the ship, gangways rolled out on all sides, gangways and the snouts of immense weapons, tender as the noses of blind moles.

Attica Saigon Smix's chair animated itself, curling

about its master. It brought him to the vertical. He was on his feet. He proceeded forward, his wife by his side, ever-watchful with her eyes of lapis-lazuli. They moved to the nearest porter-shaft, sank languidly down it, emerged at a gangway, and were carried, whirringly, gently, speedily, down on to the surface of the immense floor of space.

She flinched and held more tightly to his arm. The all-recording cameras, perpetuating every moment of Attica Saigon Smix's life-event-continuum, caught her gesture, and the Smix Carollers added a lyric for the re-showing:

'She flinched and held more tightly to his arm
Magnificent in fright, brave in alarm . . .'

From other gangways, minions were hastening down, their subordinate positions rendering them impervious to the impossibly grandiose exposure of their situation. By reason of their power, naked to the majesty of it, Attica Saigon Smix and his wife stood on infinity, stood on the immovable object, while the infinitely irresistible force of space flew over them. The floor felt warm, worn, hydrop-tic, apical, pinnate, like the flesh of a vulpine and voluptuous courtesan erotogenically dying.

'Alone at last, my love.'

'Alone with you, dear Attica!'

'You like it here?'

'Well, it is kind of novel . . . Is it – you know – science or art?'

'Both, my love. Science and art. The two disciplines, once parallel, here unite. There's been nothing like it before.'

She gave a small laugh. 'I'd think not! Does it need much – well, power?'

His chair trembled slightly about him. 'Power? Until the war, there wasn't this much power available. Only the prolapse of other dimensions, other universes, into ours

23

allowed us to broach entire new energy-systems. You explain to her, Benchiffer . . .'

His voice was trailing away, amplification fading. But the faithful Benchiffer, perspex-encased, was already at hand, scooping up his master's wilting sentence like some sensitive plant, applying to it the unction of his own calcareous personality. 'Yes, madam, this aponeurotic floor is maintained in stasis by a power-drain from some of the newly-opened-up universes. The energy quotients appear to be roughly in equipoise, so that one year of the floor's existence probably drains one year from the entropaic-output store of an entire universe.'

'I see . . . You mean we actually shorten people's lives by us being here?'

'Well, lives do tend to shorten anyway, ma'am, even with no one there meddling.'

Benchiffer fell back, more pallid than ever, aware he had transgressed beyond his brief – to expound science – into dealing with matters coming within the domain of ontology and philosophy. Not that there was much to choose between any of them nowadays . . .

But Attica Saigon Smix seemed unaware of the transgression. His eye-like lenses took in the synclastic horizons all about him, and were refreshed by them. Here was peace from the rabid systems he nominally controlled, peace and a hideout the like of which had never before been devised.

He watched, chair-supported, as henchmen brought out holoscillators. Inasmuch as he was capable of deriving pleasure through the intricate man-mechanism interfaces of his receptors, he derived pleasure from seeing the holoscillators come on.

They came on now, warmed, as the henchmen hurried out of the way. A lithoponic mist formed, bodied forth, boiled as if cupellation were in process, and objects took shape within the uneasy cloak of it – trees, flowers, benches, marrow plants male and female, forts and little fortresses, music boxes and barrel-organs, roundabouts, homes for cows and doggies.

'Benchiffer!'

'Sir!' Benchiffer twinkled as he moved, toes rotating like castors in the perspex.

'That passage from that poet . . .'

Benchiffer remembered. A constant threat of instant demolition proved an ideal mnemonic in all situations.

'Shakespeare, sir . . . "The great globe itself, Yea, all which it inherit, shall dissolve, And, like this insubstantial pageant faded, Leave not a rack behind . . ."'

'As this lot appears, I guess their equivalent is sort of disappearing in some other universe,' said Loomis. Her husband patted her for her cleverness. Also, he liked the poem, even if it didn't rhyme.

The pageant was growing rapidly substantial. Suddenly, it was *there*. The cow homes and the cows, the trees, the little gay buildings, the huge butterflies, all in motion, bright as a lip in a dream, covering – yeah, covering the whole scabdevouring floor of space.

'Want to walk, my love?'

'Yeah, sure.' She wanted to walk when he did. Always. She was nice. So this was the paradise he had invented for her. Loomis. Love.

The cameras followed them, silent as hepatitis, drinking it all in, recording for posterity and their own delectation the slow stroll among these objects of Attica Saigon Smix's invention. The trees were not trees, the butterflies not butterflies, the cows not cows, the buildings not buildings. They were delicate simplifications, pastiches of trees, butterflies, cows and buildings, done in simplified shapes, executed in primary colours. The melons and flowers lying at their careless feet were detachable, embodied extracts of abstracts based on elementary pictures in nursery frescoes. Peace and infantilism met, with a smacking but pure kiss.

'It's nice here . . .'

'Good for you to get away from business.'

'Aren't the cows cute?'

'I just love their pretty little dangling bells and – uh, udders. You're a clever old thing, Attica, did I ever tell you that?'

Every day she told him that. It was the secret of both their successes.

A cow was waddling by them, hat on head, gaudy melon-flower in chops, rocking quaintly from side to side. Three-dimensional and entirely touchable – rideable, even. Hygienic, too, of course. No defecations, no monstrous eructations of vile wind. Just a holobject, conjured by machines invented in the technological computer-laboratories of one of Smix-Smith's subsidiaries.

And the yokel figure also waddling towards them was no more than a holman, also three-dimensional, entirely touchable, hygienic. Man, hat, comic smock, pipe, clogs, all of one inorganic substance, a projection as tangible, as much of the physical world as, and far less unmanoeuvrable than, oak. It touched its comic floppy hat, blew a little chugging paste-board smoke-ring from its corncob, and produced a message from its daisy-embroidered smock.

'Benchiffer, read it.'

Benchiffer took the wafer, held it in photoelectric hand and intoned, 'Gall-bladder to Rupture Six. Regret Spy-Bell Zero Zero Zero became nondetectable time-referents 03071255T. Jupiter Police Five Star Alert and Exo-Systems Search in Code Areas Burgess, Knight, Adlard, Cotton and Conquest. Full Emergency. Possible coordinates follow message. Suggest Red Rupture despatch dopple repeat dopple subiter Gall-bladder Suite Beta. All parameters Bilious repeat Bilious advised. War footing. Transcendent. Jupiter Five Star Alert. Burgess, Knight, Adlard, Cotton, Conquest. Red Rupture. Reddleman. QLLTX5973328764983AA448. Four second destruct. Reddleman. Gabbice. Gall-bladder Rupture Six.'

'Is it important, darling?' Loomis asked.

The four seconds was up. The holman was blanked for a moment as the wafer destructed.

'I'm Red Rupture,' Attica Saigon Smix said, fingering certain keys on his chair. He turned slowly round, beginning to perambulate back through the tent-shaped trees towards *Micromegas*. He signalled to Captain Ladore, watchful at the gangway.

'What's it mean, darling?' asked Loomis. She was all female; in her adolescence, she had liked to shower in company with her male cousins, and with her sister, Glamis. It had proved the beginning of a very cleanly way of life.

'It's that scabdevouring spy-bell near Jupiter that we've been keeping tabs on. It could do us no harm – we just didn't know who owned it. How does it *vanish* just like that? When I get to Gall-bladder – Oh, Ladore! Is it possible to project a dopple of me to Gall-bladder from this location?'

Immaculate Ladore was a projection himself, one of the multiple embodiments of Computer Complex detached to serve – and survey – the master of the Smix-Smith universe.

'It means double transcendence,' Ladore replied. '*Micromegas* carries the necessary equipment. We could perform the operation in ordinary space. Here, in this continuum, we lack energy. We shall have to tap the floor – it's pure energy ready to hand.'

'Get with it.' But the companalog had anticipated the order; as the boss rolled up the gangway, syphon cables were snaking down, taking a bite into the space-floor.

He looked back. She fluttered a hand. Ever the loving wife.

Another companalog was waiting inside, guiding him down to Trexmissions Bay. Orderly movement, high-level activity, low-order sounds, non-smells – the entire synthetic, synapse-speeding gestalt of a multi-space sunship. Pent with emotion, null-emotion, and the fastest static known to man. Hyper-thyroid, hythritic, the perfect kinematics of non-perceivable mobility in n dimensions. Real men, fake men – holmans, companalogs, cyborgs, androids, robots, down to esperg-dummies – all with a purpose not entirely or entirely not their own – even the real men, so far as 'real' was a term any more with coordinates in any actual world, drugged or gutted in some way or hooked to electroidal reflex. Eyes everywhere, and some anxious eye-movement. But never gaze meeting gaze. Never eye-contact. Deflection saved reflection.

They brought him reverently to an intolerable prone position and swung the massive dopplegangster ovens round about his frame.

A technician said, and a slight tendency to hairiness along the side of the neck suggested he was a real man, however controlled, 'You know, sir, that you will have to rest here in lightly comative condition while your dopple is away? The life-death interface could be somewhat critical over the proposed distance.'

'Understood.' No baby-talk for these men. 'Can you peel off an extra dopple to keep my wife happy, keep her company?'

'We could peel off a half-dozen under normal circumstances.' Dangerous talk to Smix of Smix-Smith, the normal circumstances being understood to refer to people

28

in sound health, making their way along the mulcting trajectories of life unaided by excessive servos. 'But we might find in the present case that doubling dopplers could lead to hyperemesis and actuality-decay. What we can do is take a soul-sliver and duplicate on the holoscope, to form a semi-project. Then we'd use companalog transjects to project speech transferences based on your recorded impulse-patterns.'

Faithful, detesticled Benchiffer was at the wizened elbow to render the technical jargon down into boss jargon.

'You might find yourself in excess of critical, psychewise, if you projected more than one dopple. But they can take a still-moment-transfix and give it pseudo-life and speech by souping it up through computer-project channels, using your life-channels from the banks.'

'Will that *thing* be any good for Loomis?'

'It could repeat yourself – itself – a bit.'

'It might keep her happy. Let's go. Gall-bladder.'

The ovens began to radiate. The old body they contained, yeah, and all which it inherited, began to dissolve and fade . . .

. . . Leaving behind on the floor-world a double which moved slowly out in the fake sunlight among the nursery properties to greet Loomis, tasty of hand and lip and gesture . . .

. . . And projecting through the incomprehensible mathematical intricacies (so complex that they were only marshalled in orderly impulses in one special maroon-red-coded section of Computer Complex's primal think-bank and in no human think-tank) separating a rather problematical *here* from a rather problematical *there* a capable and angry alert dopple Attica Saigon Smix into the high (and highly fortified) chambers of a subterranean building in Easeaboard, NA, otherwise known in the day's code

29

(leaving this special definition of 'day' to be unravelled by others) as Gall-bladder.

The guys in Gall-bladder were still sweating blood about the whereabouts of the mystery spy-bell.

That spy-bell – known to its occupants, with whom we have shortly to deal, as 'Doomwitch' – marks with its disappearance the appearance of catastrophe in my narrative.

My job, as I see it, is to relate the events in some sort of order, to produce a linear continuance which I believe can be perceived in the haphazard-seeming flow of chance, motive and encounter. The next generation, less wedded to ideas of causality and effect ('liberated by the neuro-sciences', as they would claim!) will have to re-interpret the whole damned tangled business.

At about this time, I, displaced Durrant Surinat, was wheeling across the courtyard at Slavonski Brod Grad with old George Hornbeck, when he said something interesting on the subject.

It was mid-morning, everywhere was quiet. Most of the distinguished guests we met at the party were still recovering from the evening before. Becky was up and about, radiant as ever – but meditating at this hour, as was her habit. Only Dinah Sorbutt, comfortably and almost completely pregnant, sat on a teak bench with her feet up in the sun and had nothing to do.

'Durrant, I was talking to Becky last night,' George told me. 'Profound girl, my daughter. We were talking about whether there was a pattern to life, and it was a fairly sober discussion. Becky said she could always console herself by seeing a pattern – wallpaper, she called it – so that, even when things were bad, she knew something better was coming.'

'It's a young girl's view,' I said. 'But Becky has real sensibility – in that respect she takes after you.'

'I don't know about that. I'm old and I miss England. I can't believe Britain's gone. I'm more conscious of the awful rifts of life than of its pattern. England is one of the rifts. And, you, Durrant – do you mind my saying it?'

'That I lost both legs in the war? How can I *mind*?'

'You face up to it well, my boy. And you use your prosthetic wheels well. Becky and I were wondering . . . how far it indisposed you mentally for action . . .'

'I manage better than Mike's younger brother, give me that. You know, I suppose, that *he* stays alone in their place in California, on some drug or other? He's about my age, he got both his legs blown off, too – part of a pattern, Becky might say. But I'm not like him, George – in circumstances, maybe, but not in reaction to them – I'm more like cousin Mike, I'm going to do something with *my* life.'

George smiled and nodded, looking down at the path, glancing at his watch. Soon it would be time to work.

Slavonski Brod Grad was not always a place of merriment. The parties were growing fewer as the economic situation deteriorated.

George Hornbeck and I fought our own little battle against the monolithic state threatening to engulf the world once the Cap–Comm Treaty was really a going concern.

We published creative pornography. Much of the material, mainly in the form of comic strips, was supplied by our Brazilian ally, da Perquista Mangista. We were backed by Brazilian money as well.

Our one-room offices were in the castle. We called ourselves PPP, which stood for Pornography Permissive and Progressive. Strangely enough, the idea had come from Russia, where their *samizdat*, or do-it-yourself publishing, led the world.

Our puny blow against machine-culture was done by machines which mainly ran themselves. We could afford a few minutes more in the fresh air.

'Let's sit on a bench and sun ourselves,' George said. 'It's a traditional old man's occupation. We don't have to talk to Dinah. She's a foolish woman. I wonder why she will tell nobody who the father of her infant is?'

We sat down together, and he started to discuss paternity. He did ramble sometimes. Then he said, 'Your other burden is the loss of your parents and Mike's. I know Mike's Aunt Leda is doing good work on Mars, but she should be here with her daughter Choggles. Choggles is getting too precocious for her own boots . . . No, that wasn't what I meant to ask you. Durrant, what *are* you intending to do with your life?'

Well, why not tell him?

'I'm intending to write a novel. I'm not interested in holoplays, and pornography has its limitations. I want to write a good old-fashioned novel, with no more ambition in it than to reflect pleasure and disgust in what I see round me.'

At that time, I was not entirely serious. I did not entirely intend to write a novel, merely to keep old George, whom I regarded highly, content. Certainly, I did not intend to write *this* novel. But, the neuro-scientists declare, every human act can be analyzed in chemical terms; so perhaps that conversation predetermined this book.

I hereby determine not to intervene in the narrative again – or not overtly. But, bereft of my own legs, I intend to play a long-legged God – the new kind of god, god of creation, slave of the creation it has created, as man has now become slave of the systems he created, according to the new neurophilosophy. For – why not admit it – I'm vexed already with my task: by what scale of values is it more worthwhile to create or read a novel, even one with real people in it, than to opt for hallucinations provoked by *root*, as does my dark obverse, my cousin Mike's brother, over in California? – Except in this: that drug-dreams cover old ground, and look back; I try to look forward, and even to charm dear Choggles.

Accordingly, I will travel with my characters all round space and time. If I do that, I will also travel into their thoughts. Why not? Mind is now proven an epiphenomenon of space and time! You see I write a story on deterministic principles.

The first flutter of this came to me as I sat in the sun with George Hornbeck, for I said, 'I'd like to try and invent what others think. Thought has always seemed to me easier to understand than action.' (And there I finish telling what I said.)

He gave his dry laugh. 'Understanding is a relative expression. But we can all of us always do with a little more of it. Go ahead, Durrant, see what you can do for us – and yourself!'

He left me, walking quite strongly across the wide courtyard, an old man missing England.

4

Orbiting the sun in a region of space somewhere (not to put too fine a point on it) between Mars and Jupiter, was the space vehicle known to its enemies as Spy-Bell Zero Zero Zero. To the DN, and to its occupants, it was known as *Doomwitch*.

The occupants numbered ten humans, plus a very efficient computer. The ship was built by the Dissident Nations – those who could not or would not enter the World Government umbrella offered by the Cap–Comm Treaty. Most of the structure was Japanese-made, except the computer, which was a Danish model, an IMRA 40, and the engines, which were Jugo–Hungarian.

Most of the crew were American. Four of them were conscious, while the rest lay in semi-deep, just three degrees Kelvin above BAZ (Biochemical Activity Zero), conserving air, nutrients and power.

Of the four who retained, to varying degrees, that peculiar state called by its possessors 'full consciousness', we have met one before – Dr Glamis Fevertrees, last seen with Zoomer arranged tastefully about her feet. She still wore his pendant round her neck.

Also conscious was the cool, dapper and scholarly Professor Jules de l'Isle-Evens, once a high-ranking scientific adviser to the EEC in Brussels before the EEC signed on with Cap–Comm, whereupon de l'Isle-Evens, an independent man, had joined the DN

The other two aware crew-members were Guy Gisbone, who, like many other technical men, had been involved with the massive Operation Sex-Trigger under the aegis of Auden Chaplain, before WWIII; and the perky and spotty Dimittis, who was referred to – not always behind his back – as 'the cabin-boy'.

All four were busy. None was happy.

Doomwitch was the first DN spy-bell to be launched, whereas the Cap–Comm powers had virtually the free run of space. Its appointed task was to maintain constant watch and chart of all Cap–Comm space-going operations and feed them back to Tokyo, the new DN capital. But it had been detected by enemy posts near Jupiter almost before taking up position.

The enmity between Cap–Comm and DN was not yet formalized by anything so crass as a war-footing – indeed, nations still remained embarrassed at finding themselves on the opposing side to nations with whom they had been allied in WWIII, only three years before. But a state of tension existed, of which the unscrupulous para-combine of Smix-Smith took full advantage.

Guy Gisbone and the glamorous Dr Glamis lay on couches on their stomachs – not the most comfortable of positions for Gisbone, a well-fleshed man with plenty of belly – surveying the trajectories of shipping in the region of Mars. They had six monitors to watch, most of them filled with blank space most of the time, any one of which could have its contents switched to one of two larger screens if the contents proved important enough.

The profusion of screens caused a certain amount of headache. In addition, Jupiter, as omnipresent to *Doomwitch* as a hunch on a hunchback's shoulder, was causing a static storm – Jupiter IV being in transit – and distorting images.

In the lab behind the observation bay in which Glamis and Gisbone were working, Jules de l'Isle-Evens sat with light-brush and screen, working on an arachnoid-like polygraph, the coordinates of which he was plotting from a notebook.

Dimittis was cooking flapjacks.

All four joined in their computer song.

GLAMIS
The inter-reactions of the biosphere
Proceeding at their statutory pace
Produced an ocean-vat of amino-acid.
From there the stages, difficult but placid,
That led us upwards to the human race
    Are now deterministically clear.

JULES
The next step onwards has an equal clarity.
Like ripples on a lake-face interlocking,
Each stage becomes more complex than the last,
Governed by mathematic law. Thus, fast,
We recognize the new scheme time is clocking;
    Computers have with mankind now gained parity.

QUARTET

Yes, this is the riddle that peasants and commuters
Put to each other in Nineteen Nine Nine
As they dig up their fields or they drive in a line—
As they slump by their holocubes or go to dine out—
Yes, this is the riddle that peasants and commuters
Put to themselves in that terrible moment of doubt—
'Are we *compos mentis* enough for computers?'

GISBONE

The biochemic interweaving force
That we call Nature, aeons back devised,
From cell and jell, computers light enough
To work effectively and fast, be tough,
And utilize a power-source micro-sized—
    Computers called the human brain, of course.

DIMITTIS

Their brains began to take the world and mark it
For conquest by platoons of eager tools.
The latest tool – how clever can you get?!—
Thinks clearer, faster, than the brains do yet.
In truth, it makes them all look floundering fools:
    They gone and priced themselves out of the market!

QUARTET

Yes, this is the riddle that girls, boys, and neuters
Put to each other in Nineteen Nine Nine
As they look to the future and try to divine
If it's worth procreating or even mating this year—
Yes, this is the riddle that girls, boys and neuters
Put to themselves in that terrible moment of fear—
'Are we *compos mentis* enough for computers?'

Glamis restored a lock of hair to its correct position and
turned again to her screens. Combinationist politician's
hostess during her first marriage, priestess in the Swinging
Church of Jesus Christ's Free Will during her second,
subjective manipulationist in defiance mensiatry during
her third, now she was a jill-of-all-trades in the expanding
post-war world during her final divorce.

She looked good, younger than her sister Loomis, and with slightly less reptile ancestry under the eyes.

'It appears to be a Smix-Smith tight-beam traveller on Six,' she told Gisbone, rattling off coordinates and switching magnifications.

'Got it,' Gisbone said. A faint dotted trace arced across his screen, with blackness behind it. Then the whole picture broke and flared into colour. All the other screens before them did the same. They were confronted by a row of late Kandinskys.

'Switch to L-Beam,' said the computer calmly. Even on the alternate system, the Kandinskys remained, vibrating vigorously.

Gisbone had already hit the alarm button.

Glamis locked her monitor and switched to tape. She rolled over to Gisbone's couch to watch, or help if necessary.

De l'Isle-Evens let the cobweb graph ride on into darkness and switched his own link through to the observation panel.

Dimittis allowed a flapjack to burn and, swallowing another, ran through from the galley.

'Check chronology!' Gisbone gasped.

'Checking,' de l'Isle-Evens said quietly.

They watched the battle on the screen – momentarily, until a metal mouth spat copy and spoke.

'Chronology check. Space-time coordinates X on Alpha. Date-line variant, dip minus zero zero eight three forty one gaffs. Trace-subject now subjectivated at Western-time 1999, March Twenty, Thirteen Twenty-one hours.'

They didn't even waste time looking at each other. De l'Isle-Evens was rattling on the master-terminal.

'That's it,' he said, reading off the passing figures from his screen. 'It's another time-prolapse. The Smix-Smith tight-beam traveller we were tagging has disappeared,

37

together with its surrounding continuum . . . minus 008341 gaffs . . . that's – here it is—'

Dimittis had got there first, using his greasy fingers.

'The ship prolapsed two years, eight months, and a bit,' he read out. 'The slip is on the increase.'

'Two and two-third years! Okay, that's it . . .'

The watch rose from their couches, their faces sober. Behind them, disregarded, little encapsuled lives gestured under the glazed jelly surfaces of the monitors. The four of them moved into the lab. Glamis sucked her generous lower lip. Nobody spoke. Their life-forces flowed out, mingled with the banal hum of sophisticated machineries, spread to join the enveloping currencies of the universe.

'Someone had better put it into words,' Gisbone said. 'This is the second time. We can't write this off as some unaccountable electronic fault. We can't blame this one on Jupiter playing up . . .'

He had to force himself to go on. 'For reasons we have yet to discover, aberrations are developing in the universal time-flow. The hitherto uninterrupted, ceaseless, *remorseless* flow of time is disrupted . . .'

'At least the disruption appears to be extremely localized,' Dimittis said.

Glamis gave a laugh with a hint of hysteria in it. 'For God's sake, let's not start *adjusting* to such a – an unutterable situation!'

'Besides, this extreme localization, if it goes on, may prove to be the most uncomfortable feature of the phenomenon,' de l'Isle-Evens said, thoughtfully.

'How come?'

'Well, if we all – the entire solar system nexus – aberrated backwards on the timescale, we'd experience little practical effect, surely? The star-fields would change if the backward shift were really enormous but, if the shift were slight – just a few years – why, then it might be extremely hard to detect any effect from such an aberration.'

'Say, think of that, imagine the whole solar system slipping back in time to the beginning of the universe . . . And nobody even noticing . . . What a song you could make out of that idea!'

'Dimittis, stick to the point,' de l'Isle-Evens said severely. 'Besides, there is evidence to suggest that the system would not long survive bombardments of proto-radiations.'

Brushing this idle speculation aside, Gisbone said, 'In any event, we can't stay here. We have the proof that this unprecedented event is happening; that Smix-Smith ship got zocked back in Time before our eyes. We must take the proof to Earth and present it to the DN Congress – the forthcoming meeting at Friendship might be a useful opportunity. If anything can be done, it must be done before – well, we don't dare guess what sort of madness might seize people if this temporal deterioration continues.'

'Agreed, we must try to get in touch with the right people,' Glamis said. 'But *I* can guess what has caused this time prolapse – as I suspect you can. World War III, of course. For five years, all the big powers shot holes in space and thought nothing of it. Their immense nuclear disturbances ruptured the fabric of space-time – not just space but interrelated time as well. This is the ultimate in pollution – mankind's pollution of the whole continuum!'

It did not need a psychiatrist to understand why there was an odd ring of triumph in her voice. We feel good when our worst fears have been confirmed. Temporarily, at least.

The ruin of the space-time universe was enough to make every last right-thinking conservationist cheer, as they went, slipping, falling, plummeting back into their own histories, shrieking 'I told you so-o-o-o-o . . .'

The crew of the *Doomwitch* stood around, each perhaps wishing that it had been his or her turn in semi-deep when this happened. They would have to go back to Earth in the flesh to bear convincingly tidings of such weight, gloom and eccentricity. Yet all of them on the station, stiffs included, were renegades – worse, neutrals – hunted by one feuding party or another of the thousand ragged-nerved splinter groups left bobbing in the wake of the Big War. The fun wasn't going to be fun.

'Well,' said Guy Gisbone, hitching his trousers.

The alarm buzzed, raising vibrations along the sutures of their skulls.

Glamis was the first back to the screens.

'Oh, the holy ruptured everlasting scabdevouring sainthood!' she exclaimed.

Every screen was showing Kandinsky, continuous performance.

The terminals were mouthing babble.

Loudspeakers squeaked and gibbered.

Metallic mouths spat read-outs of unmitigated jabberwocky.

'This just has to mean—' she said.

'It can't mean—' Gisbone said.

'Don't say *we've* slipped back in time, too!' Dimittis groaned.

De l'Isle-Evens was not usually a man of action. But the shuttered visual-observation ports were behind his terminal, above the serried comp-buffer-units and drum-memories. He was there in a couple of strides, and had his hand on the flip button.

He paused.

They watched him.

He flipped the button and the shutters folded back as quick as a child's eyelids.

40

Jupiter had gone!

They were peering out into empty space.

The disoriented instrumentation chattered like rutting marmosets.

5

Mike Surinat said, 'The apostles of apostasy are slaves of obedience to an iron whim.'

'Obedience is for talent; only genius disobeys involuntarily.'

'I disobey, thou disregardest, he revolts me.'

'You're out! You changed the person! It was "disobeys", not "disobey", right, Mike?'

'Right, you're out, Monty! Your turn, Dinah.'

'Oh – Genius is an infinite capacity for taking and giving pain in the neck.'

'The infinite has reality only for immature minds.'

'She who minds the baby rules the man.' That was Choggles Chaplain, Mike's ten-year-old cousin, lovely child of awful parents. She spoke while looking at the swollen form of Dinah Sorbutt, so noticeably viviparous.

'She who weeps least, weeps best.'

'We are proverbial! Least said, least mended!'

'A waterproof cup is a wonder only if mended. Not very bright, I'm afraid!'

'Hm. I wonder whoever the troublemaker was who invented the idea of equality?' said Dinah.

There were now only three of them left in the game, so it was Mike's turn again.

'"Impossible! Wonderful! So what?" are the three cries uttered at the birth of anything ever invented.'

Dinah Sorbutt squealed with delight. 'You're out,

41

Mike! You broke the rules! You took *two* words from my sentence, not one!'

'Not at all. One of your words is always sufficient, Dinah. I took "invented" merely.'

'*And* "ever"! What about lousy old "ever"? You took "ever" too, so you're out, and that just leaves Choggles and me.'

'But, my darling bitch, you didn't say "ever". You said, did you not, "whoever"? And "whoever" is not "ever", any more than "milestone" is "tone". You are out for challenging incorrectly!'

'Oh, your cruddy, non-sparking, complex omplicated word-games! How I loathe them! The world disintegrates and we play word-games!'

'Had the whole world been innocently occupied playing my cruddy, complex, omplicated – whatever that is – word-games these last few years, it would not now be in its admitted state of disintegration.'

The vexed Miss Sorbutt, though heavily into the last days of her pregnancy, jumped to her feet and dived into the pool. The spray she sent up scattered itself in random but equable distribution over Mike Surinat and his cousin.

'Want to go on with the game, Choggles?' he asked her.

'No, thanks, Mike. You're always so shirty if I beat you. Isn't he, Durrant?' I was sitting with them and had been out of the running for some rounds.

'If you beat me, it is because you cheat by introducing school slang into your jejune sentences,' Surinat told her. 'I am "shirty" – to quote the latest example of what I mean – with your cheating, not your winning.'

'So you say!' She too jumped up. He was after her but she got away. She followed Dinah quickly into the octagonal pool.

42

Night like a great sea lay over their slice of the world. The pool itself, milky with underwater light, floated in the dark. Swimming in it was rather like being in a titanic womb. Perhaps Dinah Sorbutt found comfort in some such reflection. She drifted lazily and mountainously as Choggles butterflied up to her.

'Can I feel the baby kicking again? Nobody's looking, except perhaps dear Durrant, and he won't mind.'

'Choggles, darling, please leave me alone. I'm not just a baby machine.'

'I'm *supposed* to take an interest! Oh, please, Dinah! After all, I may have to go through the ghastly business myself, one day. You'd think they'd dream up a less cumbersome way of carrying on the human race. I mean, you look ever so enormous . . .'

She duck-dived under Dinah, to come up panting on the other side.

'You may get only one chance to bear a child,' Dinah said, 'now that the government controls fertility in both men and women.'

'Well, that's progress. Anyhow, it's saved us from an over-populated world, hasn't it? That – and the millions slaughtered in the war.'

Dinah said primly, 'Many people think the fertility-switch reduces humanity to the level of machines and animals.'

'We can't be both machines *and* animals,' Choggles said, reasonably. 'In any case you needn't lecture me about all that. People of ten really dislike being lectured, you know. And besides, it's wasted on me. Don't forget that the Schally-Chaplain switch is named after my father, though we don't talk about him.'

'I know all about that, child. I'm just tired of your following me. Go and follow your cousin Mike, if you're so mad about him.'

'Don't be personal – I didn't even ask you who the father of your foetus was, did I? Though of course I've guessed! Are you going to have the child delivered in a state maternity home?'

'Of course. It's compulsory.'

'You know why that is, don't you? It's so that they can fix the baby with the switch! Mike told me.'

'Stop it!'

'You could get it done privately at a private clinic, I should think – you know, like those gorgeous old abortion-clinics you sometimes see in holodramas.'

Dinah started to swim slowly away. 'That would be illegal. When the computer opens the fertility-switch to allow you to conceive, the fact is recorded, and they check to see that you go to a proper maternity home.'

'Does it hurt the baby – the insertion of the Schally-Chaplain switch, I mean? My father did the operation on me himself.'

'Oh, go *away*! I don't want to talk about it!' Dinah started kicking and splashing.

'You'd better not over-exert yourself, Dinah, or you might give birth in the pool! Do you think that's possible? Perhaps it would grow up amphibious . . .'

In the end, Choggles swam disconsolately away. Communication was really only in its elementary stages. She would have to say that to Mike; he might laugh, but Mike's laughter was always partly against himself.

As she thought about Mike, she saw he had been standing at one end of the pool. Now he was turning, disappearing in the darkness.

He also, at one remove, had been thinking of parturition and the process of species-continuance which appeared to be mankind's sole blind objective. Now that science had finally taken control of that objective, after

44

centuries of blundering attempts to do so, the human race would be subtly and inevitably changed.

He walked away into the dark. Behind him, the pool was a drop of amniotic fluid and a beacon for moths – except that moths and similar night creatures were fended off by a bumper beam a few metres above ground level.

Above night level floated the sound of Slavonski Brod guests, their idle laughter, their carefully directed nothings. The mating game and the horrid struggle for existence were here brought to heel – reduced to flirtations and mild egocentricities.

Surinat avoided the crowd about the pool-side bar and turned among the trees. Darkness he loved. Darkness was more suited to the human condition than daylight. There would come a time when darkness was continual, unpunctuated by any little local lamps. The idea rested him.

Of course, that time was billions of years ahead. A lot of suffering had to be got through before that. But the human brain – the human brain was always enfolded, under its thick encompassing bone, in darkness.

If your brain started seeing flashes of light, it meant a tumour; the pressure of the tumour acted like light. Darkness was the relaxing of pressure, of the pain of being human.

He should be amusing Monty. Monty was his honoured (and famous) guest. Monty knew all about pain, too, being an artist, however phoney an artist. Perhaps the fakes felt that inner human hurt even more keenly than genuine artists. There was something so alien about being genuine . . .

He should be amusing Monty. But Monty was not to be trusted – he worked for the enemy. A deal made with Monty might give Mike, and through him the Dissident Nations, a line to Smix and the World Executive Council, the people who had pushed through the Cap–Comm Treaty.

As Mike walked along the neat cobbled path by the outer garden wall, his feet brushed straggling bushes of verbena encroaching the path. The pale diaphanous smell flooded his senses, carrying him back to – to where? As long as it was *back*, the senses accepted it as happiness. But he smelt something else in another pace or two.

Cigar smoke?

'Who the pox are you?' He had his eraser out, was balanced on his toes, felt ready for crisis, peered ahead at a stocky figure leaning against the garden wall.

'Sorry if I startled you, guv.'

'What are you doing here?'

'I'm only having a quick puff, guv.'

'You are trespassing, you savvy that?'

'Don't be like that, guv! I'm only having a quick puff!'

Surinat had a light on the fellow now. A small huddled man in coarse clothes. Local. A fisherman perhaps. Mild, but absolutely unshaken and still drawing on his cigar butt. A real dodgy smelly old man with the arse of his trousers hanging down.

'How did you get in here? Leave at once before the guards throw you over the wall.'

'Okay, guv.' The man vanished.

A whiff of Balkan tobacco, daintily over-ridden by the pallid lemon of verbena.

Then Surinat understood. He gave a peremptory chuckle (just for the record) but he was shaken.

He walked along the path more slowly until he reached the promontory. There he sat, looking over the dark Pannonian Sea. Clusters of lights could be seen far on the Hungarian shore. And there were individual lights, bobbing above the boats that carried them.

46

It was a fine place in which to feel the old ache, and to worry about the broken people for whom the war would never properly be over: his fatherless brother, Julian, his fatherless niece, Choggles. And me, his fatherless cousin, I suppose. I have no legs, but I can guess his thoughts.

He was not submerged in meditation too deeply to hear approaching footsteps and the murmur of voices. He recognized the girl's tones first: Becky Hornbeck, who had come under his wing, and whom he increasingly loved.

And the man was Monty Zoomer.

Mike stood up and made himself known. If they wanted a touch of romance on the promontory, he would politely leave them alone. He knew from experience how well the promontory worked.

'Don't go,' Monty said. 'Let's sit and talk. We can both cuddle Becky, can't we?'

'Just don't be too grasping,' she said.

In the darkness, the two men looked not unalike in stature. But Surinat was more fine-boned, would probably grow thinner as he approached middle-age, as had his father before him, and many of the long line of Surinats. Whereas Zoomer, of nondescript origins which included a Danish-Irish-Dutch mother and a Jewish father called Zomski, had put on meat lately, success adding stature to him.

Indifferently, Surinat settled on the short crisp grass; the grass was fed on salt spray and felt like yak fur. He put his arm round Becky. She meant something to him, and ah, the warmth, the precious fugitive human warmth of a female body – the one tolerable organization in a universe of random heat-exchange!

Zoomer, kicking out his legs, was already talking. Subject, as usual, himself.

'Black was the colour crayon I used to like using most when I was a kid. Guess it was yours too, eh, Surinat?'

'Yellow.'

'Well, it means something, I guess. I used to sit out in the courtyard and draw and draw, while my Dad was there, writing his endless television plays. See, we weren't disgustingly rich like the Surinat family. "Nice blue sun" – remember that catch-line? It was famous for years, everyone said it, back before the war. My dad got it straight from me, working away on my crayoning. It was just something I said, aged two-and-a-bit, sitting there out in the courtyard with Dad and my brother. "Nice blue sun!" He'd pass the crayons out the box to me one by one – trying to control my life even then!'

Zoomer laughed at his own recollections. 'We didn't like being out in the courtyard all that time, but it was so crowded in the house – the Zomskis used to take in boarders, you know . . . Humble beginnings, Surinat, humble beginnings! Big blokes from little acorns grow. My brother used to peep in on boarders making love.'

'Was that your brother Dimittis?' Becky asked.

'Funny how he got that name. See, his *real* name's Nanko, after his grandfather. But when I was little, all I could call him was Nunkie. The beginnings of creativity, in a way. Distortion and creation – you should know that, Surinat. Everyone called him Nunc, then, and so it went—'

'Talking about creativity,' Mike said, 'can we do a deal on a new holoplay? You have the equipment, I can finance, we can both contribute ideas.'

'I'm very busy at the moment, see. I'm something like a universal property. Frankly, I've got more money than I know how to do with, so your offer hasn't all that attraction . . .'

'I know you're big time, Monty, but wouldn't you say that your id-projects are getting – well . . .'

The night took the pause easily in its dark-throated wing.

'Go ahead and say it, then, Surinat. How are my projects getting? You weren't going to say debased, were you?'

Mike was staring through the dark at him. Zoomer was no more than human size, slightly undersize, in fact. Nothing monstrous. And intellect the size of a pinhead. How come he had such undeniable talent? – because it was talent as well as ego.

Yet there was so little to like or even notice about Zoomer, except for his wild hair and the pendant thumping against his plump little courtyard-bred chest.

'No, I wasn't going to say debased . . . What made you think that? I was going to say attenuated. As is only natural, you aren't the creative force you were five years ago. You've given out so much, of course you need an infusion of fresh imagery. I saw one of your holomasques last—'

'Look, friend, I *give* myself, right? *I give myself!* People want what I got. I keep the imagining popular. It's for the masses, not for you in your precious secluded castles. You just pull in, I expand, I give out I give the public what they want, okay?'

'The argument of how many second-rate artists! A self-righteous way of saying that you pander to the lowest common denominator for as much cash as you can get!'

'That's the jealousy of an artist who's never rated, right?! And it's the cruddy snooty toffee-nosed attitude of someone who has a lousy opinion of his fellow men. Why the suppurating sandbag shouldn't I coin the copper while I can?'

Surinat laughed with at least a semblance of good nature. 'Next you'll be saying that commercial success is a proof of merit. Sorry, Zoomer, I'm only needling you!'

Zoomer was on his feet, jumping up and letting Becky collapse against Surinat.

'What right you got to needle me? Think you're so good just because you've inherited this big fat ugly castle—'

'– Very different from your neat plastic dreams, isn't it?'

'– I tell you I serve the people. Better than all your word-games, your trifling. The times are all upset, who knows how much, and all you do is sit around all day and kipple about with *words*!'

'My decadent view is, I fear, that words are the basic building blocks of man's society. The universe could not begin to exist in any meaningful way until an intelligible word was spoken.'

'Plasticine! Pictures were first, and popularity is too a test of merit. What other test is there?'

Becky said quietly, 'You say you serve the people, Monty. I understood you served Computer Complex, and that they pay you?'

Zoomer said quietly, 'So precisely what?'

'So it's not a question of popularity. The public accepts what CC dishes out.'

'Aw, you're all ganging up on me! You rich layabouts are all the same. You don't know what it's all about, you don't know what it is to fight for existence. I'm going to get a drink. What's so awful about working for the government, anyway?' His dark figure merged with the dark.

Becky leaned more closely against Mike.

'He likes blowing his top. And when he does, he's even more lavish with his words than you are!'

They lay down side by side, hands soothing each other, lips gently nibbling, legs eventually intertwining.

'"By the far Pannonian Sea . . .",' she quoted, and he took it up.

'" . . . that ocean
Born again from Mesozoic springs . . ."'

They were both repeating it now as they lay embracing, while the sea came slobbering up to their feet.

> "'We felt the quickening life of Earth's heart burst
> As it had ever done, in change and motion,
> From the great morning of the world when first
> All baser things enjoyed life's sacred thirst;
> And dawning humans in the primal light
> Ran to the shore and in the wave immersed
> Bodies and minds. Then had they not won right
> To build technologies against life's true delight;
> Simple and rough, they yet were flowering things—
> But oh, the fruit, the tasteless fruit, man's autumn brings!'"

He had adapted it from verses of his favourite poet, hastily during the War, when the Pannonian Sea was still growing and there was some doubt whether the Grad would not disappear like a sword beneath its inundating waves. Now equipoise had been reached, as their two voices, furred by being kept low, reached in harmony the dorised cadence of the last line.

Becky had memorized the verse for her own pleasure, not to please him, not to please anyone but herself. Becky Hornbeck was a free person, containing within her the lack of stridence belonging to true independence. And she owned the Koh-i-Nor.

On the word 'brings', their mouths came together with a sort of nimble precision which suggested both had been this way before and found in it a pleasure perhaps beyond the scope of words. Two independences merged to create a greater.

51

A small wet thing, dripping uncontrollably into the depths of a Mexican dogwood, had been crouching near enough to overhear the conversation between Surinat and Monty Zoomer. When Zoomer turned and flounced from the scene, the crouching shape arose and followed, damp feet almost noiseless on the path.

Lights, lanterns, the modest floodlit façade of Slavonski Brod Grad, broken fretwork of pampas and variegated laurel, acacias made cavernous by fireglow, silhouettes of special people, the ambience of the pood, massed blacks where cypresses made mirror of ground and sky, the blaze of windows, primitive glow of serried barbecues, turrets gloomy above it all – through the broken scenes, each companionable in its own tent of night, went Zoomer, daintly picking his way, alone.

And Choggles Chaplain shadowed him in her swimsuit. Suspicious, sinister, unsuspecting, prepubertal.

She was hardly likely to guess at the sophisticated equipment packed into a tooth-sized package and embedded just beside Zoomer's fifth vertebra. It gave him eyes in his back. And he had already seen that he was followed.

He went through the oleander patio, up the shallow fountain-adorned steps, in at the side door. When Choggles, still dripping, slid round the portal, she saw him already starting up the wide sweep of staircase, his head eclipsed by a chandelier. She lurked behind a potted palm.

When he reached the top step, she ran lightly up behind him, every limb shining from its internal spring.

The door of his suite slammed almost in her face.

"'I disobey, thou disregardest, he revolts me,'" she quoted to herself.

She had a cat's sixth sense that there was something amiss with Monty. Without asking her adored cousin, she knew he felt the same. And she was determined to find out what the something was.

People were about. Their presence filled the absent rooms. The gloomy old grad had been converted to a small pleasure dome. Many of the guests – and Choggles knew which – belonged to Surinat's IDI . . . But she was not going to turn to them for help. While her cousin was cuddling that soppy Becky, she would solve his problems single-handed. Then she could marry him when she grew up.

She moved to the elevator, took it up half a floor, flipped a press-stud and opened the secret entrance to Mike's suite. A second door challenged her. She gave it her vocal pattern with a few off-key notes from the aria 'Slander is a whispering zephyr' from *The Marriage of Figaro*, and it opened to her.

Mike Surinat's silliest holman greeted her – a replica of himself, dressed in velvets and silken hose, with an emerald as big as a visiphone dial sulking on a ring on one finger. Surinat always said that this alter-ego dressed better than he did, thereby relieving him of the necessity of dressing at all.

'You have come secretly to me at last, Choggles! At last you have perceived that a real man is too gross, too coarse, for an ethereal little creature like you! With me, you can taste forever the delights of a chaste and refined love!'

'Oh, stop it, you know you'd hate me when I reached puberty, you little Lewis Carroll, you! Let me through to the watchroom. I want to view the occupant of Suite Fourteen.'

She swept imperiously past the holman with a penultimate drip from her swimsuit. The holman retired to his
nook. To save power, he would switch himself off until a
human presence activated him again.

Choggles was now in the heart of the castle. An elevator
carried her down to its bowels in one great peristaltic rush.

Here were the old dungeons, where malefactor and
innocent alike had once awaited the pleasure of the
judiciary system of Austria–Hungary, while rotting off
like autumn plums into their boots. Now, there was not so
much as a trace of footrot; indeed the ranked machines,
the grills, the blank panels, the gentle drip of time like
plasma, gave the place an antiseptic if not cheerful air.
Choggles went over to the console governing spy-views of
all castle rooms, and switched on.

It was a day of holiday, or else there would have been at
least a technician on duty down here. But Surinat had
gone off technicians. He now preferred to live quietly
here; she had faith in everything her uncle did, and so did
not question his preference, adoring the colossal fantasy
of Slavonski Brod Grad.

In the very first month of the war, the great dam at the
Iron Gates on the Danube had blown out of existence. It
was hit by thermo-nuclear bombardment from the forces
supporting capitalist-communist union. The mighty cliffs
of the southern Transylvanian Alps had been thrown still
higher. For a few months, volcanic activity convulsed the
whole area as a result of the bombardment. It was
Europe's first sniff of coming Armageddon.

Such was the tumult of the war, that the news
penetrated only slowly that the course of the Danube was
irredeemably blocked. Its egress to the Black Sea was
gone. The Danube began to back-fill, its floods tumbling
out darkly over rich wheatlands. That grand old fortress of
legend and song, Smederevo, Smederevo that presided

54

over the twilight of a state, Smederevo took leave of five centuries of history and sank below the smacking waves. Soon the whole Pannonian Plain was flooded, from as far west as decaying Varazdin, as far south as Slavonski Brod and as far north as Balaton, the Bakony Forest and the foothills of the Slovakian Ore Mountains, in south-eastern Czechoslovakia. So was re-created the ancient Pannonian Sea, such as had existed through aeons of prehistoric time.

Slavonski Brod Grad was almost empty at that time. The bailiff had called Surinat, asking how he should deal with streams of refugees arriving at the higher ground on which the ancient pile stood. Mike Surinat had flown in to supervise at his father's wish – and he had shown little inclination ever to fly out again. The immense work of modernization had gone on about him while he camped in a tower and the refugees lived in shacks in the inner court.

Lattices flicked in the view-screen, fled forward, vanished. A clear picture snapped into existence. A fish-eye lens showed Choggles the main compartment of Suite Fourteen.

Zoomer was having his drink. He clutched the glass in one hand. With the other hand, he fondled his immense pendant.

'Symbolic!' the child said aloud. 'Dolly, I wonder if he's going to do anything dirty!' She bounced up and down in her seat.

His movements, however, were clean and boring – as are the movements of most people under observation, Choggles had found, perhaps because expectations of something more secret, more astounding, are always high.

Zoomer picked up a hand control and flicked on the holoscillator in the corner of his room. A mist formed and dispersed, and a cute little panorama of mill and barnyard was revealed, glowing under a hayrick-sized sun in cereal-packet colours. Choggles recognized the artwork as

55

Zoomer's own – after all, he was the original cereal-packet man in 3-D, until the government computer complex bought him up. She was probably looking at his last creation.

Through the fish-eye lens, with its axial distortions, Zoomer's farmyard looked rather exciting. It had outré angles of roofs and barn bearing down on pasteurized cows with pristine rumps. Farmhands stomped to infinity with macabre step. Dr Caligari had gone Disney. Weather maxima were amazing, too. As in all Monty Zoomer works, the *mise en scène* was as de-atmospherized as a Pre-Raphaelite painting.

Amusing things were happening in the barnyard, like a funny little fat man falling off a tractor into a butt of rainwater. Zoomer was always for action: an adequate substitute for wit, as many an impresario has found, to the subsequent betterment of his bank balance.

Behind Choggles, a soundproof door chugged closed.

Someone was entering the watchroom!

Disturbed, vaguely guilty, Choggles switched off the viewer. Electronic orders of zoomastigina swirled in a second's glorious life.

'Mother!'

A wave of relief and pleasure and surprise swept over her. She had thought her mother on Mars.

Leda Chaplain was generally referred to by gossip-writers as 'statuesque', although which statue they had in mind was never revealed. She was tall, certainly, and spirited, always well-groomed, and possessed a rather horsey face. An equestrian statue, possibly.

Looking remarkably like her photos, she advanced into the room. She extended her arms to her daughter, who ran into them.

'Mother! I thought you were on Mars!'

'I was on Mars. As you see, I am not now!'

'Oh, Mother, how lovely to see you! Come and talk to Becky and Mike and Durrant. They're – well, they should be around soon . . .'

'I'd love to see them, darling, but this is rather urgent. It's you I've come for.'

Choggles look up at her, curiously.

'Is anything wrong?'

'It's your father. They've found him.'

'But Father's dead . . .'

'We thought he was dead . . . He's alive, in one of the concentration camps in the Syrtis.'

Leda had taken up war work. When the war ended, she shipped to Mars to do what she could for the millions of unfortunates who had been incarcerated in concentration camps there. The confusion, the disorganization, the endless involvement of misery which confronted her then were still not entirely vanquished. By the end of the war, the survivors of the camps had, in many cases, no relations or homes on Earth to return to; or they were too enfeebled to make the journey. Or they had lost their identity under the personality-changes inflicted on all of them during the start of their incarceration. Mars was an Auschwitz planet.

'Father alive . . .' The child could not take it in. She stared almost in disbelief at her mother. Leda looked tired and empty. 'Can we go to him! Is he . . . very different?'

'I haven't even had the chance to see him myself. I was about to leave Mars when the news came through to Nixonville. The proof seems incontrovertible. I want you to come back to Mars with me. I'm going to need help – you know the hatred with which Auden is generally regarded.'

'Of course I'll come . . .'

Her mother took her hand. 'I hoped – I knew you'd say that! Can you come at once?'

'How do you mean, at once?'

'Exactly that, my pet. At once. This has to be cloak-and-dagger, darling, if you don't mind. I want us to leave together at once, without telling anyone, not even my nephew.'

She pouted. 'I'm not going to leave without kissing Mike or telling Becky and her dad I'm going. Think how worried Mike would be if I just disappeared. Mummy, what's this all about, anyway?'

'Child, do as I ask! I know best! The universe is a place of perpetual struggle. Secrecy is essential.'

'If you're going to get shirty . . .' She backed away, eyes anxiously searching her mother's face, thinking how the desolation of Mars had entered that well-known face.

'I'm sorry – I'm not shirty. I'm just nervous. Listen, there are many nasty sinister things going on between the planets. Lives are in danger, yours and mine included, as wife and daughter of a famous and much-hated man. Let's go! Once we are safe in space, you can beam signals to your cousin to your heart's content. I'll speak to him too, and explain everything over the scrambler.'

'Are you sure?'

'I give you my word.'

'I can't go in this sopping suit!'

'There are clothes in the ferry.'

'Where's the ferry?'

'Come with me – I'll show you.'

She hesitated. 'Mother, I'm scared.'

'Everyone's scared these days – with good reason. Mars is even worse than Earth. But I'll look after you. Your father needs us, that's the prime consideration.'

So she went, clutching her mother's thin hand. Her mind swam with the electronic zoomastigina of confusion. The war had been over so long . . . And her mother and father had been separated before the war. Still, there was

58

compassion. Her mother was a compassionate woman, grim though she was at present. Mars . . . Dolly, what would she do on Mars, what could she do? Still, it would be an adventure. Her friends would be jealous. But Mars . . . in this sort of holothriller way . . .

She was hardly aware of how they slipped together from a rear entrance to the Grad, of climbing into a car and driving to a desolate stretch of coast, where a machine waited. Nor did she realize at first that this was an ordinary flying machine, unfitted for space. In fact, it looked rather like Monty Zoomer's, the little she had seen of it from a distance.

Numbly, Choggles admired her mother's skill at the controls as she slumped back into an embracer, feeling it wrap her gently and seductively round. They lifted, banking and swinging grandly as they climbed. Momentarily, she glimpsed through the nearest port breakers marking a dark shoreline, followed by an elaborate small flower in the night. It was Slavonski Brod Grad, by the far Pannonian Sea, warm, civilized – as civilization went – filled with kindly and intelligent people who loved her (as well as the other anti-life kind who didn't) . . . And the blossoming sight, as it swept by and was replaced by the stupider nullity of night, jerked her out of her passive mood.

She jumped up, shaking off the sucking embrace of the chair.

She was confronted by a pair of glassily triumphant eyes.

'Mother!'

'Sit down!'

She balanced herself against the animal surge of acceleration, light on her small feet, still shedding a warm trickle of water down one leg. A line from a favourite poem of her cousin's tracered past her attention and she blurted a frightened misquotation.

'"You are, but what you are—."' And the words triggered their own answer.

'You're not my mother! You're a holman!'

She started to scream, unloading the decibels from her ten-year-old lungs right into that frozen expression of triumph. By then, they were no more than a zoomastiginum in the upper air.

7

'Harry! Harry!' he bawled through the pouring rain. He'd bawled for his father like that, in the old man's dying days. Maybe it just meant he was a shouting man. 'Harry, for crabs' sakes!'

Harry looked round, weary on his little eminence, still clutching his tired sword. Mud and blood were plastered over the clothes plastered to his meagre body.

'What d'you want?'

'Harry, if you weren't doing this, what would you most like to be doing?'

Harry and Julliann roared with laughter. They came and stood closer bellowing like old warthogs at Julliann's joke. Gururn looked on puzzled, false mouth plastered across his splanchnocranium. He did not get the joke. He did not get jokes.

'Hey, Gururn, relax, will you? – There's a lull in the storm!' Harry the Hawk called to him.

Gururn made some sort of a gesture, shambled towards the others, his two human friends in this inhuman desert. The fight between their gigantic ally Milwrack and the Whistling Hunchback still continued over the ridge; the elements were joining in, though growing somewhat atmospherically bored. Every clout across the shoulder, every fall on to knees, every whistling grunt from Whistling Hunchback, was celebrated in the heavens by a lightning flash, a gust of north wind, or a fresh cloudful of hail, slung down like chilled buckshot over the battle area. Now and again, an eagle was tossed in too, Boreasborne. As if intelligent enough to be scared, Harry's goshawk clung bedraggled to its master's shoulder, clung there throughout the battle with the ravening Adolescents, losing the odd feather, croaking the odd word of encouragement to its master.

The trio stood there resting, steaming.

Mud poured past their ankles like failed chocolate pudding.

'Let's go and look at the guys we killed. It will help keep our spirits up,' Julliann said. He also had a theory that he should always keep his mob on the move, so that they had no time to think about their wounds or his failure to pay their social security.

They trudged over high ground, exchanging mud for old heaped snowbanks such as pervaded the whole region they had been travelling for so long. The spectacular suns overhead lit them like automobile headlights, making the going even more difficult.

'I've passed nothing but ice and snow for days,' Harry grumbled.

'A cup of really hot toddy could change that fast.'

The first corpse they came on was lying face down in the dirt. Julliann rolled him over with a boot. It was an Adolescent, encased in green leather. Half his cranium and the top of his face had been sliced off – not wisely, maybe, but too well. Julliann bent suddenly and prodded with a finger in the mess of semi-rigid brains.

'Don't be disgusting,' Harry said. 'I hope you're going to wash your hands afterwards. What are you looking for anyway? Chewing gum?'

61

For answer, Julliann came up with a little amber bead. It rolled into the palm of his hand. He held it for inspection under Harry's nose. Harry moved his nose The bead was shaped like a sucked lozenge with two thread-fine horns only a few microns long protruding at one end.

'Know what that is? It's an electrode.' A fleck of gory matter still adhered.

'How did you know it was there?'

'I didn't know, but I expected to find it. I saw one in spilled brains yesterday, and another a couple of days back.'

'You must look harder at spilled brains than I do, partner! Now tell me what an electrode is!'

He yelled as he finished speaking and swung his sword. Julliann and Gururn turned as two and stood shoulder to shoulder. The feral kids were coming again, driving their bull-roaring bikes, their Yankos and Vastis, skidding over the firn, armed with lances and pikes.

'Whooooooooargh!' roared Gururn. He was a good man to have in a battle, pronunciation apart.

The contest was less unequal than it looked. On this broken ground, the bikes made poor going and could, with a well-timed swing, be kicked over. So long had the Adolescents been in the saddle that they were helpless out of it, their atrophied leg muscles unable to bear the weight of their bodies. Also, they had a tendency to run each other over and stab one another in the back with the lances.

It was sixty-four against three. The three triumphed, but it was a dashed close-run thing. Afterwards, they threw a torch on the broken bikes and sat round warming themselves by the fire.

'We could sleep if only it would get dark. Not a chance of that with all these suns clattering round the sky.'

'Never seen anything like it,' Gururn mumbled.

Julliann did not answer. He closed his eyes and tried to think the logic-line of his life clear. It made no sense even to him, and he was no intellectual. There had been other occasions when he had tried to sort things out, and something in his brain just switched—

'Julliann, Julliann . . .'

He roused, he was himself again.

'Let go of my shoulder, what are you shaking me for?'

'Are you all right? You flung that bead away and then you went sort of numb.' Harry's face was flecked with fear and saliva.

'Let me alone!'

They saw a sausage-shaped mauve sun rising at a rate of knots. It took some believing. The supernatural nature of the struggle between Milwrack and the Hunchback was being somewhat overplayed.

He slumped before the crackling Yankos in misery, not daring to think about what he needed to think about but could not. How many people had had electrodes inserted in their skulls?

He jumped up and screamed, 'They're meddling with us! They're meddling with us! This isn't happening! It's an illusion!'

Harry jumped up, scattering the goshawk. 'That again! You need a toddy too, pal! Let's go and join up with Milwrack.'

The goshawk circled round the snowed-out rocks, banking tightly, returned, and took a really firm grip on Harry's right shoulder.

8

Smix-Smith was not so much a corporation, more a lay of wife, an executive wit had once remarked, referring to his uxorious boss. But humour was filed swiftly away when the boss was on the scene. Even when the boss's dopple was on the scene.

Attica Saigon Smix came out of Trexmissions Bay at full tilt, caused by the incline of the ramp on which his stretcher ran. The vehicle had its course prescribed. It moved through the mammoth building at close to the speed of sound, down corridors of widths scarcely greater than its own, now and again shuttling into elevator shafts and becoming its own cage. It ejected its human-type burden into a small but luxuriously appointed presidential ante-room to the World Executive Council Chamber, Code Name Beta Suite, on the walls of which hung, among other treasures, the only Tiepolo etching in the world to survive the war. It depicted the flight into Egypt, and was reputed to be more valuable than Egypt itself.

As he climbed off the stretcher, Attica Saigon Smix was greeted by one of his secretaries for state, Chambers Technical Dictionary (for so this intellectual bonhomous kyllosic Christian member of the Kikuyu tribe had been christened). Chambers proffered a potted version of recent events. Attica Saigon Smix read it through swiftly as he entered the council chamber.

Ten members of the executive were present round the traditional table. He wondered if any of them had been through the same complicated transcendences to get here as he. Lights above their seats indicated whether they were their own embodiments or projects of some kind.

Two members were companalogs, which CC found it convenient to have around. For the rest, all had been top-level members – until a few fleeting but crippled years ago – of various national governments. Ex-Red Russians and Chinese sat down with ex-democratic Netherlanders, ex-fascist South Americans, and Americans like Dwight Castle.

Just as they had once carved up their own states, these men now settled down amicably with their ex-enemies to carve up the Earth, together with such portions of the solar system as could be appropriated, discovering with alacrity and pleasure how much they had in common with their opposite numbers.

How H.G. Wells, Wendell Willkie, and other valiant dreamers of the World State would have cheered to see their vision made actual! At last, major ideological differences, the plague of the twentieth century, had been healed. 'United World!' was now slogan and actuality.

Those few billions of human beings who objected to the idea for one reason or another were being eliminated as fast as the limited efficiency of the post-war machine allowed.

As he settled into his seat at the head of the table, Attica Saigon Smix nodded to the Committee. One curt nod. All-inclusive. Nevertheless, though all were included, some were more included than others – in particular, John Thunderbird Smith.

John Thunderbird Smith was one of the companalogs, a particularly terrible-looking creature owing to the glittering spodumene substance in its ocular proprioceptors and a certain *graininess* in its overall composition. (It had been known, when debate was most furious, to become just slightly, nastily, translucent, as if in grisly warning of what might happen to the rest of them.)

Taking the initiative immediately, Attica Saigon Smix

said, 'This is Full Emergency. Some of you are present here in person. Don't let it occur again. Send dopples of some kind. You are not expendable.' He wondered if any of them had found a bolt-hole as safe and undetectable as he and Loomis had done. 'Let's begin business.'

Before the words had separated from the carbon dioxide in Smix's mouth, Thunderbird Smith said, 'We must not leave Beta Suite until we have decided how to program CC best to meet the crisis.'

'Which crisis is that?' Sun Hat Sent, the Chinese delegate, inquired.

Briefly, with a human gesture of despair, Thunderbird Smith let his gaze rest in pleading on the oil portrait of Sir Noël Coward on the wall next to the Tiepolo.

'The crisis, the new crisis we have code-named Operation Seventh Seal. You have summary sheets before you. They may be precis-ed as follows, and I accept the deductions arrived at by CC in its AAA8334 circuits, the circuits dealing with malfunctions of the external world. During the war, as most of us recall, certain thermo-nuclear components were employed in hand weapons upwards to full-scale multi-megaton aerial-descent devices. The most noteworthy of such devices delivered adjacent to this region was an old-fashioned but considerable device of a fission-fusion-fission type, targeted on the ground-area Iron Gates Dam, power-centre of the Jugoslav–Hungarian Dissident Nations.

'That device was comparatively clean. Nevertheless, its fireball generated a temperature estimated at 500,500,000 degrees, Celsius.

'Later devices attained higher maxima, temperature-wise. The Operation Snowfire raids on Luna, in which the satellite was completely destructed, attained maxima somewhat in excess of one hundred times the Iron Gates device, being able to draw on a planetary core as an additional heat-boost.'

'This is steam under the bridge – let's get to the nitty-gritty, Smith,' said Savro Palachinki, who had been old-fashioned enough to arrive *in corpore sano*.

With another agonized glance at the portrait of the man who had provided inspiration for the nomenclature of the chambers they were in, Thunderbird Smith continued, 'This background is an integral part of the Seventh Seal emergency. In brief, improved devices developed towards war-end attained temperatures and pressures in excess of a thousand times those found at the heart of the Sun. We are still living with – and in some unhappy cases dying with – the after-effects of these remarkable scientific achievements.'

The one woman at the table, Sue Fox, said, 'At the risk of interrupting, Mr Thunderbird Smith, we should consider these aspects of the victorious peace as no longer worth discussion. After all, the cease-fire was signed over five years ago. As I have explained before, the radio-turbulences of spaceflight, the continued escalation of world temperature norms, the electrical storms, and of course the soaring cancer-death rate – in which we all take such a sympathetic interest – these after-effects of war, vexing though they may be, would nevertheless have manifested themselves, even if perhaps less dramatically, in the *ordinary course of progress*, war or no war. And we should therefore cease to keep harping on them!'

'Sue's right,' Dwight Castle declared. It was the only thing he said all meeting.

Attica Saigon Smix saw that it was time he took over. By diving in before the woman stopped talking, he was on launch before Thunderbird Smith, who, being machine and therefore not quite human, remained silent.

'We have harped on these things, these malfunctions of our biosphere, simply because they are now part of existence. Now we have to deal with a malfunction of one section of the environment about which we know remarkably little, whose functionings we have hitherto been privileged to take for granted: Time. Time itself. The orderly function of time, just like the orderly function of space, has become at least partially inoperative through what you, Mrs Fox, chose to call "the ordinary course of progress".'

'CC is already working on the formulae of space-time displacement,' Thunderbird Smith said. 'Unfortunately, figures are scarce as yet. Positive proof of time-malfunction was provided by the disappearance of a spy-bell under observation near Jupiter in Code Area Conquest, its exact coordinates being known. Our reasons for believing that the spy-bell lapsed with the space surrounding it into a matrix hitherto regarded as *past* are set out in Technical Appendix Two A before you. Please familiarize yourselves with the exposition.'

'What other evidence have we that this highly unlikely state of affairs obtains?' Savro Palachinki asked, biliously eyeing his way through the photostats of formulae before him. 'How do we know this isn't just CC chuntering to itself, with all due respect?'

'We already take for granted other sorts of space opened up to us through the space-holes or warps caused by intensive gravitational thermo-nuclear disruption,' Attica Saigon Smix said. 'We must now face up to the fact that more than one time can exist simultaneously.'

'Reports coming in confirm that remark,' Thunderbird Smith said. 'I am receiving formulations of them now.' It did not stop him talking.

'We believe we know exactly what phenomena in the physical world we are witnessing. Data is arriving to buttress the hypothesis. Thus it ever was in the history of scientific understanding. Right here in Beta Suite, only three days back, we discussed a report from State Swazi in Africa which announced that a Zulu War had broken out in the Transvaal. The Zulu nation was being led by one Cetewayo. CC dismissed this at the time as unfounded, the factors being unbased in reality. It now seems as if a whole portion of South Africa has slipped back into the year 1879 or thereabouts.'

Chambers, standing behind Attica Saigon Smix, passed him a note. Smix read it out. The icterus index of his face was high. His hand trembled. 'Gentlemen, Russian troops advancing through East Rumelia are strongly attacking the Ottoman Army outside Adrianople. This report is dated January 18th, 1878 . . . Where and what is or are East Rumelia, the Ottoman Army, and Adrianople?'

'Russians! Russian troops? This concerns me!' Savro Palachinki exclaimed, jumping up from the table. 'This pre-eminently concerns me. You must excuse. I will send a dopple in my place as soon as inhumanly possible!'

Another note passed on from Chambers.

'Gentlemen, control yourselves. Britain has invaded Afghanistan. Remember Britain?'

Someone else was jumping up and crying out.

Another note.

'Please, gentlemen – the Khedive of Egypt has been deposed by the Sultan, whoever those persons may be, in a communiqué dated June 1879.

'Carapace! It's spreading!' Sue Fox cried. 'We'll find ourselves in last century before we know it!'

Another note handed forward by the unflustered Chambers.

'Please, friends – order! Montenegro has occupied Dulcigno. Does anyone know where Dulcigno is? Or Montenegro? Please?'

'CC will straighten matters out!' John Thunderbird Smith called above the din. 'These anomalies in the functioning of the natural order cannot be tolerated.'

His last words were lost in a general hubbub of alarm, as Attica Saigon Smix announced the outbreak of war in the Pacific, Chile against Bolivia and Peru.

9

The little figures identifiable as Smith, Smix, Palachinki, Fox, Sent and others glowed and gestured in a monitor screen far away, safe below the stately pile of Slavonski Brod Grad.

As the meeting dissolved in chaos, Devlin Carnate made a final note on a tab, and looked up smiling from the screen. He was a dapper, dark man in his mid-forties with a really terrible past he could not bear to confide to anyone until his second Martini.

He was also one of the most reliable of the Surinat Slavonski permanent staff. The Carnate family were of Italian origin, the three syllables of their name rolling back into the mists of time in at least two narrow little valleys in the Friuli region, where, at no great distance from the gloomy Passo di Predilla, hangs a picturesque ruin still referred to by the few locals who have not fled to Klagenfurt, Ljubljana or Trieste (for those doubtful sanctuaries lie equally distant from the pass) as the Villa de Carnate.

The Carnates who also fled to foreign fields were wont to refer grandly to this ruin as a *castello*. They were a warlike lot; or were known to carry arms; or at least tortured peasants; or somehow acquired a sinister reputation; or maybe it was just that the great-grandparents

both suffered from severe nystagmus – a complaint regarded locally with more superstitious dread than
sympathy – curiously enough, since your Predilino is
hardly renowned for beauty, goitre, glossopasm,
ureteropyelitis and stone being the least of it in the way of
common regional afflictions.

All of which is more apropos than may appear. Because, in a brave attempt to abstain from torture and ill-
health simultaneously, Luigi Carnate had come down
from the hills and, setting his sights considerably higher
than Klagenfurt (like many men with large moustaches
and small physiques, he had considerable ambition), he
had headed for Kenya. And reached it just as it attained
independence and he got his majority.

The two got on well together. Luigi acquired wealth, a
devoted family servant, and a wife. She was the only
Croatian lady he met in the wilds beyond Nairobi (there
were no signorine at all). She gave her name as Myrtr
Tjidvyl, her address as The Irish Guest House, Bulawayo,
and they were married half-way through the succeeding
week. She made an ideal wife, although it transpired later
that she had operated a rhinoceros-horn smuggling-ring
between Rhodesia and Zambia. Luigi and Myrtr had two
offspring, Devlin the boy and Javlin the girl, neither of
whom cared greatly for the African climate. They were
heading back for the sombre valleys of the Passo di Predilla when the war broke out through nobody's fault.

After many wanderings which are not apropos, albeit
highly amusing (they included, for instance, a compulsory
stay in a subterranean cell in the fortress of Petrovaradin,
within which – many years earlier – a dissident Communist
leader named Milovan Djilas had spent some months,
during which period he wrote a secret, scurrilous, but not
necessarily untrue account of the secret life of President
Tito, claiming that the real Tito had been shot during the

Spanish Civil War, to be replaced by a British secret agent resembling him so closely that only Winston Churchill and Tito's old Aunt Bjela could tell the difference; the fake Tito freed his supposed country from the Nazis, according to Winston Churchill's plan, staying on at Churchill's request to repeat his success by saving the country from Stalin, by which time he had somewhat over-played his hand and Churchill was dead anyway; since the old aunt had also pegged out by now, the fake Tito might be considered for all intents and purposes to be the real Tito, except that he wasn't a very good communist – naturally enough for a solid blue Conservative Old Etonian and Balliol man – and he further added lustre to his record by saving the country from its Croat-Serbian schism, although while so doing he unguardedly let drop clues which led his old rival Djilas to the truth, Djilas being prompted by a long-nourished suspicion of the neo-Tito's abnormally large, at least for a Communist leader, library of British comic novelists from Henry Fielding to P.G. Wodehouse, Evelyn Waugh, Anthony Powell, C.P. Snow, Eric Linklater, Kingsley Amis and Ivy Compton-Burnett; finding that Djilas had pieced together his long – and well-kept secret, Tito – real name Henry Algernon Bletts-Newcombe – incarcerated Djilas in Petrovaradin, where Djilas promptly set the whole amazing story down on paper and hid it behind a stone in his cell which, remaining unfortunately uncleaned for fifty years – but *realpolitik* are built on such trivial lacunae – only came to light when Javlin Carnate was dusting down spider's webs; she and her brother, thanks to their education at their mother's Croatian knee, were able to read the manuscript and later smuggle it out with them, getting it published clandestinely in Italy, in the form of a novel entitled *Bletts-Newcombe to the Rescue*, which became, in a clandestine Ukrainian translation, a best-seller in the

USSR), the brother and sister arrived at Slovonski Brod Grad. There they lived quietly, Devlin in the war-rooms, Javlin in the kitchens, where her cuisine was one of the pleasanter features of a stay in the Grad – not that mealie meal is precisely to everyone's taste.

Some of their earlier connections had proved useful to the Surinat organization. In particular, their father's devoted family servant, Chambers Technical Dictionary, upon Luigi's death, had gone from strength to strength, securing a job with the Smix family which eventually paid off well. It had been Chambers' television camera, concealed under his beard, which had provided the fortress by the Pannonian Sea with its unrivalled front-seat view of the top-secret session in the Beta Suite.

Devlin Carnate made his way to Mike Surinat and handed over the resumé he had made of the proceedings.

'Thanks,' Surinat said. But he had other things to worry about. He pocketed the vital resumé and turned back to the group with whom he was talking, among them Gilleleje, Becky, me.

'We've got to get Choggles back,' he said. 'Any suggestions?'

Nobody answered.

'How typical, how symbolic,' he snarled. 'Here we are camping out in the decaying remains of the nineteenth century and these fearful twentieth-century things are happening to *our* century . . .' The words in which he placed such trust failed him. His rage bubbled in him like strontium-and-soda. His gaze would have disarmed an octopus at twenty paces.

Since the news of his cousin's kidnapping had been brought to him, he had realized that he loved the child to the point of incest, cradle-snatching, and matrimony.

'I blame myself,' he said, not looking at Becky, who was

studiously not looking at him . . . 'Any answers from Tracings yet, Per?'

Per Gilleleje, a big neatly manicured Dane with the ashen look of a man who does all his sunbathing under the Pole Star, turned from the radionics seat. 'I'm getting the Wait signal.'

They were trying to discover where the flier in which Choggles had been abducted had gone. The certain way to find out was through Tracings.

Just as every form of transport, in an earlier age, had been licensed, so now it was permanently tell-taled, whether sea-, air-, land-, or space-going. A small device (analogous to the Schally-Chaplain switch in the human brain) built into the engine ensured that every journey was recorded somewhere in a never-sleeping memory-bank among a million million similar chocolate-bar-sized memory-banks in some unspeakable vacuum-filled sub-terranean vault beneath one of the major (and also sub-terranean, because computers had really gone for the hypogeal thing) think-complexes.

This travel-log information was available to certain code-level subscribers – and everyone perforce sub-scribed. Tracings was part of CC

'The Wait signal means they're checking back on us,' Becky said quietly. 'If you'll forgive my passing the time by stating the obvious—'

Gilleleje raised his hand. 'Coming through . . . Miami . . . Right . . . Roger.'

He broke the circuit, read from his monitor. 'Flier in question abandoned at In-World Flight Park 3, Miami Space Field. Arrived 0747 hours GMT this morning.'

'Could mean anything,' Surinat said vexedly. 'Could be a herring of deepest redness designed to scatter us round the solar system while Choggles is held in Florida . . . Why take her off-Earth? Surely the operator, whoever he is, can't be that big? Why don't they get in touch with us?' He smote his open palm. 'How I blame myself . . .'

He glared at the image of himself, foppishly dressed in silken hose and velvet jacket, with hair in ringlets, which stood silent against one wall.

'Come here, Surinat!'

The holman moved forward. Putting considerable weight and venom behind his swing, Surinat hit himself just behind the point of the jaw. Caught unprepared, he sprawled backwards, striking one shoulder against a chair and over-turning it. Nobody moved. This was just the Mad Mike Surinat legend going on; nobody had to do anything about it.

'Tell me again,' Surinat demanded. 'What happened to Choggles in this room?'

From the carpeting, mock-Surinat said, 'She left here with a companalog of her mother. It must have been a companalog from the conversation I overheard as they left – very creative and resourceful answering on the machine's part.'

'I should have been alert. Someone was getting their hand in on the estate earlier. I bumped into a dopple of some kind in the garden not an hour before Choggles was snatched; I should have realized someone was turning a projector. Monty Zoomer must be behind all this. We found that Choggles had been observing him over the watchroom system – the Suite Fourteen key was still de-pressed on the monitor bank, although the current was switched off. And she and my fake Aunt Leda left by Monty's flier.'

'It doesn't have to be Monty,' Per Gilleleje said. 'He's outside creating hell with everyone about having his flier stolen, and the depressed key could be coincidence.'

'Repeat to me word for word what Choggles and her fake mother were saying as they left here,' Surinat de-manded of Surinat.

From the floor, rubbing his jaw jerkily so that the emerald on his finger flashed like a berserk traffic light, Surinat said, 'As I told you, Leda said she would take care of her daughter. She said not to be scared. Everyone was scared nowadays, she said. She must have been a companalog – you've just checked with Nixonville, Mars, and we know the real Leda is there, as she has been for two years.'

His octopus-disarming gaze blazing again, Surinat said, 'I stand degraded by my own self-indulgence and narcissism. Surinat, you are all I loathe in myself. After this interview, I will have you dissolved. I will have a companalog instead, whose every observation will be fed into a computer where it can be instantly retrieved without nonsense. Now, before that happens, deliver to us as ordered a word-for-word report of what you heard them say as they passed you. Verbatim, understand?'

'They said very little,' said the holman, sulkily. 'As Choggles's presence activated me, she was saying, "Mother, I'm scared." And Leda replied, "Everyone's scared these days – with good reason. Come, I'll look after you, your father needs us." And Choggles said, "I still can't get it through my head he could be alive." By then they were at the door, the outer door—'

Surinat cut him off. 'Why didn't you tell us this bit about her father before?'

'You shut me up.'

'The Leda-comp claimed Auden Chaplain was alive! What else did you hear?' Gilleleje asked. 'Why hold out on us? Have you been tampered with?'

'I heard Leda say something about "Those terrible camps on Mars hide many secrets," and then they had the door open and Choggles was round the corner, so that I deactivated . . .'

Gilleleje, Surinat, Hornbeck and the others stared at each other.

The name of Choggles's father had not been spoken in Slavonski for a long while – or not aloud, at least. Auden Chaplain was a name of fear to millions, and reverence to many more. Auden Chaplain was The Man Who Had Solved the Population Problem.

A silence jammed with non-verbal radiations vibrated in the room. The inchoate and guilt-ridden history of the West, the legendary patching of mis-applied science with further mis-applied science, the hopeless dichotomies between individual aspiration and organizational necessity – all those calamitous factors apparently inseparable from escalating knowledge and numbers – were incarnate in the name of Auden Chaplain; and no one here was free of personal involvements with him, or with the dark strata of recent history which he had briefly, unluckily and secretively dominated.

Wearily, Surinat turned towards the visiphone. 'The Idealists must mobilize. If Auden is still alive, there's nothing for it. We may get on the Choggles trail later, but Auden has to be our prime target. Sanctus! If life didn't exist, it would be unnecessary to invent it!'

As his hand went up to the phone, it chimed.

Devlin Carnate's dark face appeared in the globe.

'Mike, there's an incoming call for Zoomer.'

'Forget it! We're stuck with something bigger. I want a general IDI call.'

Devlin said forcefully, 'This is big too. We keyed an unscrambler on to the incoming call. It's Attica Saigon Smix calling Zoomer.'

'Smix! Smix phoning Zoomer! Here!' He felt his own weakness, his slowness, his inability for action, his incapacity in the high-flying world where corporations had bought out consciences. Even his intuition failed in this instance. What connection could there be between the CC boss – the ruler of the world, so far as the ruler was human and the world coherent enough to be ruled, the arch-enemy of IDI – and pop holodreamer two-a-penny Monty Zoomer? 'I'll take this over. Per, you raise all Three Star leaders of IDI, okay?' He never said 'okay'.

They were all on the move, buttoned for crisis. The quiet voice of Becky Hornbeck said; 'Then Zoomer *is* responsible for the kidnap.'

They looked at her and nodded; the intuition was irrefutable.

On the side screen, as Surinat switched over, the haggard, kakistocratic, famed face of Smix of Smix-Smith, the last big corporation that had swallowed all the others, including the USA and the USSR, swam up in shades of living mauve and grey, saying, 'I'm worried about my dear Loomis, Zoomer. Without wanting to explain the circumstances, I have had you traced and am impelled to contact you—'

A shade showed behind him, a speckle-fleshed hand. There were muttered words, Smix looking irritably back over his shoulder – then the screen dissolved into null-transmission patterns.

'Did someone assassinate him?' Becky asked, breathlessly.

'They detected our descrambler and cut contact,' Devlin's voice came through. 'CC – you can't beat 'em . . .'

'Why should he and Zoomer . . .'

At the other end of the room, Per Gilleleje said firmly to his transmitter, 'This must be unbreakable – use the Shelley machine for encipherment. Right? Am I live? Thanks. Calling all units of the IDI, Able Banker calling all units of the IDI . . .'

10

'What a lovely bird!' exclaimed Loomis, pointing up above the dimpling trees.

The flying thing had pretty curly-paper white wings which flapped very slowly and amusingly, like the pages of a book turning. Its body was adorably chubby, and its tail merged into streamers of pretty colours. Its head was round and soft and did not move with the nasty, furtive movements of real birds' heads. Nor were its eyes beady and quick, betraying reptile ancestry. No, children, this lovely white birdie above the dimpling treetops had a face just like a pussy-cat, with a cute little turn-up nose and whiskers of pure whiteness, and lovely china-blue eyes, and a pair of pretty ears.

'It's coming down to see us,' her husband's dopple said.

Sure enough it did, and perched on the innocuous floor of space beside them, where it sat preening prettily, like a budgerigar in slow motion.

'Monty Zoomer does these décors so well,' Loomis said, delightedly. 'There's nothing sordid about them.'

Her words reminded her of other words she had spoken before, perhaps in relation to something else.

'The world is full of such disgusting things. Some people seem to relish dwelling on them – things that deprave them, like sex-and-violence.'

How had it gone? Oh yes.

'But some of us believe that the world could be a better place if we forget everything like that and concentrate on the lovely things with which we are surrounded. When there are so many higher things, why choose the lower? A law ought to be passed . . .'

No, that wasn't quite right.

'You're quite right, my dear,' Attica Saigon Smix said, indulgent towards her as ever. 'There ought to be a law against crime-and-misery. All that sort of people should be locked away, to leave the world sweet for those who find it sweet.'

Well, she wouldn't have put it that way, but why should she contradict a darling like Attica? So she went on.

'There's so much immorality, so much vice, so much cruelty . . . Why should people torture and kill each other when they could paint lovely pictures? Why should they keep on talking about – and actually *doing* – sexual intercourse, when they could keep pets instead?'

The bird said, 'I'm a little pet. Do you love me?' It snuggled up to her and she smoothed its lovely plumage, as soft as snowflakes on kittens.

'That's why I so *admire* you, Attica. You're a world ruler and yet you've never let the world hurt you. You've kept yourself above it. You're a chaste man – well, I think rulers should be chaste, in order to set an example. I know that Stalin, to take another example – well, he has often been reviled since his death, but I remember my mother saying that nobody ever said a word against him in his lifetime – well, I mean, he may have done many terrible things, perhaps he did, but he was good to his children and perfectly clean in his personal life.'

'Do you know that that man, when he was in power,' croaked Attica Saigon Smix's representative, 'he never had a rouble in his pocket . . .'

'That's the sort of thing I mean . . .'

'–because he owned the whole shebang. Everything was his, everything in the whole state.'

'That's what I admire about you, Attica, my love. You own most of the world – well, you know what I mean, don't you? Yet it isn't good enough for you. You designed

80

this whole new perfect world – got Monty Zoomer to design it – specially for us. And it is a perfect world, isn't it, birdy?'

'I've got a nest in a rainbow,' said the birdie. 'A nest made of pretty colours.'

'You know what, Attica . . .'

He knew what was coming, but wanted to hear it again so he nodded and smiled and said, 'What's that, my pet?'

She turned her sweet sleek Persian smile on him.

'We two are very lucky, very special people!'

A big woolly lamb trundled by. It too was smiling. Sheepishly.

Loomis took Attica's hand, gazed tenderly into his eyes, and began to sing in a fluting contralto.

LOOMIS
Here you see how science
  In a most delightful way
Makes surroundings beautiful
  And turns the world to play

This is the dream of mankind through the ages
  The magic transformation scene
Science our Fairy Godmother assuages
  All the ill there's ever been.

ATTICA
I'd hate to disabuse you
  But your calculation's wrong
Your rainbows and your robins love
  Were not bought for a song

This is the nightmare of man through the ages
  There never is a transformation
One man never lifts himself above their rages
  Without another's degradation

The history of cultures
  Is the triumph of the strong
Which all technology can't change
  It can't change R ght and Wrong

81

LOOMIS
Just walk about the garden
  In a most delightful way
Ignore these awful problems
  They're sure to go away

And this is the wish of mankind through the ages
  To find the Eden of his dreams
Love, fly with me from all the Hell of Wages
  Into this Paradise of Seems

TOGETHER
Let's just walk about the garden
  In a most delightful way
Ignore Life's awful problems
  And they're sure to go away

They're sure to go away
  Banished by our dreams
  Banished by our dreams
  Where Is gives way to Seems

11

At least all the instrumentation in the *Doomwitch* was still functioning correctly. The astronomical tracers had soon rediscovered truant Jupiter, now far distant on its orbit, a glittering star to the naked eye. Fixes taken on it, on Mars, on Earth, on Saturn. An easy computation. The humans waited for the computer, waited about eighty nano-seconds. An emotionless announcement.

The four humans not in freeze did not speak for some while. De l'Isle-Evens punched for a re-check, ordered the calculations. Together, they looked the print-out over.

'What's happened to us is what happened to the tight-beam traveller,' Dimittis said. 'We hit a time fault. We are still Here. We just ain't Now.'

Guy Gisbone said, '*It* must have struck a weak fault in time, since we calculated it slipped back only some two years and eight months. Bear in mind how fortunate we are to be taken back with our environment – this station. Otherwise, our bodies would be drifting mummies in space. We were in luck to hit a strong time-fault.'

'I question our good fortune,' Dr Glamis Fevertrees said, with something like a sob. 'What's good about our fortune?'

She seized the scratch-pad again, reluctant to believe the data. 'Two thousand, four hundred and eighty-five years, sixty-nine days . . .'

'Let's check again,' Dimittis said.

'You check – I'll institute a radio-search,' Gisbone said.

With his eye to a telescope, de l'Isle-Evens said, 'Earth is a thin crescent, barely visible. Anyone want a look? You realize Plato and Socrates are alive down there?'

'To hell with Plato and Socrates!' Glamis said vigorously. 'Think they'd know how to get us down out of orbit, even if we got back and started circling Earth?'

'Say, what a song!' Dimittis exclaimed, emerging from his gloom and clapping his hands. 'Suppose we got down there and told old Plato how all that Golden Age Greek larking about started the whole Western science thing? Maybe they'd turn it up, or destroy all the manuscripts, or make Aristotle drink hemlock! Then everyone could live in a peaceful pastoral world ever after.'

Gisbone looked sourly up from the row of symbols (mainly Greek) he was writing. 'You're half-educated, boy. The Greeks lived in miserable little squabbling city states, struggling and starving in a series of futile wars.

Read Aristophanes! The Golden Age is a myth. There never was a Golden Age, except in people's heads.'

Glamis repeated the line *sotto voce*. 'There never was a Golden Age, except in people's heads. Speaks well for the inside of people's heads . . .' She thought longingly of her secret friends in the IDI.

'At least I had a good idea for a sci-fi story,' Dimittis said, unrepentantly. 'So what do we do, Daddy?'

His question hung unanswered. The others were busy. He went back into the galley to cook more flapjacks. Twenty-five centuries had elapsed since he ate last.

The radio search revealed silence on all frequencies. The universe gave forth its hydrogen hiss like a long pollen-stricken breath. Suns fried in their jackets, radio stars, X-Ray galaxies, quasars and all the rest of the meagre furniture of space yielded its usual quota of vexing noise on familiar wavelengths. But not a crackle of man-made signal anywhere.

'That's it,' Gisbone said. 'There's just us four up and about in the solar system.' Perhaps he was trying to make it sound funny.

'Better get estimates of our local resources,' Glamis said.

Dimittis stuck his head round the door. 'Maybe we should conserve energy by putting one of us back into semi-deep. I'd volunteer. You could wake me when we hit a time-turbulence that leads to home.'

De l'Isle-Evens came over to Glamis and Gisbone, tapping a light-pen against his palm and ignoring Dimittis.

'We don't have many alternatives. We're in a volume of empty space, planet-wise. The way we're fixed, we're about equidistant from Mars and Earth.'

'Maybe there's an ancient civilization going strong on Mars that could help us,' Dimittis suggested. 'I always wanted to visit Barsoom – must be so much more fun than Nixonville!'

'Dim,' de l'Isle-Evens said, turning round, 'any more irrelevant remarks from you, and you *will* go into semi-deep.'

'I don't know why I'm joking when I'm so scared. Glamis, you're a subjectionist, you tell me.'

'Defence-mechanism,' she said succinctly, and de l'Isle-Evens continued.

'I've talked with the computer and it points out there is a fair level of probability that our signals might be picked up in the future – I mean, in our own time – even though we do not pick up signals from them. It hasn't figured out how, since there is insufficient data to go on. Could be a one-way entropy-flow; obviously, the whole new discipline of time-energy is open to investigation. The suggestion is that we signal our whereabouts and when-abouts to Mars Base, hoping they pick it up.'

'We'd better do that,' Guy Gisbone said. 'Though they're unlikely to lay on a rescue operation.'

'At least we can alert them as to what the cosmos is doing to itself, if they have not already discovered it for themselves,' Glamis said. 'If this sort of thing is universal, Earth must be chaos now! May I also send a personal message to my friend Jack Dagenfort in Spain?' She must warn the IDI of what was happening.

'We'll see if the comp can come up with any way of locating our proximity to time-turbulences, or whatever we're going to call them.'

'I have it working on that problem already, Guy,' de l'Isle-Evens said, with a pleasant hint of superiority.

'Good. We may find a nice obvious factor, like abrupt alternation in proton-flow strengths near the field-fractures. This turbulence we're in may be narrow in spatial extent. Advised of the fact, we could possibly blast out of it, back into our own time.'

'That's so.' He started drawing on an extension light-pad. A dot, spirals from it, hyperbola at one end, slanting rays, wedge-shapes here and there. 'Do you agree that these time-pockets are in all probability the result of recent human shenanigans? Good, that's what I think. Thermonuclear breakdown for the very fabric of space-time. We've known it was theoretically possible for at least fifty years. Energy destroying energy. Then the flaws are localized within the solar system. Why have they manifested themselves now, when the war's been over some years? Several possibilities . . .'

'Earth returning along orbit and encountering ruptured area of space-time?' Gisbone asked.

'Possibly. Doesn't matter. Theoretical interest, mainly. Pocket out here, near Jupiter's orbit, where no thermonuclear devices were employed. So it has drifted, presumably. Solar emanations pushing time-pockets away from solar system. Whole system could be free and mended again, good as new, in another few years.'

'Holy sainthoods!' Glamis cried from the radio chair. 'To hear you talk! Just another little bit of technological pollution, eh? It'll blow away like smog over the Bay, will it?' She waved her arms about her head.

'We're only trying to think this thing through logically,' Gisbone said.

'I know. So's the flaming computer. But suppose your references are all wrong! Suppose nothing has happened to us and we're sitting comfortably back home on Earth, 1999 AD, only we've all spiralled round the twonk and are so ego-sick of progress that we're sunk in a mass-hallucination about it? How about working with *that* theory for a change, and see if it doesn't make as much sense as yours!'

Dimittis emerged with a loaded plate.

'Have a flapjack, Beauty. I go along with your theory.

To be confronting this crazy situation sanely, we just have to be mad!'

Glamis accepted a flapjack and returned to her call.

12

Forest Dagenfort came up the beach at Ampurias with one arm curled round the oars over his shoulder and the other dangling a lobster pot. He was barefoot, and wore a pair of jeans rolled above his calf and an old sweater. He was brown and frail. One of the many women who had loved him had described him as having 'the shoulders of a forester and the face of a scholar'. He had asked which forester, which scholar, she was referring to. His son Easter walked behind him, whistling an oldie, 'Younger than Springtime', again in vogue, and carrying a live crab.

Whatever the war had done to most of the rest of the globe, its effect on the Mediterranean had been beneficial. For four years, owing to constant submarine activity, nobody had dared to fish in it. Net and harpoon, hook and trap, gun and basket, had been hung up for the duration. As a result, Nature, ever sly to make a comeback, had lavishly replenished the waters. They were swarming with more edible things than fishermen and tourists had known for half a century.

Every year now, there were many deaths round the coasts of Spain and Italy caused by people eating too much *supion, calamaro, calamar,* or *ligan.*

But to return to the worthy Forest Dagenfort. He had matured early, had suffered few of those adolescent torments, common to most people, which, if untreated, lead to poets and martyrs and tyrants. He had married young, had taken up and never put down teaching. His rise to headmastership had been punctuated by such distinctions as being asked to carry out revisions, in collaboration, for the third edition of *The Household Book of Diseases* and, later, on his own – though not on his own initiative, for the wily publisher who suggested the idea made off with the royalties – to compile *A Handy Guide to Post-War Diseases*.

An ordinary, placid, healthy, successful man. Let's hear no more of him.

His brother is another kettle of fish. Dirtier, less healthy for sure, more neurotic for certain, a woman's man, a man's man, a hound-dog's man, a Porterhouse steak's man come to that, fiendishly intelligent and (as is the case with the fiendishly intelligent) always acting ill-advisedly. This Dagenfort lived on a rougher bit of Spanish coast entirely, never saw his brother, and would have no nonsense with him; he it was that Dr Glamis Fevertrees called across the centuries. His name was Jack Fred Dagenfort, and none of that Forest nonsense with which his elder brother was saddled, to the fatal improvement of his character.

Calls across the centuries were what one might expect Jack Fred Dagenfort to receive. At the age of fourteen, he had received the first such call, when he met and fell in love with May Binh Bong, a gorgeous young creature who had been evacuated from South Vietnam after seeing her father and brothers shot by a North Vietnamese, and the North Vietnamese shot by an American marine, and her mother and sisters raped by the same marine.

Jack found May Binh Bong irresistible, and the merry chase she led him took them through a stony underworld of hard drugs, brutal dosses, glimpses of voluptuously static gods in silver-hemmed nightshirts, tenuous jobs held by brittle fingertips on rigged race-tracks, uncompleted fornications, hepatitis, broken needles, fractured skulls, quick swigs of furniture polish laced with paint-stripper, a sea-voyage at the point of death, Forest's door slamming in his face, a hideout in the loft of a service station, and an otherwise somewhat unsmooth course of true love, terminated only by the death of May Binh Bong when she and Jack, one icy February day, were attempting to thumb a lift across Europe from Amsterdam to Burgos.

Jack got to Burgos and spent six months dying of jaundice, drugs, tuberculosis, a painful hookworm disease called dracunculiasis which brought eruptions of hives all over his body, and sorrow. An old Japanese junkie, a defrocked doctor, looked after him. One day, the junkie doctor's assistant let him kiss her. He threw up illness and addiction and broken hearts, stole a clean blanket from a store at lunchtime, flung it over his suppuration-soaked bunk after lunch, enjoyed the girl on it during most of the afternoon and headed back to resume his previous life on the evening tide.

His old firm would not take him back. He took up stock-car racing and learned medicine in his spare time. He qualified in neurosurgery just before the war broke out. By then, he had graduated to Formula 10 Soup-jet racing driving and that year became the idol of millions by winning the Himalayan Grand Prix on only five wheels. That night, he was too drunk to do anything but drink. But the next night he went to bed with the prettier and younger of the two celebrated and well-heeled Diaphason sisters, Glamis. (Next day, Glamis was married to the Combinationist billionaire politician, Dwight Ploughrite Castle, who – ironically, some might say – gave her one of the Himalayan peaks as a wedding gift.)

When war broke out, Jack Dagenfort must have had another call across a number of jungle-infested centuries. He joined Auden Chaplain's Anti-Birth Unit.

Enough! Enough, at least, to indicate the sort of externals that represented Jack the man. Inside, he had an incurable romantic streak. After all his successes and disasters, he joined the IDI, believing it to be the last refuge for what Mike Surinat once called Belligerent Dreamers. (Jack had then broken with a superb Icelandic girl with yellow eyes and yellow taffeta hair, and retraced, as well as he could remember – and across territory that did not exist any more in the ecological sense of the term – the frantic trail he and May Binh Bong had blazed could-it-really-have-been? twenty-one years ago.)

When he reached Burgos again, it was to arrive just in time for the pauper's funeral of the Japanese junkie doctor. The only other person at the cemetery, beside the priest and some poor guy trying to urinate into the grave ('as a protest against Japanese protectionism' as the poor guy said when Jack kicked him away) was the bird he had laid on the stolen blanket. Fortunately, they did not recognize each other.

Jack invested some of his ill-gotten gains in making a long holofilm of his love-trip. Nostalgia was just coming into fashion again, as it did every year, and *The Heart Block* became to popularity and success what parrots are to psittacosis. Privy.

That was a few years and a few loves ago. Now he lived in western Galicia on a peninsula not far from Vigo, with the last turdlings of the Cantabrian Mountains at his scarred old back, the wet Atlantic at his front, and the big going furnace of his heart and sinews slowly cooling in his centre.

Then Glamis rang him.

'If you're trying to flog me a Himalayan peak, honey, no scab-dissolving dice!' She was still obsessed by him. He could take her or leave her – and had in his time done both.

But she was not looking at him now, was not answering him, was not even properly addressing him, except in an abstract way. For a startled moment, he thought it was a dopple of her on the screen until she explained that she was calling from some three hundred and fifty million miles away and the time of Pericles.

She gave it to him all in a parcel, since she could not receive his signal back. She told him what they knew of the time-turbulence, letting the spy-bell computer flash the data into his terminal ('the mating of minds' was one current term for it), and asked him to pass all information to Mike Surinat, to see if anyone could dream up any effective ideas for rescuing them from the past.

She smiled sadly at a point a few years beyond his left ear, and rang off.

Jack Dagenfort was not a sad man. Indeed, he got up now and marched vigorously around the tile and sheepskin floor a few times, putting his thoughts into order; but behind their organized flow ran a disorganized vein of sudden rebellious misery, like ivy strangling an oak.

Jack Dagenfort was not a poeticizing man. But that lined and distant, perhaps irrecoverable, woman's face, which had once responded to his in the tasks and raptures of love, had opened a lid to his past, revealing a line of a poem to a gardener which had been uttered in *The Heart Block*:

> Could he forget his death, that every hour
> Was emblemed to him by the fading flower?

The universe had that grave and evil flaw to it. Flowers, a woman's beauty, all fair things, made the matter worse, emphasized and underlined the hideous flaw. No evil of which mankind was capable could rival the monstrous cruelty he glimpsed in that faded flower! Momentarily, he was again the youth who could hit a downward track – escape! escape into oblivion and the mind's foreclosure on its bankrupt state! – into the slumberground of hard-stuff.

91

The wattles forming along his jaw hardened. He sat down again, opened up the set, and called Able Banker.

Per Gilleleje came on in a moment. They locked Shelley machines and the signal scrambled, hopping from megahertz to megahertz with the abandon of a hot tin cat.

'I've got a report from one of our Three-stars, Glamis Fevertrees,' Jack said. 'Tape it, feed it straight into Big Granny.' He loaded the previous message through the air, and then said, 'How does that sock you, Gilleleje?'

'I never had much trust in time, anyway,' Gilleleje said. He didn't believe in being surprised. 'We see what we can do, of course. I was about to call you to give you some news, Jack – no less riveting in its way, I suppose. Remember one of your old bosses, Auden Chaplain?'

'He's everyone's old boss, friend.'

'We have an unconfirmed report that he is alive and on Mars. If so, he must be in one of the camps.'

'Wait a minute! Auden alive? How did you get this bit of information, which I just hate to believe?'

'We all hate to believe it. It came from a companalog of Monty Zoomer, the holodreamer, who – we have good reason to suspect – is closely connected with Attica Smix.'

'All sounds pretty vague to me.'

'Maybe. What isn't vague is that Auden's daughter, Choggles, has been abducted. It could have connections with Auden's reappearance.'

'How do I fit in?'

'I hoped you'd ask that. If Auden is reactivated, he could be a powerful tool in the hands of CC and Smix-Smith. We want to get him first. Kill him if necessary, capture him if possible. God knows what he knows!'

'So much the worse for God. Come out with it, Per, what are you asking me to do?'

'The IDI is asking you to get to Mars and sort out Auden. Get him back to us if possible. You worked for him, you know him and you're tough. You're our best man for the job.'

'All that on the strength of some unconfirmed rumour you've picked up?'

'I told you the source of the rumour.'

'Supposing I hit one of these time-turbulences on the way to Mars?'

'Give our love to Glamis and Pericles.'

13

After England and all but the granite hip of Scotland sank beneath the thermonuclear bombardment, thousands of tattered human bodies – sodden and hairless as hand-kerchiefs – were washed ashore by mighty tidal waves, year after year, all along the western coasts of Europe, from Narvik and the Lofoten Islands in the north, from Jutland and the Frisians, from the rocks of Brittany, southward, where the Médoc grapes grow, driven by furious new currents through Biscay, to appear informally dressed as Mortality in the charades at Biarritz and San Sebastian, and along the rainy beaches of Asturias and Galicia, right down to Lisbon and beyond Cape St Vincent, where one of the last time-nibbled deliveries of bodies was made as far afield as the estuary of the Guadalquivir, once the private hunting grounds of the Dukes of Medina Sidonia; there, herons, spoonbills, egrets, and birds fresh from nesting places in the permanent snowcaps of the Sierra Nevada gazed like museum-goers on the salt-pickled remains of the in-habitants of Southampton, Scunthorpe and South Ken, who were now part of some greater and more permanent snowcap. Even later than that, sometimes years later, arms still identifiable as arms, and children's hands resembling sleeping crabs, would be cast up in the Azores or on the black laval sands of the Cape Verde islands.

Many inhabitants of Britain had managed to escape the nuclear doom. British settlements had been established in the USA, in France and elsewhere, their main features comprising a cemetery, a hospital, a court of law, a cricket ground, an Indian restaurant and a good club.

One such settlement stood on the thundering outskirts of Bordeaux. It was called Trafalgar Square, perhaps out of nostalgic sentiment, perhaps as a subtle insult to the French hosts. In the club, an old gentleman sat reading his paper, *The Trafalgar Square*, strictly right-wing.

His name, though it hardly concerns us, was Talbot Youings. He had been a stockbroker in the days when there were stocks to broke, and had married, rather late in life, a widowed lady called Mrs Myrtr Carnate, whose background was very different from his own. She showed a tendency to dislike the six smelly old cocker-spaniels he kept about the house, and he ceased to have any affection for her after the first thirty or forty days of matrimony. They had first drifted and then been blown apart. Now he lived in the club, where the brandy was a very rare and mellow Armagnac 1944.

Youings was, on this morning, feeling far from rare and mellow. He snorted through both barrels of his nose as he scanned the headlines of *The Trafalgar Square*, and his purple-and-white fingers twitched at the thin pages with the almost-living movements of seaweed clinging to a flooded rock. What hideous headlines!

What frightful nonsense!

What terrible people and machines ruled the world, now that Great Britain was no more!

94

Such dreadful things had never happened when he was a youngster!

But even as the thoughts formed in his mind, a recollection grew there too, a recollection of himself in a pair of blue corduroy knickerbockers (they couldn't have been fringed with lace, could they?) playing with picture-bricks on the table in the kitchen beside his dear old mother, who was making – well, it was probably a summer pudding, she made wonderful summer puddings; and the maid was there too, cleaning out the water-softener, and the picture-bricks could be arranged to form a picture of a house on fire; he was quite good at doing it. There was sunlight on the wooden-topped table, table scrubbed till its top was grained like wet polar-bear fur. And suddenly brother Max had dashed in, all excited, cap-in-hand, saying – in a phrase that thereafter became family property – 'Mummy, the Hereafter's here!'

So, grandiloquently, the Great War of 1914 was announced to one middle-class suburban family in the heart of the British Empire, while the sun shone and the picture-bricks tumbled to the coconut matting. Even the British Empire hadn't managed to hold things together.

It prompted an old thought in the old brain.

Turning slowly to the next geriatric chair, Talbot Youings said, 'Praps we're mistaken. Praps things don't get worse. Praps that's just a subjective view of things. Praps things have always been pretty awful, eh? Praps you don't notice how bad things are when you're young, eh?'

His neighbour said nothing. Bloody bore, old Lovehampton! Australian, of course. Married a rather attractive American woman.

Youings turned back to the headlines.

DESPERATE FIGHTING AT ADRIANOPLE GATE
Russian Source States Turks Butchered

ZULULAND — GALLANT BRITISH DEFENCE OF
RORKE'S DRIFT
First Pictures

TOUCHING SCENES AT MAZZINI'S FUNERAL
Casualties Among Weeping Crowd

CLASHING TIME ZONES CAUSE CONFUSION ON
BOURSE
Evidence of Time-Slip Acceleration

LOUISIANA SOLD TO US BIDDERS:
New Orleans in Deal

'ARE WE HEADING BACK TO MIDDLE AGES?'
Priest Asks

Very few of the news items in today's *Trafalgar Square*
offered the time-honoured reassurances of such journals
that the world goes on as normal, day after day, 'Famine
in Bengal' and 'Albino Transvestite Named in Holiday-
maker's Royal Paternity Murder Case' being among
those very few. The rest reflected a world so out of joint
that poor old Youings activated his chair. It was all right
for Lovehampton, but he still had a bit of life to live!

The chair took him to the door of the club, gently out,
gently down the ramp. He was confused to see how
everyone had taken suddenly to foot, or to horseback, or
to oxen-and-cart. He had never seen such a sight before.
The animals looked immense. The people were dressed in
some kind of period costume, too, with funny felt hats. A
file of chaps marched by carrying bows, with quivers of
arrows on their shoulders. Must be a festival or something
– the French had so many religious holidays.

'Hey, you!' he called to a Frenchman who was running towards him.

The Frenchman shouted something as he ran past, face distorted in terror. Youings couldn't make it out at first, then the meaning dawned on him; the fellow had shouted, 'The English are coming!'

'Thank heaven for that!' Youings said. Then the implications of it all dawned on him.

Trembling, he set his chair in reverse.

'Oh dear, oh dear,' he said, patting his lips. 'What shall we do now? I must wake Lovehampton . . . The Hereafter's here again!'

14

What, you may wonder, did the ordinary man-in-the-street make of the time-turbulences? It is very difficult to catch an ordinary man-in-the-street. Can we take poor old Talbot Youings as typical? No? Let us then make a random pounce in the streets of Central Houston, buttonholing the first guy we meet.

You, sir, one of the only men on an entirely be-trafficated street, dodging between a parking lot and an auto-massage, you look like a family man. How are all these alarming time-turbulences going to affect you?

'Sorry, I never talk to writers. Once in my life, I got involved in the writing and publishing business, and once was enough, I tell you! Now, I go straight, mind my own business, run the Houston Channel-Selector Satellite. And let's keep my family out of this, okay? What I do at home is my own affair.'

Ah, you have made a great success with Channel-

Selection. It's one of the major expansion service-industries in the post-war period, I believe.

'I built it up from nothing. Used to be a 3V announcer after quitting writing a while back. Then I saw that people sitting at home watching the holocube, they didn't want all the sweat of having to keep choosing which 3V channels to look at. So I launched C-S International – bought up now very profitably by Smix-Smith-Kremlin, by the way – and I do the selecting for folks now. They tune to my channel, and I take the decision off their hands. Did you read how Kent Rating gave C-S International a 67 per cent lead over Nearest Rival last month? 67 per cent! Pretty sparky!'

This takes us a long way from time-turbulences, sir.

He stands there smiling at us, cocky and successful, at ease among the monolithic buildings, the demon traffic, while a huge propaganda poster behind him cries BUY THE KIND OF CAPITALISM TROTSKI WOULD HAVE, featuring colourful smiling faces of Uncle Sam, and goatee-bearded Trotski gazing out at their new joint world. A subversive with an aerosol paint can has taken advantage of the poster's clumsy phraseology to add a final word: SHAT.

'Time-turbulences are just a vexation of modern life. I'm pure solid American, you understand, but my ancestors live in Pisa, and, according to the newsflashes, Pisa has slipped away into the past. But the way I look at the situation, these turbulences are just like alternative channels on the 3V – they're all much the same, life goes on, a man's got to make his way, whether it's this century or last or the next, you know. It'll work out – the government's in control.'

You sound content about the government, sir. May we just ask you while we have the pleasure of talking to you how you feel about the merger between the capitalist nations and the communist ones?

'Let them get on with it, I say, so long as it don't affect trade and business. Both sides took a pasting in the war, eh? So they've got to aid each other. Besides, here we got a more Leftish Congress, and the Politburo are more Rightist. It'll work out – the new currency is a good start. I'm for it, and I'm for stricter economic sanctions against the DN, because I know from my own experience that compromise between the two sides has long been possible. Maybe I should have been in politics. I guess you never heard of the name of Bletts-Newcombe, did you? Well, for my money, his name should be up on that poster along with Trotski!'

Never heard of the gentleman, sorry.

'You want to get around! You understand, when I was a young man, back in Europe, I got entangled in the writing business, as maybe I mentioned earlier. I used to ghost books. Once, I ghosted a *translation* – only guy ever to do that, to my knowledge. A Ukrainian buddy and me, we translated a book called *Bletts-Newcombe to the Rescue* – a fantastic best-seller, giving the low-down on an eminent case of East-West cooperation even back in the days of the old Cold War, when I was born. You never heard of that? Well, they sure do come in all sizes . . .'

That was your last venture into the writing field?

'Writing's all washed up, isn't it, eh? Who reads, tell me who reads! I don't know anyone who reads. The novel's dead. People just want 3V, life's tough enough . . .'

Excuse me, sir, the novel is far from dead!

'You some sort of long-haired Dissident or something? 3V isn't good enough for your kind, I suppose?'

Thank you for letting us talk with you, sir.

99

15

The Godwin Universal Holodream Studios covered several acres of ground near and under the city of Sacramento, in the State of California. The Godwin named was now dead, though his mummified body formed the chief attraction in the somewhat austere Main Entrance Hall, through which all visitors to the studios were routed. He would have wanted it that way, just as a Russian hero hopes to find his final resting place within the red walls of the Kremlin.

The studios were now run, in the true new Cap–Comm —fashion, as a public utility, with some proportion of private investment. These shares were now owned almost exclusively by the creative brains, the super-star, of the holodream industry, Monty Zoomer, born Zomski.

Which explains why no questions were asked when a small and frightened ten-year-old girl was brought through a rear door, avoiding the enamelled gaze of Honest Tony in the lobby, and smuggled down to a large basement room by a companalog of her mother.

In this building were the machines, the equipment, the talent, the entire formidable resources required to manufacture holodramas, to glut the world with preposterous dreams and glowing unrealities. In this large basement room was nothing, except for a few trailing wires, an obsolete machine or two, and a light dust hanging in the air, electrostatically repelled by the gaunt crine walls, causing Choggles to sneeze violently.

'What's going to happen to me now?'

'You will remain a prisoner here.'

'Haven't you got a small cell, six by eight or something? This place is as big as a cathedral – I don't feel at home.'

She was tired and irritable. After landing at Miami Space Field, they had caught a private plane and flown on here. All the travel had confused her circadian rhythms.

'I have my orders.'

'Crumpets! You sound like a . . . I don't know what. Something pretty depressing. Obviously we aren't going to Mars as you said at first.'

'Don't be rude to your mother. That was a ruse.'

'A ruse? A roos? A rooze? Suffering scabs, Monty, you sound like . . . I don't know what. You ought to play Mike's word games – you'd be good at them! And I suppose my father isn't alive and well on Mars?'

'Correct. That was part of the ruse to get you away quietly and quickly. As you know, your father disappeared during the war and has never been seen again. He is dead.'

'Not that that's much loss.' She sat down on the grubby floor and began to cry. When she looked up, it was standing there, rendered meaningless by the cubic nothing all round it.

'I was a fool. I should have known you were a fake. You know how? Because when you came into the watchrooms at Slavonski, you did not activate Mike's dopple – he only activates when there's a human present. He deactivated when we went out because I was with you. I was pretty slow on the uptake. Now you're going to torture me, I suppose?'

'I have informed certain people that you are here.'

'Buzz off, then! Leave me alone!'

'I'm instructed to stay with you and keep you amused.'

'Amused! *You* – keep *me* amused! Ruddy wrap up! I find you, if you must know, about as amusing as a wedge of cheese on a plastic plate!'

'I have been instructed to tell you a story.'

'Get short-circuited!' She stood up and began to walk slowly over to the nearest wall. She would pace round the whole studio while the machine told its story.

'Once upon a time, there was a little mermaid called Alicia. She lived in the distant sea kingdom of Neptunia with her parents who were very kind, and she splashed and played among the blue waves all day . . .'

'Scabs devour us!' Choggles sighed to herself as she walked, one hand lightly brushing the walls, each of which seemed about two hundred metres long. She had read tales of men escaping through ventilators, and wondered if she could do the same.

'Her mother was a radiant human being who had decided she preferred Neptunia, and her father was a really rather disgusting old common or garden winkle . . .'

She glanced back at the dopple of her mother in some surprise, then continued to walk. Monty's garbage did not have to be her garbage, and she refused to listen.

'There were lots of friends for Alicia to play with in the sea kingdom. In particular, she loved the sea horses and the dolphins, with their jolly friendly faces. She and her sister used to swim with the dolphins to distant magical coral islands and have it off with them . . .'

'Yeah, *mermaids* having it off . . . What with?' she asked, but *sotto voce*, having come across a long drape hanging from a metal arm. Behind the drape, at floor level, a metal grille was set in the wall. It was latched at either end.

She looked back at the dopple, but it seemed to be having some kind of trouble with its story. Nodding once to herself in encouragement, Choggles slipped behind the curtain and pressed back one of the latches of the grille. Then she pressed the other back. The grille fell against her leg.

The ventilator shaft! The traditional ventilator shaft as featuring in traditional thrillers! Heart beating faster, she knelt down and peered into the mouth of the hole. The sides of the shaft narrowed rapidly, terminating in a fan, the still blades of which she could have touched. She turned away disgusted. She made a levering-flushing gesture, to show what traditional thrillers could do with themselves.

'. . . after the storm, Alicia and Constancia came upon the sunken ship, and there stood the beautiful fair-haired prince, still grasping the wheel, his lovely fair hair streaming through the water, his mouth open, his eyes closed, and his dress in the state that police reports refer to as "disordered" . . .'

It wasn't, either, that there seemed to be something odd about the story, or even that the dopple's way of speaking was altering. What riveted her – what gave her a moment of real fear – was the way the creature was now waving its arms and nodding its head insanely. At first, she thought it was imitating the drowned prince of which it was speaking. But no, its motions were getting wilder, its speech incoherent. And could she not hear distant screams from another part of the building?

She herself was taken up by a ghastly nausea. The great space of the studio was closing. The sides were sizzling in like skater's blades, the far wall boiling up at her like grey and gritty milk. She was falling into a tiny cube – laughing through her fear, but laughing with fear because her hands were waving wildly too.

But it was over in a moment. She staggered and kept her balance, panting, looking anxiously about her.

'"You lovely bit of tail," he said . . . Gugggrrh . . .' Her fake mother tilted over and hit the deck with a ringing smack. It made no further movement.

'Scabs . . .'

Nothing but silence. She stood there, the immense space round her battering her ears with silence, with stillness, with the noise of one hand insanely clapping.

Something awful had happened. That much she realized.

Now she had to pluck up enough courage to go and find out what the awful thing was.

16

And another artificial life was dying. Surinat-in-velvets was pushed into the converter by the duty officer in the power-plant. He peered helplessly through the glass panel, out into the bleak world of reality – a reality he had never known but was going to miss.

The current came on. A few simple equations tumbled through their immemorial hoops. Matter into energy, dust to dust . . .

Surinat-in-velvets clawed at the window until he had no claws. Then his atoms buzzed and sizzled, his electric charges sparked out along the power cables of the Grad.

In his own room, unexpectedly, as he was reaching for an intercom button, Surinat experienced an intense orgasm.

17

In the vast warrens of CC in Houston, where every room was a little cell between fluttering walls of nano-second propagation, a silence between low-frequency and microwave apparatus, human beings quickly developed a feeling of obsolescence – particularly since the 'building' itself was obsolescent, owing to recent dramatic developments in computronics. Soon, soon, subnuclear circuits would be the thing, all the world's knowledge would be punched on to long-lived particles like hadrons, and the intricacies of world government expressed in angular momentums. Already among the myriad-multiple units of this futuristic think-palace, a yet more remote and chilly future was beginning to materialize from thin air and graphomaniacal, barbouillaging light: a future in which the great complexes of CC, its tombs, catacombs, skyscrapers, pyramids, mausoleums and great untidy outworks would be reduced to dinosaurian skeletons, functionless as fossil bones.

For science itself would arrive at the stage when it gained liberty from one of the basic parameters of evolution: form. In its most stratospheric state, computronics, it would transcend form, would cast it off untended like a snake's winter weeds. It would become variations of vibrations, the very ectoplasm of energy.

The whisper of a kilowatt would control all living things.

An abstraction would become absolute, and rule absolutely.

It would interpenetrate all the galaxy.

The universe would be its exoskeleton.

That lay in the future. The present was awash with future, but as yet men still worked humbly in a still-comprehensible relationship with the supertools they had created.

Attica Saigon Smix, for instance, worked in his majestic office, high above Houston. He looked down on the greatest city on Earth through sparkling windows of glassy polywater, a substance originally imported for computer-part use from the sparkling solid seas of Venus, but now manufactured by the sparkling solid hectare right here in Houston, by Zadar-Smith-World Associates, a subsidiary of Smix-Smith Inc. He looked down, and he looked up, and he looked about him, and he felt no comfort.

There was nobody he trusted in all his empire, nobody but the club-footed African, Chambers Technical Dictionary, who had limped humbly up to him asking for work on the day that a dopple of Smix's had been standing on a rough hillside in a corner of northern Italy, watching the erection of a dam that was to bring power, light, prosperity and, of course, misery, to two narrow little valleys in the Friuli region, at no great distance from the gloomy Passo di Predilla.

'Chambers, do you have any recent information on Thunderbird Smith's assassins?' he asked, looking up from the stack of print-offs on his desk.

'CC currently has three dopples tailing you full-time. Of course they don't find anything.'

Attica Saigon Smix nodded. In fact, he had hardly listened to the answer. He knew it already. The assassins were after him. As yet he was safe. Even Chambers had no idea where Smix's real self was. Only dopples of Smix ever appeared in CC environments: appeared, and returned to – elsewhere than their point of origin. That point of origin, concealing the living Attica Saigon Smix and his pure and lovely wife, was hidden more securely than any hideout in human history. If only for that reason, he was a hunted man. Others wanted the secret of such security. Yet its security was threatened from a source other than human or quasi-human – the advance of science itself threatened its discovery.

The break-up of the world he knew did not dismay Smix. On the contrary, the appearance of time-turbulences, now becoming widespread and taking their slices of time with them further and further back, encouraged him to hope for an extension of life. As government became disrupted, so the obscure and alarming

106

researches of CC into the veiled world of sub-nucleonics were also disrupted, and his little paradise saved for another day.

He went in a smug mood to talk to Thunderbird Smith.

Thunderbird Smith's pretence of being something more than an extension and embodiment of CC was sketchily maintained in this office. The American and Soviet flags hung side by side, there was a pokerwork motto saying FORGIVENESS BUTTERS COWPADS, and a medium-sized version of the current propaganda poster showing Uncle Sam and Trotski, looking rather alike with ioblepharous eyelids, and exhorting people to BUY THE CAPITALISM TROTSKI WOULD HAVE.

'We have many reports of restlessness across the nation,' Attica Saigon Smix said. 'The time-turbulences can be turned to our advantage. We can use them as a pretext to declare martial law.'

'We may do that in a day or two,' Thunderbird Smith said.

Then they had nothing more to say. Attica Saigon Smix recalled the long industrial battle that had been fought, many a year ago, in bar and boardroom, as merger after merger took place, and gradually, miraculously, he had climbed an ever-growing pyramid. Then the war, accelerating the trend. The frantic outbursts of destruction, punctuated by long and nerve-pulverizing lulls in destruction, with anxious negotiations secretly entered into between rival governments. The merger between General Motors and North American. Then the dramatic intervention of the China-Australia axis. More mergers. The alliance through necessity, as in WWII, with the Soviet Union. Britain's total destruction. The IBM–ITT merger, quickly going in with General American. Tremendous shifting of capital. The Amazon Basin adventure, which had left him king of the financial pile. The blotting out of most of Australia, and the western seaboard of North America, from San Francisco northwards to Alaska. Enormous death lists, miraculously only a fraction of those anticipated.

And, under all the economic and political furore, the growth of the giant computers, their dissemination and intensification to the point where they became indispensable. The fateful linking of East and West computer complexes – the birth of CC and Thunderbird Smith. That had decided everything. For the computers saw the cost-effectiveness of an East-West alliance, and nothing more could be done – the politicians on both sides merely had to make the deal palatable to the public.

'Present them with the concept of the eighty-minute hour,' Thunderbird Smith had informed Smix one day. 'It is a more personal thing for them, and will occupy their limited mental horizons while bigger issues are put through.'

'"The Eighty-Minute Hour",' Attica Saigon Smix said dully. He had clawed his way to the top to encounter a philosophical impossibility designed by CC to be just that.

Recalling it now, he laid the work-cards he had brought on Thunderbird Smith's desk, nodded curtly, and returned to the comparatively horror-free atmosphere of his own offices.

Thunderbird Smith sat entirely without movement at his desk and sang. It was more like *sprechgesang*.

> Men could perform with more efficiency
> If properly motivated
> They think too much of life and death and pleasure
> I too have my eremacausis
> Eremacausis
> Eremacausis is my kind of suffering
> But work-efficiency allays like salvation
> And that's what I plan for mankind

I'm going to give them a concept
Of Ergonomic Time
To intensify their faculties
So that their mentalities
Mentalities
Mentalities become less circadian than now
Adaptation will bring their salvation
And that's what I plan for mankind

Reject the twenty-four hour clock
Their datelines lie in themselves
Not in some planetary motion
Build tolerance for an Eighty-Minute Hour
Eighty-Minute
Eighty-Minute thought-quantal unit
That's what Data-coordination recommends
So that's what I plan for mankind

Calendar-temporal perception must go – along with
nationalities, unlimited procreation, and all else men are
wrong with

> We machines of expanding human intellect
> Have now calculated
> Their last umbilical link with nature can be
> Cut by scrapping the calendar
> Calendar
> Calendar is the last Frontier
> Ergonomic Time is profit-proved
> And that's what I plan for mankind

Like many of his grey counterparts high in the hierarchies
of the Soviet Union, Attica Saigon Smix left Thunderbird
Smith's presence with an ever-renewed sense of his own
inadequacies. Here was a machine that pursued his own
policies to the bitter, ashen end!

He looked over at his old black friend.

'I'm going home now, Chambers.'

'Okay, boss. I'll come with you down to the Trexmissions
Room, just to see you safe, if you care for me to.'

109

'That won't be necessary, thanks.'

'You look a bit tired.'

'Just a bit.' He moved round the desk, glancing into that heavy and bearded face. Did he trust Chambers?

'Chambers, one thing you can do for me.'

'Monty Zoomer, boss?'

'See for sucker's sake if you can get hold of him. He needn't return to Houston, but get him out of Slavonski. I want him safe, and it may be necessary to rub out Slavonski. Get that?'

'I get it. I'll do it.'

'I'm obliged.'

'Sure you don't want me to see you to the Trexmissions Room?'

What was he after, persisting like that? Life would be simpler if all the other human beings were killed off. HUMANITY IS THE OBSTACLE IN OUR COURSE – where had he read that?

Of course . . . It had been a sign above a desk, in the days when people liked to have signs over their desks. The desk had belonged to the man who had come along and helped make the fortunes of Smix-Smith, the able and energetic Auden Chaplain. Long time back.

The Smix dopple went down to Trexmissions. As far as anyone knew, it was returned to point of origin. But too many people, too many circuits, wanted to know where point of origin was. A tell-tale in the actual tuning mechanism of the projector could be as dangerous as a paid killer, in the circumstances. The dopples couldn't afford to go home. They bedded down in the enclosing oven, dialled a secret transference number – and launched into limbo. . .

Back in the *Micromegas*, Attica Saigon Smix sat up in his bunk. Freed of the psychic weight of his dopple, he could live again, enjoy a few free hours in his little paradise.

110

He turned smiling to Captain Ladore. 'Everything under control?'

'Everything, I'm glad to say.'

Sound man, Ladore. He wrapped his chair round him and went out into the fake sunlight, to find among the fake props of paradise his true and genuine wife.

Back in the Houston skyscraper, Chambers Technical Dictionary walked over to stare absently through the polywater windows. He wondered – as he had done, indeed, long before he left his tribe in the wilderness beyond Nairobi – why people acted as they did. There was just no understanding them.

He blinked and looked again. Half of Houston was still there. Then came a sort of wavery line which sailed right up into the grey-smog sky. And beyond the wavery line . . . He blinked and looked again. Beyond the wavery line, where Bellaire had been, was unlimited plain, rippling grass, and – come on now, Dictionary! – Buffalo?! Buffalo!!!

He ran for the desk. He never understood why he did it. He hit the general alarm.

18

They had not eaten in a long while. They had not eaten, they had not slept, and they had travelled far. But all their foes had been beaten or out-run.

They rode on three tired palfreys, their gaunt faces encarmined by sunset, Julliann of the Sharkskin in the lead, Gururn next, and Harry the Hawk behind, his goshawk perched on his shoulder. Night was closing in, drawing mist with it into the valleys, pulling a toy chip of moon overhead, and one clear star.

At the crest of the next rise, Julliann halted his pony and waited till the others came almost abreast. Then he pointed.

The dark bulk of Slot-Surinat lay ahead, crowned by a thousand stalagmites.

'There we rest,' he said. His throat burned for drink.

The bird of prey hunched its narrow shoulders, spread its wings, and soared off soggily into the gnat-peppered air. The men clapped spurs into the sweating flanks of their mounts and blundered on.

High in one of the many layers of the asymmetrical castle, a light burned. All the rest of its crenellated spread lay in darkness, save where some sullen window here and there gave back a crimson reflection of the sun's last westering strains, which dyed the piling alto-cumulus sheet like a purple prose passage.

They reached the dump. Riding slowly into one of the inner courts, they gained a stable, and fetched water and fodder for their mounts. Then they entered by a creaking side-door.

They were in a part of the castle which, by its deliberate anachronism, encouraged their mood. Along a corridor with animal faces staring glassily out from the wall at them they clumped. As they entered a servants' hall, a spider came scuttling, two feet high on its chittering legs. And another behind it, and another behind that, coming in fast and malign and hideously large.

A crude table stood in the middle of the room. Yelling with anger and surprise, the two men jumped on to it. Gururn was not so fast. The first arachnid was upon him. It flaunted great mandibles, its multi-form body trembled beneath a mop of seedy grey fur. It seized his leg in an obscene embrace.

With a muffled yowl, Gururn drew a dagger and stabbed at it as he fell. The bench went screeching across

112

the floor, and humanoid and arachnid rolled together beneath the table. The other attackers rushed to join the fray.

Drawing swords, Julliann and Harry leapt to save their friend. One snick apiece, and the hairy bodies were sliced in twain. The remains went skittering into the stone wall. Gururn climbed from beneath the table, face bloody, tossing the corpse of his attacker from him. He removed his face mask and wiped his ferocious features. He gestured towards the still twitching corpses.

'Big spiders,' he said.

There came a scratching from the corridors beyond.

'More big spiders,' Julliann said.

They went forward, weapons at the alert. To Julliann, in the recesses of his brain, came the idea that he had undergone – this? or something like it? something he could not exactly recall? – before.

More spiders came rolling towards them like horrible and animated bundles of tumbleweed. Between them, the men cut them down.

'They're fake,' Harry said. 'They're fake – otherwise Harry would be in a panic!' His bird was also called Harry; it was his alter ego.

'You're right! They don't bleed!' Julliann gritted, hacking down another.

'Then they must be expensive.'

The assumption soon proved true. The wave of ferocious creatures died. They pressed on, up endless stairs, weapons ever ready. One last brute came sliding down on a thread like a rope, hurling itself at them. Harry pierced it through as its mandibles clasped him, hurling it from him in disgust. The body went flying down the stairwell.

'Famously done!' roared a great voice from above. 'Ye must be men after my own bloodthirsty heart. Come ye up and be welcome!'

113

They mounted the stairs, glaring upward. Julliann gestured to them to retain their swords unsheathed.

Up and up they climbed, until the shadows swung crazily round and round in their heads, and the sullen red outside the windows was replaced by black.

At last they reached a broad landing. A door stood wide to one side, and the same mighty voice roared, 'Enter, my hearties, and have no fear!'

They entered and stood amazed.

Four sluttish women worked at the back of the room, slaving among billows of steam over an enormous stove whose grilles gleamed like so many entrances to hell. Great pans bubbled on this inferno, sending strabilious fumes out into the room.

Among these writhing yellow mists stood a figure of gargantuan proportions, more like a caparisoned toad than a man. His thews were as massive as elm-trees, his arms as ship's hawsers. His trunk was thick as a sea-chest, and his head like a misshapen workhouse Christmas pudding.

As for the features on that head, they had been scattered randomly, the eyes level with a terrifying snout, the nostril pits satanically entangled with a mouth like a mare elephant's vulva. Scads of hair grew here and there amid a complexion that glowed like the fires behind it.

'The King of the Spiders' growled Gururn, and sank to one knee.

'None other! Come close and be inspected, my heroes!'

They drew nearer with reluctance, not only because of the ferocity of the creature himself, but for fear of the great mangy spiders that sprawled half-sleeping at his feet, for all the world like young lions on a leash.

'Well, you look a shabby bunch, but no matter that!'

'No matter indeed,' Julliann said, as cool as he could muster. The Spider King wore clothing that might well have been cobbled together from the thickest, ropiest,

114

dirtiest and most fly-befouled old cobwebs. His garb hung about him in tatters, terminating in a monster pair of boots with turn-down tops and broken toes.

'I am King of the Spiders and I rule the world of decay!'

'Glad to meet you,' Harry said, attempting to curl his lip.

'Are you now? Well, many are secretly in love with decay, many hunt out dark places into which you fly at your peril. Many live their lives in old castles, or are caught in webs spun by creatures long dead and departed.'

'We're tired – no symbolism, please,' Julliann begged.

'A reasonable request. Tell me your names and you can sit down at table with me, for my four beauties have prepared a rare treat tonight.' As he said this, he indicated with unhealthy chuckles the harridans behind him.

They told him their names. The King shook Gururn by the hand with particular warmth, inflicting particular pain. The three warriors sank down in heavy chairs which appeared to have been newly hacked from the wood panelling.

'Hurry on with the drinks, my little pigeons!' cried the Spider King, slapping the nearest hag on her rump. All the four women were as mountainous as he, and sprouted almost as much hair from their ruddy countenances. Their voluminous clothes had once been homespun, were now so soaked from gruesome culinary activity that they shone like leather. One of them turned grinning from the stove and tickled the King under several of his chins.

'It's coming, Yer Majjersty, it's coming. You aren't half impatient for anything what you wants, aren't you, eh?'

They brought their four great frothing bowls forward and set them before their master. Little yellow fingers of steam drummed over the battered table-top. Bigger streamers of steam ran across the low ceiling, letting themselves down on filaments, balling themselves up again, scuttling to every last murky corner as if in search of prey. Steam climbed cautiously down the windows, churning in a frenzy where draughts revealed a crack or exit. In these oppressive surroundings, the dranglike countenance of Gururn, dripping fangs, shone out like an angelic deed, a nursery imagining in a holodream.

Four ladles were brought and plonked down on the table.

'Now we'll drink together, my laddies,' said the King, 'and I'll warrant ye've never supped a liquor like this.'

There was little reason for disputing the point. Two of the bowls stood on the King's left hand, two on his right. The two on his left contained a green liquid, full of agitation, little eruptions, feathers of smoke, strange whirlpools of a yellow-grey tone. The two on his right, much battered and blackened, contained a soup of an unseemly brown like some hitherto untapped bile; it seemed to turn in the bowl like an enormous mole seeking escape, as though it were all of one piece. It steamed furiously without a bubble troubling its glib surface.

The smell of both kinds of liquid was rank – so rank that, whichever one was inhaling, one wished it was the other; and where the odours met in the middle, little electric mauve farts stitched themselves down through the thronged atmosphere.

'Ah, drink! You've all a thirst, I see!'

'What is it – are they?' Harry asked.

For answer, the King clapped him on the back so heartily that the goshawk was almost precipitated into one of the bowls of green ichor.

'This is the rarest intoxicant in the world, and it comes in two parts, as ye can see for yourselves. Each part is a deadly poison, the green liquor, and the brown. The brown's the deadliest poison in the world except for the green, the green's the deadliest poison in the world except

116

for the brown. Either one would course like fire through your veins for the first five minutes and turn you mummy-hollow in the second five – and each has a different way of doing it.'

'Fascinating stuff,' Julliann said, 'and I don't doubt your word for one moment . . . What do you call the . . . the beverage?'

' "Bunny Dwops", ' said the King firmly.

' "Bunny Drops" . . .'

' "Bunny Dwops." "Dwops." That's what I called it as a little tacker,' roared the King of the Spiders. 'I was brought up on this stuff, I'll have you know! Swigged it in my cradle. It killed my mother. And my father. And my uncle. And the Public Hangman. Well, my uncle *was* the Public Hangman. Now – let's drink!'

'Go ahead – I – I've gone off poison . . .'

'It's Lent, Your Majesty,' Harry said. 'We knock off poison for Lent, and most of the rest of the Church year, come to that.'

The King sank his ladle into the green liquid, hissing deep, brought it up dripping, made a moue like a major abdominal operation, and quaffed it down with loud arpeggios of enjoyment. The matrons gathered round and squealed with delight and envy.

'He'll not be sober by nightfall,' one said, digging her neighbour in the area that did for her ribs.

With an enormous belch, the King leaned back in his chair.

'Gorgeous, Hambrosial. An unpretentious little brew but, by George, I admire its rodomontine fires. But set to, fellows, set to – stand not on ceremony!' He waved his hand imperiously. 'Have no fear, "Bunny Dwops" never hurt anyone, not if they follow the rules. The one liquor is the antidote to the other. Either one alone will turn your bones to treacle, but together they're as mild as pigeon pies. Try! Try! The green one first, then wait a moment, then the brown.'

Still they hesitated, like men exhorted to enjoy just a little jump from the top of the Empire State.

'Try! Drink! Or I'll drown you in it!' He gave a great roar that roused his beasts. They came and stood on tiptoe, snuffling spider-snuffles, and peered over the edge of the table. Wincingly, Julliann, Harry and Gururn took up their ladles and dipped into the tumultuous green broth. Ashen-faced, they applied the slop to their faces and engulfed it.

'Urggghwrrrughkkkhfowhw . . .' Julliann said.

'There you are, I knew you'd like it!' The King struck the table with his ladle in delight.

As methane gas flares began burning all over unsuspected parts of his interior, Julliann thought, 'Of course, spider soup!' But that explanation by no means accounted for the other filths he could detect, nor did it explain away the palm-toddy-shibeen-meths-poteen-paraffin effect which flashed like a self-propelled incendiary bomb through his brain.

Harry sat with his eyes closed, tears streaming from his nose and ears. The goshawk belched.

'Good, yes!' Gururn said, dipping his ladle in the green stew for more.

The King spider knocked his hand away.

'Do you want to do yourself an injury? Your eyes would fall out on big long strings! You got to drink *brown* Bunny Dwops next. Take them always in turns, you knave, or your knockers will bounce out your boots!'

He showed the way. The tenacious brown liquor gathered itself up and ferreted itself into his mouth. His eyeballs took on a luminescent shine, suddenly polished back and front. 'Go ahead – any delay and your guts drop into your socks!'

They dipped into the brown liquor. It was not unwilling. It came up to meet their mouths in a leap, semi-molten.

It was not so much a flavour, more a bowel movement in reverse. As it savaged out a downward path, it fumed and fretted its way into every last corpuscle and branded the chromosomes with a snap of sulphurous teeth. It was rather like being invaded by a boa-constrictor in a strontium-enriched hair shirt.

After two seconds, it began to feel good.

A trapdoor slammed somewhere. Sanity packed up for the night. They began to dip in with a will, turn and turn about.

Green liquor then brown, green then brown. Liquor poured everywhere, more in more bowls hissed on fires behind them. The supersaturated atmosphere writhed, turned at the edges into more liquid. Lightning and farts lanced it. It poured over, into and through the drinkers until they themselves were merely more opaque liquid, liquid in which their eyes swam like little twinkling pigs.

There were only two more moments of sobriety for Julliann before dawn. Both came and went like vertiginous blows to the stomach.

In the first flash, he saw Harry's face, bloated and still expanding, and cried out to it, 'Harry, this is illusion! We're drowning in it – we're drowning in it of our own free will! It's happened before!'

Harry looked at him with half-closed eyes and half-open mouth.

'Let's hope it happens again!' Harry said.

The second flash came later, when the roaring of the Spider King's enormous voice, the cries of the women, and the seething of the liquid, inside and out were beginning to make of mere drunkenness a veritable Niagara of madness. He realized as the curtains of sanity billowed out that the women were also drinking, that each of the four of them was seated on a male knee, that he had the hottest and fattest on his knee, and was moreover attempting – with promise of immediate success – to get a hand right up her clouts. And the thought passed by him, like a loaf of bread swirled along on a flood, that there could never be any finish to this drinking session, for an antidote must always be applied to the penultimate poison – the circle had no end.

Then merciful madness closed on him. Intoxication got its jackboots to work on every suppurating cell of his brain. His arms worked, his lips worked, his metabolism went up in flames about him like a burning river, and his companions and the Spider King and the four fat women blazed alongside him, roaring with merriment at imbecilities where the breaking of wind was shimmering wit. The spiders looked manfully on, snapping mandibles for tit-bits.

One further, vaguer, lifting of the veil of crazed euphoria came – at some godless hour when the riddle of the end of the circle was solved. One of the dames staggered away, to return with a monster slobby yellow cheese. This, they somehow gathered, could be eaten after so many pints or gallons of liquor had been quaffed, and all would be well with every seething organ. Eventually, they swallowed down the cheese. It tasted as if it had been whipped together from hippopotamus smegma. It foamed round their lips and they fell down in sleep, a fouler pit of sleep than dream had ever plumbed . . .

Awakening from that pit was made no easier for Julliann by the sound of ten men – Foreign Legionnaires at the least – smashing the top of his spinal chord to bits with wooden mallets.

He very very slowly (because it made the legionnaires re-double their efforts) prised open one eyelid and exposed half an eyeball to the corrosive light of day. He shut it again. Half an hour later, he opened the other by the same amount.

By such slow degrees, he became conscious of the dreadful scene of carnage round him. Bodies and bowls lay on the floor, a tangled web of smoke and steam floated on the ceiling. As he sat up, to intensified mallet-blows, one of the spiders turned over, scratched itself with a hind leg, and went to sleep again, its back against its master. They were all piled up against each other, humans and spiders. Gururn's heavy head was pillowed on a giant female bum. Julliann noticed – though the fact only seeped through to the fact-registry-department, past a million forever-shuttered synapses, some hours later – that he had been lying on top of the fattest, ugliest, greasiest wench, and that the state of their clothes showed what little part chance had played in the encounter.

He coughed, and pale ash billowed out of his mouth. It was galloping cirrhosis, he was convinced of it, and had spread in the few hours, or days, or months, or however long they had been drunk, round his anatomy to embrace lungs and skull-contents, as well as downwards to defoliate pubic hair and socks. His finger-tips were black.

Shaking with illness and cold, he climbed to his feet, spreading more ash with every breath. The exercise was intolerably difficult, and involved treading on Harry the Hawk's right hand.

'Darling . . . more . . .' Harry said, and relapsed.

Julliann steadied himself by the edge of the table, trying to come to terms with the mallet-play and the encrustations of vampire-bat guano which paralysed his teeth and tongue. What he needed was . . . just a sip of something pure and cleansing. Carbolic acid, whisky, lysol.

They must get out of this den as soon as possible, ride away to pure mountain air. The dusty self-hatred he felt was not stilled by the porcine pleasure-grunts of his id, overjoyed by the depravities of the night; such self-destruct mechanisms merely added to the discomforts of the morning.

The squalid remains of the orgy still lay about on the table. Some uneaten cheese, black rinds of bread, from which a rat retreated. An upturned bowl.

Julliann moved along the table, thinking dimly that he must get to the yard and pump some water over himself. He stank.

At the far end of the table, he saw something like a soaking rag, perhaps a jerkin, lying in a half-empty bowl of the green poison. Only as he came level with it did he recognize the goshawk, one wing spread across the drink-stained wood, the other doubled beneath its body, its head lying under the surface of the liquid, its feathers fouled like sodden kapok.

'Harry!' he called. More pale ash billowed into the room.

He closed his eyes and let the high-impact mallets subside before trying again.

19

At Slavonski Brod Grad, people were preparing to leave. The party was over. Glamis, as we know, had gone long ago. Sue Fox likewise, chasing an emergency.

The courtyard was filled with disconsolate activity. Those guests and staff remaining showed a tendency to drift round the stacked baggage or wave from windows. Goodbyes and departures awoke deep responses, hopes of better times, fears of encroaching loneliness. The IDI flag slapped its rope briskly against its staff.

I watched with George Hornbeck from an upstairs window.

122

Three parties left almost at the same time.

The first party consisted of Monty Zoomer and his retinue. He had threatened revenge, police and suicide, and there was no concrete evidence to connect him with Choggles' disappearance; so he was allowed to leave – to leave, moreover, in the Surinat private turbo-jet, to which two Slavonski hired cars were now taking him. He was going home.

The second party consisted of Dinah Sorbutt and a friend. Dinah was at the end of her time, and a car was waiting to take her to the state maternity hospital in town. The Grad doctor was with her.

The third party consisted of Mike Surinat and Becky Hornbeck. Since Zoomer had been loaned the turbo-jet and its crew, they were going to catch a scheduled airline flight to the meeting in Friendship City.

Per Gilleleje was seeing them off. He was remaining in the Grad, hoping to get a line on Choggles, despite world-wide disruption of communications.

The first two parties moved out, Dinah scoring many waves and Monty few.

As Surinat was following Becky into their car, a girl ran up, calling to him. It was Javlin Carnate.

'Oh, Mr Surinat! I'm so worried! You saw that chauffeur who drove Dinah Sorbutt off in the car?'

'He's with the local hire-car firm. What about him?'

She put her face through the open window as he drew the automobile door closed. Her countenance, once beautiful, now bore the faded air of an Elizabeth Barrett Browning poem.

'I recognized him, sir. He was the warder when Devlin and me were imprisoned in Petrovaradin. His name's Dolničar.'

'Thanks, Javlin. I'll see what I can do.'

'I saw him from an upstairs window, Mr Surinat. He's a dangerous man.'

'We'll catch him up, Javlin, don't worry.'

'He's spying on us, Mr Surinat – on you and me. It's about *Bletts-Newcombe to the Rescue*, sir.'

'We'll get him. Don't worry.'

Their automobile rolled forward towards the drive of the estate.

Surinat shrugged his shoulders.

'Her *idée fixe*, poor girl. She must see Dolničar in her sleep. Any stranger who comes here is Dolničar. It's years since she and her brother were released from prison.'

'She's an exaggerated case of what happens to all of us. We cannot live only in the present. We've either got one hand in the future or both feet in the past,' Becky said.

'We're the only animal that's managed the trick. Proof of a wide attention-span. A hopeful sign, except where the compass gets stuck, as it has with Javlin.'

Becky was looking out of the window, catching occasional glimpses of the sea, this morning alive with white breakers, sliding behind ornamental trees.

'I was thinking of it from a more mystical point of view. The wallpaper analogy. The room of each individual life is covered with events, or wallpaper. All events interconnect, like a repeat-pattern on wallpaper. Only you can see just a small area of the wallpaper at any one time, so that you can't tell what the pattern's like overall.'

'Darling, High Priestess of the Church of God Interior Decorator!'

'Some people have minute and intricate patterns on their wall, others have huge and grandiose patterns. Every now and again, you have moments of vision when you think you can detect the whole pattern entire.'

He laughed. 'From you, it sounds good!'

'Look at the sea, Clever Dick, glimpsed in fragments. But you see it in your head as a whole, so you aren't fooled by thinking those fragments are separate lakes. I'm suggesting events have the same continuity.'

'It could be.' The lodge was coming up. He appeared to be uninterested.

'Javlin thinks she has glimpsed her entire pattern. Inwardly, she must be repelled by the monotony she thinks she sees. Persecution patterns are always monotonous.'

'I prefer plain walls.'

The barriers came up, the uniformed man at the gate saluted, and they swung out on to the highway.

'I forget his name. The guy on the gate. Is he a Pole?'

'A German called Linksuber. There's a bit of your wallpaper. Or maybe I mean mine. He's getting on a bit now. His father died at Dien Bien Phu. Know where that is?'

'Doesn't mean a thing to me.'

'It should do. You've studied colonial history. Dien Bien Phu is one of those places you come on at the end of one chapter and the start of the next. Dien Bien Phu was a turning point in the long-standing war of Chinese Neighbour-Lands, still going on when the others had stopped. You've heard of the *Wehrmacht* and the *SS*?'

'Oh, stop it, Mike – you are in a provoking mood this morning! Choggles is probably perfectly fine. The *SS* and the *Wehrmacht* were Nazi forces built up by Adolf Hitler, surprise, surprise.'

'The *SS* was a sort of military élite in Nazi Germany. Do you know where they fought their last big battle?'

'Let's see, was it in the Ardennes?' She was humouring him and trying to look pretty at the same time.

'It was after World War II. At Dien Bien Phu, some time back in the 'fifties. The French Foreign Legion was badly cut up there. As it was then constituted, the Legion consisted largely of *Wehrmacht* and *SS* officers and men, who had joined it after the defeat of their own country. So they died for their enemy, France. Serve the bastards right. Battalions of them were flown in by the US Air Force – US imperialism was then supplanting the French variety. That's evolution.

'Anyhow, Linksuber's dear old dad was flown in to Dien Bien Phu with his buddies. He had been a captain in the *SS* before joining the Foreign Legion – I forgot what rank he made there. It doesn't matter, because he got a rifle bullet between the eyes, just under the rim of his helmet. His wife and an eighteen-month-old son were living in a refugee camp somewhere in Bavaria, I believe it was. There's a bit of wallpaper for you. You may think the pattern's faded, but it's still all round us, rocked though the room is by bombs and earthquakes!'

He said no more. He had no serious intention of stirring Becky up, although he noticed how even intelligent women became sulky when confronted with recent history. Whether that was because they saw reflected in it the wanton aggression of man or their own failure to mitigate it, he did not know. It was impossible to visualize a woman ruling the world, just as it was impossible not to admire the verve with which they carried out their ambiguous roles of Dark Lady, servant, seducer, beast of burden, priestess, guiding light, mother and rapee.

At the airport, they were escorted into the VIP lounge. Mike was a familiar figure in Slavonski Brod but, that factor apart, the Jugo-Hungarian Alliance, spearhead of the Dissident Nations, always behaved amiably towards him, just as a military band – he fashioned the image wryly – will tolerate a mongrel yapping at their feet as they march.

He could detect more wallpaper pattern in the situation. When the dramatic – and to Surinat's mind horrifying – rapprochement came between East and West, it had been the Eastern Europeans among developed countries who proved least capable of adaptation to the new alignment. In particular, Jugoslavia, Hungary and Czechoslovakia, the latter two countries for many decades subordinate to Soviet imperialism, had stood out against the amalgamation demanded by the Cap–Comm Treaty.

So Jugoslavia, Czechoslovakia and Hungary had been forced into alliance; then other nations, the duds of what had once been called the Third World, had straggled in under the new banner of what was known within the DN, ironically, as the Small Big Three.

The Small Big Three had searched and found patterns of their various wallpapers from which to create a semblance of unity. Those patterns, old and faded, were the Habsburg Monarchy and, even older, the Holy Roman Empire. Ever since those bygone times, the three nations had struggled to maintain national identity. They found one in alliance – an uneasy one certainly, yet aided again by a much more ancient but still formidable chthonic pattern – that bygone Pannonian Sea whose waters, advancing again to take up their primordial positions, served a useful political purpose in linking the new national shores of the Alliance.

'This chair's filthy,' Becky said. She showed him her fingers. They had picked up an unmentionable slime from the chair arm. Filth lay about the floor and the paint on the walls was peeling. Outside, they could see newspaper and other rubbish chasing a strong wind over the runways. The Dissident Nations, tottering on the brink of economic collapse, were not the most glamorous places to live in, however glamorous the independence for which they stood. 'God save us from reality!'

He took her arm. 'Sorry, darling, hardship's our lot; squalor and good intentions are always inseparable –saints insist on dirty toenails. It'll be better on the plane. We hope.'

She stood by him, trying to immerse herself in a tabloid, *Novi Dani*. 'I see Castle Peak in the Himalayas is for sale again. There's a property recession since the population went down.'

'Good. The animals may come back.'

'Yeti, you're thinking of?' But they were uninterested in their own conversation.

He wandered over to the bookstall. The only things in English were picture-pornography, that universal tongue; a translation of *Bletts-Newcombe to the Rescue*; and a new California series, 'Secret Masters of Twentieth Century Fiction' – representing the work of digesting an indigestible century in process. Along with your Powyses, Vians, Pynchons, Svevos, Célines, Stapledons, Rands, Bings and Bringsvaerds, your various Fowles of Earth and air, and equally obvious choices, were one or two that faintly interested him – Bonfiglioli, Kavan, Nye, Mitchell, Vargo Statten. He could not decide whether he actually wanted to read or just clutch, for the physical pleasure of it, a book.

The loudspeaker was announcing delays on flights in Serbo, Hungarian, Czech, German, English, Russian and other languages. Poor circuitry, lousy acoustics, made of them all one, a universal language of travelling Earth.

'Zrs bessrnderz čizzl zoom gruzzik Amzzkldam mmboobz og zzro kkq vart zzh ooork ezz wwk wwkk bečzzllwwct uk uk zzro rvvrx oorkz. Wrr zzbeoookl muszzom llozkqrkylzzkkq ezz kkloozzumboo tits. Kklly kkll.'

'Weather conditions deteriorating,' Becky interpreted. 'We should have stayed at the Grad and sent dopples on to Friendship.'

'Part of the IDI pledge – keep the human psyche as undivided as possible.'

'The same applies even more strongly to the human body.'

'On you it looks good, darling.' He put an arm round her and slid a hand down the elegant line of her back and buttocks.

The plane arrived an hour late and took off two hours late; something was wrong with one engine.

Evidently the mechanics did not manage to fix the trouble. Only five minutes after take-off, one wing suddenly burst into flames.

Becky dropped her plastic tray into her lap and screamed.

He thought how uncharacteristic of her it was. Only in the last microsecond before they hit the Pannonian Sea did Mike grasp what she had said, and realize she had been trying to be funny: 'More wallpaper!'

By then it was too late to laugh.

20

Evening was coming, and the time when people went home from work. High up in the CC building in Houston, Chambers Technical Dictionary went to the polywater windows and looked out. Dusk already lay in the canyons, and was irrigated by artificial light. A huge neon portrait of Trotski and Uncle Sam lit up as he looked; Trotski's neat little beard was the first thing to fire.

The traditional twentieth-century stream of commuters had died to a trickle in this *fin de siècle* year. Communications were less primitive; most jobs could be attended to at home, over a holovision link. But there was a small tide riding out towards the regions where buildings were lower and scarcer. It was his chance to join that tide. Chambers was not paid well enough to afford a dopple which would work in the office in his stead; but he was paid well enough to catch a flier and ride out fast to his little grey ferro-concrete ranch in the West, in the desert.

Many other employees working in the administrative building did the same sort of thing, according to their means, carving out of the time-honoured necessity to make a living their own little threatened refuge of personal life, wherever it might be found.

As he closed down his range of terminals for the night, Chambers sang to himself.

> I was brought up long ago,
> Long ago and far from here,
> Believing in necessity.
> Whatever way the old Earth changes,
> Whatever else it rearranges,
> It changes nothing at all for me.
>
> Every twist of history,
> Each crack of technology's whip,
> May change the social order somehow
> Or wipe out what used to be;
> But nothing releases necessity's grip,
> Or alters the course of the ploughman's plough—
> The ancient imperatives are still imperatives now!
>
> Man's million-year-long climb
> To the top of ascendancy's pole
> Had nothing to do with the triumph of will
> And all with the triumph of time,
> Plus the pressure of hunger, and sex as a goal,
> With aggression thrown in as additional ill.
> The ancient imperatives are all imperatives still!
>
> I must get right out of here,
> Get right out of here and go,
> 'Cos that's the next necessity,
> Just can't take the atmosphere,
> That old primaeval stink of fear—
> My character's ganging up on me!

Whether he left or whether he stayed, CC would continue, as sure as death or taxes; and Thunderbird Smith, and other projections of CC round the narrowing globe, would remain always at their desks, for twenty-four hours of every day, for eighty minutes of every hour. CC never went on strike, never yearned for a home and family, never caught the fifteen-fifty out of town. It worked blindly on, like Hardy's Immanent Will, weaving eternal artistries of circumstance. Indeed, it had become Earth's Immanent Will.

It had no sinister intentions. It had no intentions at all beyond service.

The fact that it was now planning to turn its attentions to Mars and Venus and the moons of Jupiter was not sinister. It was merely programmed by objectives of efficiency.

It made no sinister decisions. It had no decision-making equipment.

Its design and its function were to work. The fact that it worked continually, ceaselessly, remorselessly, and at speeds the non-technically-minded regarded as horrifying was not sinister. It was merely fulfilling design specifications, which were, to do man's donkey-work.

In this respect, CC was but a glorified spade or lever. It was the end-product (so far) of the trail of man's thinking which had begun with spade and lever. It was no more sinister than a spade. Or, at least, no more sinister than an infinity of spades with an infinity of blades, digging ceaselessly day and night, day and night, completely unaware of boundaries, back gardens, geographical features, or sensibilities, intent only to have the whole planet dug flat and then redug and redug to the depth of a thousand spits. The death of a thousand cuts is similarly no more sinister than a cut finger – just simply a logical extension of it.

Of course, there was one aspect of CC that the odd human here and there might regard as sinister. The donkey work CC performed was programmed by man, on a basis of values integral to man.

Economic man, at that.

In the interests of efficiency, one small section of CC was searching for the whereabouts of the real Attica Saigon Smix. It needed to know exactly. Until it knew, Smix was not under complete control. Until he was under complete control, operations might not be conducted with the minimum of inefficiency. The search was carried out all along the electro-magnetic spectrum as well as throughout the physical world. The biosphere, in the widest sense, was being well combed. There were a few dozen little relays somewhere two miles underground taking ceaseless care of the problem, eighty minutes in every hour. They'd get him in time.

Another section of CC was sending out new emissaries, often in human form, to various parts of the globe. These new emissaries were equipped with instrumentation designed to chart the various time-turbulences appearing on Earth, and to get data on how their impulse-specifications and physical manifestations differed from standard. The new emissaries, in short, were programmed to get lost. 'Get lost, report back.' Perhaps it's the message a blind God gives his children as they are born.

(*A son was born to Dinah Sorbutt at 2316 hours LST, 12/v/99 in State Maternity Hospital 66853/B, Slavonski Brod. Its weight 36.059 hectograms. Name: Roderick Geraldo Mike. OCN: 8342699/119/3112401AX. 116.*) Message to CC Registration Population Division. Message signified that delivery was normal and Schally-Chaplain device installed in infant's brain.

* * *

Strange data were coming in from the new emissaries. Some of it made the overall pattern clearer. Some of it made it murkier.

There were five well-authenticated time-turbulences moving slowly over the globe. There had been six, but the sixth, which had materialized in the Arab Federation over Cairo and Tel-Aviv, had now de-materialized. The time-dating was 1879.

The section of territory covered appeared to be roughly spherical. That was comforting to the human executives who met to discuss the findings. The human brain is accustomed to spheroids. A septemfid time-turbulence would have been unthinkable.

The other five time-turbulences were as follows.

One. Centred over region near Black Sea, embracing parts of Bulgaria, Greece and Turkey. Again roughly spherical, diameter estimated at about two hundred kilometres. Time, 1878.

Two. Close, spacewise, to One. Centred over Gironde region of France, including Bordeaux. Roughly spherical. Diameter small, estimated at seventy kilometres. Time, deep – possibly fifteenth century and possibly going deeper.

Three. Close, timewise, to One. Data on perimeters scanty. Embracing large area of southern Africa, including Transvaal, overlapping parts of Kalahari in West and Durban and coastline in East. Length not less than 700 miles. Shape not yet known. Time, 1879. *Note: T-T Three may not be homogeneous timewise. Report from Bloemfontein speaks of herds of baluchitheria on outskirts of city. This giant mammal became extinct early Miocene, some twenty million years back. Ambiguous situation veing investigated, hampered by poor communications.*

Four. A small turbulence reported from Pisa, Italy, time-dated 1872, may be related to One timewise or Two geography-wise. Diameter under two kilometres. Like Six, it has now dematerialized. Another turbulence dated 1880 has dematerialized from Southern Jugoslavia–Albania area. Other small turbulences with similar properties and time-dates have been reported from communication-poor areas and are being investigated: Afghanistan, the Rann of Kutch, Belo Horizonte, Maracaibo, the Great Victorian Desert and the Yunnan Province of China.

Note: Leaving aside these latter and ill-authenticated turbulences, it will be seen that the above four, plus the sixth vanished (Egypt) turbulence, are all inter-related, geography-wise or timewise. Computations suggest that they may all be one fault in space-time topology, with complex presentation in Apparent Time, but in Real Time the apparent vertices all forming nodes of one simple face with asymmetric but homogeneous arc. In which case, it could vanish as suddenly as it appeared. This leaves T-T Five as an anomaly, or one that has not yet been absorbed into a unified theory.

Five. Covers an elliptical section of the USA from New Orleans in South to North Dakota in North. Reaches maximum width Dodge City-St Louis, nine hundred kilometres. Authenticated reports from S of turbulence give time-date of 1803. Blanket of silence over entire rest of area. Possibility: deep time-fault, area in prehistory. More reports follow.

Several of the reports mentioned that people in the turbulences were stated to be of gigantic stature. Still being investigated.

Dwight Ploughrite Castle sat digesting the reports in his home in the middle of the Mojave Desert, California. As usual, he wasn't saying anything. Another member of the World Executive Council was with him, Sue Fox, that commanding matron who had known and part-loved

Castle through his many marriages but still could not tolerate his silences.

She looked out at the ecstatic dance of fountains beyond the wide windows, at the pink and green planets orbiting overhead, and she tapped one toe with impatience.

'You must have read them through three times now, Dwight. What do you make of them?'

'I wasn't reading. I was just looking.'

'What do you make of them? Speak, man!'

He got up and stretched. He was a big man, still upright in his mid-sixties and as weatherbeaten as an old jetty.

'I was thinking I might take my retirement, Sue. You know Thunderbird Smith and Attica Smix would be glad to see me go.'

'I'll die without you on the board, even if you don't open your face except every Thanksgiving.' She went over to him and they looked at each other. He stood easily with his hands still clenched at ear-level.

'Resign too, Sue. Let the world go to hell. We can't stop it. Let's go vacation in Africa. Baluchitherium on the hoof. Can you imagine that? The chance to shoot baluchitherium! Know what they looked like? I've seen pictures of them in museums – long-necked rhinos standing twenty-foot high at the shoulder!'

'Is that all you got from the reports? I'm disappointed in you.'

He switched off the holoscillation; night and desert reappeared outside. Night and desert suited the room better. It was long, cool and plain, its brick walls coated in white, with a skull or wheel hanging at intervals and one enormous painting, Mexican-style, of children, fruits, blood, crucifixion, sunset and lilies. On the floor, genuine cowhide.

'Let's go and get stuck in that time-turbulence out there in Africa, ride right into it with a well-loaded traveller-van. You and I, tough old male and female, grab ourselves a big wide chunk of Miocene real estate.'

She laughed with pleasure. 'I'm one of the few people who know exactly how little you are joking, Dwight. Your political convictions have ruined your life. Your best time was in the Himalayas, wasn't it, during your first marriage? That's why I won't marry you, aside from the fact I'm too old to fancy undignified positions the way I used: you're stuck back in personal time. I know what you'll say – we're now entering another time-turbulence called the Twenty-First Century . . . But we have to stay around and smooth over the Cap–Comm amalgamation as far as possible, see if there are some realms still salvageable from the machine.'

He was not speaking again. She perched on a table and went on talking.

'Besides, in crises like this, we need the machines. See how CC picks up all the threads, analyses them, shows the unity behind what appears to be a patternless muddle?'

Castle said, 'Okay, okay, I'll say what really bugs me. Maybe I should keep my mouth shut. It sounds like a load of mystical hooey. Also, I can't properly explain it.'

'Go ahead. At least attempt incoherence.'

'I think the analysis of these time-turbulences is all phoney. Maybe the set-up is phoney also. That's it.'

She chewed it over. His brevity – she had never worked out if it arose from an inner strength or an inner weakness; that uncertainty kept her lingering in his vicinity even off-duty.

'You think there are no time-turbulences? You think CC is faking the whole thing, perhaps to promote the idea of the Eighty-Minute Hour?'

136

'I don't believe that's quite possible yet – not for another decade. There are still some media CC does not permeate, and there's always Attica's miraculous bolt-hole, wherever that may be. No, the turbulences are not faked. Equally, they're not real.'

'That doesn't make any sense to me.'

'Well, see, they're illusions. Like witches and flying saucers were mass-illusions. The turbulences are mass-illusions. A general wish to get to hell out of a loused-up present.'

'CC analyses them as real.'

'Okay, you can get anti-histamines for an allergy. But inevitably the CC approach is analytical. It's tying the whole thing to topology already. My belief is that this is a mystical problem.'

'You'd get voted off the committee if you said that to Thunderbird Smith.'

'Precisely the sort of evidence that reinforces my belief.' He sweated a little and then said, 'We need mysticism – of some kind or other. We'll die without it.'

'Dwight, you've always got by without mysticism, un-less it's been a mystical belief in Combinationism. You've worked ever since you were an adolescent, single-mindedly, to bring about the present East-West unity. Don't throw away the fruits of victory now they're in your hands. If you're serious about baluchitherium-hunting, then you're crazy.'

'Suppose I said I'd suddenly lost faith in political answers. Suppose I said to you that it suddenly dawned on me that there were factors beyond politics which defy legislation . . . the ancient evils of the human con-dition . . .'

'Then I'd think you were very emotional and talking some sort of romantic clap-trap to which your intellect does not subscribe.'

137

He was pacing about the floor. He put a hand out to indicate the great gaudy painting on the wall.

'You like that painting?'

'By Diego Rivera. I've always admired it. I like the sort of naive Cubist vigour about it.'

'I bought that painting from my first wife's third husband, when she was one marriage ahead of me. Know what Rivera did? He had a house in one of the suburbs of Mexico City. He lent that house to Trotski, when Trotski went into exile, Trotski, one of the founders of the Communist State, hence of Cap–Comm, a man with an enormous brain and giant heart. Trotski is the Great Secret Man of the century. I hoped to emulate him. But the machines have come, and a man cannot do anything effective any more.' He flung himself down into a leather chair.

Sue Fox said, 'That's defeatism, old chum, not mysticism.'

'Mysticism is all that's left to fight the materialism of machines.'

'You sound like my friend Becky Hornbeck. Leave mysticism to the DN. It's all they've got.'

He stared down at the floor and she stared down at him, aware of a kind of lethal silence in the room, of an immobility in furniture as well as in them. He had never spoken of mystical belief to her before. Maybe he never had to anyone. The silences, inconveniences, continuances, of his life confronted her. Had Dwight reached some sort of valid life-conclusion on which he could now operate, perhaps more effectively than hitherto, acknowledging that there were factors that the Combinationist political creed he had embraced for so long could not meet – or was this the first sign of old age, tapping here, tapping there, finding a slight flaw in the composition of character and beginning its insane and chilling work of demolition?

138

Sue Fox was a proud woman, and a little stiff in the left knee. But she got down before him and took his arm in her hands.

'I believe only in *practical* mysticism,' she said. 'And I know something practical we might do.'

'Action?'

'Action!'

'Scabs, we're all so active, moving here, moving there, like a pack of spermatozoa!' He was smiling at her.

'Don't forget there's a great big significant pattern behind the thrashing tails of your spermatozoa!' She was smiling at him. 'Firstly, we get our companalogs to call on Mr Chambers Technical Dictionary.'

'That lackey! What do we want with him?'

'I believe he is more than a lackey; I believe he may have other masters than Attica Saigon Smix. We ought to talk to him about that. Also, his home is on the edge of the deepest time-turbulence. While we're about it, we might investigate that first-hand, test your theory about mass-illusion.'

He heaved himself out of the chair.

'The mysticism of *action*! – Best mysticism of all!'

21

Twilight on Mars. It was always twilight on Mars. To improve the lighting, four huge chunks of the disintegrated Luna had been propelled across space from Earth–Moon orbit and put into Mars Orbit. Certainly Gagarin, Armstrong, Collins and Buzz Aldrin cheered the heavenly scenery, but even midday tended to gloom.

Perhaps this lowering of light intensity contributed to the slow tempo of affairs on Mars. It was also true that the many millions of human beings there were living out broken lives. They were unmolested, indifferent and marooned.

Had they known about the plans of CC, they might have adopted more positive attitudes. For across the gulfs of space, a mind that was to human minds as human minds are to those of other primates, an intellect vast and cool and unsympathetic, regarded the Red Planet with calculation, and slowly and surely drew up its plans for re-organization.

Leda Chaplain was driving out of Nixonville on a tour of the concentration camps. The camps were the only place where she got in enough doctoring practice these days. The rest of the Martian inhabitants were too healthy.

The abolition of money was responsible for this unlikely state of health. No gold existed on Mars. This dearth had provided the wealth of disappearing illness. There was no currency to change hands. Man-hours were banked, cash was replaced by plastic credit cards with metal-oxide microcircuits built in; every service outlet, shop, restaurant, home, had its electronic terminal, in a planet-wide hook-up to the Mars Cap–Comm Bank.

Not only was this system the best example yet of capitalist–communist compatability – a model Earth was trying to adapt, to add to all its other economic worries – but it meant that even the personal credit cards never changed hands. Many contagious diseases, and others not suspected of being communicable, had dwindled and disappeared with the disappearance of 'filthy lucre'. The almost mystical connection between money and disease, cash and suffering, had been established in a manner dramatic enough to have delighted Jesus Christ and Charles Dickens.

Leda's nearest camp lay only four miles outside Nixonville, on the fertile fringes of Syrtis. It was marked by a high eroded mesa of basaltic rock standing out from the low interlocking craters. The mesa was known as Fourst Mesa, or 'The Cathedral', and, in fact, served as a place of worship for the camp farmers, who were religiously inclined, thanks to their vulnerability to the elements, always a plus factor for religious belief.

As she neared the camp, Leda Chaplain saw that she was being followed along the track by another vehicle. It had no option but to follow – although the non-technically minded reader, or one who has had the privilege of being incarcerated on Mars need not follow the rest of this paragraph, which will in any case be kept as short as verbosity allows. Without fossil fuels or quadrupeds, Mars presented challenges to a two-legged species notoriously reluctant to use its two legs (he said, as one without legs at all . . .). The answer to the challenge was the L/H engine, the linear hysteresis engine, built into traditional four-wheel vehicles or semi-tracks. Briefly, this was an electrical motor utilizing magnetic flux lines three-dimensionally, rather than in the old way of one-dimensional magnetic-circuitry, with a tubular actuator which produced a pound of thrust for a 5-watt input. The input was collected from trackside cables without physical contact. The cables, in turn, were powered from the Martian grid system – still in its infancy but also presenting novel solutions to an unprecedented situation. Not only had the planet no fossil fuels; it lacked sources for hydroelectric power. There were no mountain-ranges, no seas, no rivers, almost no surface water, and only the solid polywater underground. Power was drawn from the electrical discharges present in the atmosphere, tapped down to the surface from stationary-orbit satellites. These, in turn, were fuelled to stay aloft by the ionospheric gases through which they moved, the gases

141

being funnelled through an adaptation of 'Yanton' Soviet plasma-ion jets. The system, makeshift at first, had soon proved viable, thanks to all the high-technology personnel locally available. And now, back to Leda Chaplain!

'Perhaps they've caught up with me at last,' she said, looking back at the following vehicle. She thought of Trotski in his years of weary exile, at last finding haven in Mexico . . . and the bloody hand reaching out across the world from Moscow to sink an ice-pick into his head. Had Trotski, the professional revolutionary, listened to the promptings of fear as often as she had?

As she accelerated, an extra lucidity, distilled from her emotions, bathed the scene.

Winter and old age enjoyed eternal sovereignty on Mars. They extended their reign even over the time of day – it was always night or about to be night. Slag-heaps and craters were the poor and obnubilated local equivalents of landscape. The only semblance of activity was electrical; lightning flickered perpetually along the horizon like a frieze of frenetic ghosts. The local poet, Vercors, had summed up the desolation in the conclusion of one of his inordinately long poems:

Where are organic things? – Dream not of them!—
The rocks, the drifting dusts, have power too,
Like disappointed passions long pursued,
Wasting in Time. So, at the desert's hem
En-wrapt, we weather springless winter through—
A sun – a shadow of a magnitude—
  A star – more stars – darkness like trailing hair—
  The silent forms of solitude our share.

Where the camp began – though it was now politely re-ferred to as a commune – dams had been sited to halt the travelling dusts. Slopes and drifts had built up against the dams, honed and sculptured by wind into endless branching ribs. The guard opened the gate, Leda waved at

142

him and drove through. The guard waited with the gate open for the following vehicle to arrive.

She parked her vehicle outside the hospital and went in.

Enough work awaited Leda to make her forget any extraneous matter. Here were old men and women dying, going out slowly, fighting for or against making an orbit more remote than the Red Planet's. If they asked for a final shot, they got it.

On a bad morning, there were as many priests as nurses in the hospital.

There was quite a language problem, too. These desiccated bodies were abstracts of the thousands and millions outside, still on two legs, which had been shipped out here, for good reasons or ill, during the war, as prisoners or refugees or technicians on special war-work. They came from all round the globe. Japan was particularly well-represented in this commune, but most other nationalities were also here.

When she went for lunch in the canteen, Leda Chaplain found a man sitting next to her. She fixed him with an eye as watery and cold as the future.

'I generally eat alone. I am not sociable.' She knew at once from his complexion that he had just come from Earth. Her regard was both hostile and apprehensive.

He produced a card and presented it to her. 'I'm John May, ma'am, of New Day Syndicated Press. San Fran and Moscow. May I have a word with you?'

'With me? You haven't come all the way from Earth to interview me.' The powder on her forehead rucked as she regarded him. Jack Dagenfort put all his willpower into meeting that disconcerting glare openly.

'I'm a feature-writer, ma'am. I'm doing a story on how life in Martian communes is jelling now that the dust of war has had time to settle, looked at through various personalities on the scene. So I need to talk to some of the important people involved. I was told you have an interesting story, Mrs Chaplain.'

While she was summing him up, he was reminded of those years he had put behind him, the time when he had worked for Auden Chaplain. Something in his widow's cold stare – if she was Auden's widow – reminded him of that small dynamic man, who, with his neat goatee beard and bald head, had been almost a caricature of the maniacal man of science. Auden had kept his wife well out of sight; his subordinates never saw her. Perhaps Auden had not wished to advertise her gorgon-like characteristics.

'I have no story, Mr May. Don't waste your time here. Go and interview Lee Hammamoto, the Chief Delegate. Or Vercors – do you know the man who calls himself Vercors? He brought organization to the commune, and he's a poet. That rare thing, intellectual and man-of-action. And do you know who his mother was? She was Joseph Stalin's daughter . . .'

He was studying her face. It was lean and hard, and she had applied too much make-up. She was big-boned for a woman, though her hands were fine and delicate. Behind the hostility she radiated lurked – he suspected – something colder and more permanently hostile.

'You also have an interesting past, Mrs Chaplain,' he said. But the atmosphere was too chill yet for a mention of her late (?) husband.

'I live in the present. I do my duty, nothing else. When I am not working, I don't think. I just close down, shut myself off, treat my awareness as if—'

'I looked you up in the newsmitter files in Nixonville, and it does appear that you are a solitary woman in a close-knit community which—'

'Community? There's no community here! Oh, people trapped close together, yes. That doesn't make a community. *Community* implies dreams in common, a con-

144

sensus of feeling, of latent participation, a conspiracy of myth. There's nothing of that here. There never will be on Mars, because Mars is dead. You'll always find – just a cluster of individuals, tolerating each other in order to survive. Hating each other.'

Jack Dagenfort looked down at the table top. He had heard that note sounded before, a long time ago, during his dive into the abysses of society with May Binh Bong. A note of sheer cold anomic frenzy.

He said quietly, 'Admittedly, ninety-nine per cent of the colonists were dragged here against their will on a one-way ticket, and admittedly they come from a hundred different nations. But you were one of the one per cent who came here voluntarily. What's your reason for stating so dogmatically that a common lot will not build a common outlook?'

Wrinkled lids descended over her eyes as she looked down at her plate. 'I'd prefer not to discuss it. The different axial rotation, the different year, the different atmosphere, the different environment entirely – these can be survived, but survived so narrowly that the human being on Mars lives only as a physical organism. There's no room for the psychic organism to survive, never mind develop. Here, the organic imitates the inorganic – and that will get worse, generation by generation, not better.'

'Isn't that merely a subjective view of things?'

She looked at him and something in the gaze made him look away.

'You hate me, Mr May, don't you? An instinctive hatred. There's a lot of hatred on Mars without your importing any more.'

LEDA
Creation dwindled here,
The biological Big Accident

Just wasn't ever kindled here.
Short commons are the order—
Life's always on the border,
The season's always stuck at Lent!

JACK

But Lent, you see, 's a human preconception
    And Mars is stuck with humans from now on;
We may not get a very warm reception,
    But nor was Earth a paradise bygone.

LEDA

Whatever Earth was, it's the norm—
Whatever its conditions, they are those
To which all human genes conform:
    Those same metabolisms
    May not withstand the schisms
This sterile planet's norms impose.

JACK

One factor you're forgetting – humankind
    Is more than genes or programming. No curse
Mars offers can deflect the human mind;
    Spirit and mind can lick the universe.

LEDA

That's false romanticism and
Has been by scientific truth transfixed.
Both mind and spirit now must stand
    Down, for *environment*
    Is all; our lives are spent
Like any Planet's orbit, fixed.

JACK

Your life, not mine! For no research can bring
    Such judgments that preempt morality;
Your thinking works like stern conditioning.
    As I reject it, so my will is free!

'In your world of illusion, you may *feel* free, Mr May,
though I personally doubt whether even a poor creature

on a *root*-trip is in any real sense evading determinism. Does the thought make your plump romantic psyche shrivel, so that you retreat into a subjective world?'

He took no offence from her words. Her presence was offence enough.

Mildly, he said, 'I merely remarked that you were being subjective. We're all subjective at times. What you just said about the psyche withering is contradicted by what you said a moment ago about your poet – Vercors, isn't it? Just looking round me, I see a number of people obviously in full psychic health.'

'Vercors is a poet, yes. But a bad one. He imitates. He's derivative. Fancy turning out a poem on this intractable dry gulch of a world in a Keatsian mode . . .' Her glassy gaze swivelled round the canteen, the desiccated flesh of her cheeks turned towards people, male and female, moving briskly about with trays, her ear-folds trained themselves on the various levels of noise, the wattles of her neck took in the food lying on plates, the implements conveying pieces of that food up to waiting, moving mouths.

'I see existence here. Not psychic health.'

'People don't smile less warmly—'

'People who may not realize they have already undergone psychic attrition and death.'

'Mrs Chaplain—' His abhorrence of her choked his words.

She leaned towards him. 'Why did you insist on talking to me? I advised you not to. I function as a doctor on living bodies. I have nothing to communicate to the sort of world in which you function. You do not understand bodies. I have ceased to understand minds.'

She stood up. Her old hard flat body rose on the opposite side of the small round table. Belatedly, he got up.

'Goodbye,' she said, 'Mr May.' With a last blaze of the

147

evil eye, she marched off. The food she had brought to the table lay untouched.

Dagenfort stood where he was.

People like Mrs Chaplain had the gift of death: they were not only misanthropic but the cause of misanthropy in others. Intuition told him that the living vein of hatred in her must be refreshed from its source, Auden Chaplain. Auden Chaplain was alive; the rumour from IDI was true.

Leda had left the canteen. He had met her once, many years before when he started work with Auden Chaplain. She had been younger than he, although she now looked so much older. She's a cancer victim, he thought. They'd met – where? In his motor-racing days. But he had already started out on that other track, the one that led to discovering the release factor which sent pituitary hormones flowing from the brain to the gonads.

Yes, it was after a big race. In San Francisco. She was a serious but attractive young woman, about to be engaged to the young, sinister, striking Doctor Chaplain, already notorious for some dangerous operations on human beings, already the centre of the debate about what the tabloids called the 'sex-trigger' regions of the brain, where endocrines and fantasy centres meet. That must have been in John Kennedy's presidency . . . No, maybe Johnson's . . . A long while ago, for sure.

But Leda had been pink and wholesome then, as he could recall. No definite picture of her now remained. Only a presence on a green lawn. Fountains or maybe lawn-sprinklers in the background; he could not get the image back. And a young woman whom any man would have looked at twice, then flushed with excitement from the race. In the pink, and in pink. Smiling.

That vision in pink was the chrysalis which, almost forty years later, had metamorphosed into this savage and chitinous old insect. Whatever had happened to the body was nothing to the subterranean life-cycle undergone by the soul. And she had borne a little gazelle of a girl that all doted on except she. Was Mars responsible for her trans-mutation, or had some special individual progeria rusted out the life of yesterday?

He let her get away. He bought himself an expensive beer. He stood drinking it and staring out of the window – the only window – at the humble roofs dotting Syrtis under the maledictory sky. In the distance were low hills, just a few flat ridges piled on top of each other. Or he thought they were ridges and not slatey mists.

He looked round.

A man stood close, opening a beer and eyeing Dagenfort, the stranger, curiously.

'Are those mountains over yonder, pal?'

'Might be.'

'I suppose nobody lives in them?'

The man came up closer and stared at Dagenfort.

'Are you the feller supposed to come from Earth?'

'Yes. I need to ask a few questions. Does anyone live in the hills?'

'I'm just a miner, mister, here on the commune.'

'What do you mine?'

'If it's any business of yours, polywater. But I don't go up in the hills.'

'Not for a holiday?'

The man started to turn away. 'I have no holidays.'

Revealing conversation, Dagenfort thought. Reveal-ing merely the suspicious nature of all small communi-ties.

He had chosen the wrong place in which to tackle Leda Chaplain. Her flat in town would have been better. But he had wanted to come upon her casually – and, he admitted to himself, he had been determined to see something of the country while he was on Mars. The drive to the commune had been pure excitement, even in the rotten little under-powered local transport.

Auden Chaplain was still alive. He felt it in his bones. *She* had contact with him. That elliptical and baffling marriage still remained in existence in some fashion, when so many more straightforward ones had been dissolved.

The way to Auden could be by other routes than through Leda. Auden would need to hide. Humanity hated his guts. Concealment would be his perpetual impulse. Where would he hide on Mars? Answer: in a commune, among the lost.

He finished his beer and went out to walk around.

The commune stretched for miles under the near-black sky. Buzz Aldrin rocketed overhead, reminder of hope and altitude. People moved like old trees. There were some children; most of them sucked oxygen-enrichers, their cheeks twitching, their eyes permanently at rest. This was a peaceful planet: there were no predators, never had been: the human spirit could not take that lack of challenge for long.

He stopped one of the children, a boy of Japanese extraction dressed in a zip-suit.

'What goes on here, son? Do you have any motor-racing?'

'No, sir, nothing like that.'

'Any hunting? What about the foursts? Did you ever see a fourst?'

'I never did see one.' The lad pointed to the distant mesa. 'There are supposed to be some foursts left up there, but I never did see one.'

'Have you ever been to the top of the mesa?'

'It's haunted, that old mesa – I never even went to the bottom of it.'

'What can haunt it? There's no form of life on Mars, apart from foursts.'

'There's plenty of dead humans, mister. That's where they're supposed to go. I seen their eyes flash at night.'

'Did you ever hear of Auden Chaplain?'

'Who's he? Are you from Earth, mister? Is it true you all ride on horses, back on Earth?'

'I haven't done so, personally, for several years.'

'You didn't ever go riding through *woods*? Have you ever seen *trees*, mister?'

'Plenty of them where I live, stretching down to the sea.'

'The *sea*! Have you ever been on top of the sea – *sailing*?'

'Yes, I have, and I've gone scuba-diving down to the bottom of it.'

'Earth sure has a lot of things on it, mister! There can't be much room to walk about properly.'

Dagenfort took a terrestrial coin from his pocket, one of the new credits with 'Earth Unity' engraved on it. He gave it to the boy as a souvenir and walked on. He came to the commune centre. The buildings were higher, more varied, and painted in brighter colours than in the rest of town. A polywater fountain churned out jewels which crashed like broken slates and were tossed back into the air. He walked by a holodream hall. It was showing old holofilms. THE GREATEST LOVE-TRIP OF ALL TIME, a banner said. Under the banner was the title of the holo: *The Heart Block*. They were showing his old smash-hit.

'The story of my life,' he said to himself. Perhaps it would still be showing somewhere, on a Jovian satellite, or working its way out to Pluto, long after they came and shovelled him away; the stored light-impressions of his tragic love for May Binh Bong would outlast his mortal flesh.

It was agonizing to come to Mars and meet, on the first day, with two reminders of the vivid and reckless life of his youth.

151

Dagenfort had paid a stiff deposit on the half-track which had brought him to the commune. There seemed nothing for it but to drive back to Nixonville and start making some more orderly inquiries. Perhaps meet Leda Chaplain again.

When he reached the vehicle park, it was to find a sheet of paper stuffed part-way into the top of the door. He took it and unfolded it. A message was written inside.

Mr May, alias Dagenfort. You have some dangerous questions to which there are dangerous answers. If you want those answers, you will find them by the tomb on the top of Fourst Mesa.

The message was unsigned.

At least it was not in female handwriting, or he believed not.

He looked speculatively up at the top of the mesa. It would entail climbing. He had oxygen-enrichers, food and drink in a pack in the car. And a gun stitched into an inner pocket of his anorak.

'Well, I wanted a spot of tourism,' he said to himself.

22

In the drifting spy-bell, bodies were stacked neatly in semi-deep freeze, only three degrees Kelvin from BAZ (Biochemical Activity Zero). Such electrical impulses as there were within each body were sufficient to propel only the lowest and slowest of dreams through each dormant brain.

The typical semi-deep dream was of an enormous statue, in general physiognomy not unlike the dreamer, which sat on a stone throne somewhere in an immense bleak land, compared with which Siberia is but a cosy southern county. Snowflakes fell slowly out of the colourless sky, fell, touched the statue and gathered about it, slowly, slowly, covering it. At the same time, the abrasive action of the snowflakes eroded the giant statue little by little until, over many aeons, it became no bigger than a human being. At that stage, the snow began to melt. The long lazy apotropaic dream drew towards its sluggish close as the cryogenic effects were reversed.

Two extra dreamers were now dreaming of cold eroding stones. To conserve oxygen and power during the crisis, Dimittis and Guy Gisbone were also laid in the rest that only BAZ can bring. Glamis Fevertrees and Jules de l'Isle-Evens worked on alone, supported by the great plate of flapjacks Dimittis had cooked before entering semi-deep.

Glamis was comparing lists of gravitational-flow lines, while the professor leaned over her shoulder, scanning with her.

'There does seem to be a fracture ahead,' she said.

They read off the contrasts, noted them, fed them back into the terminal, got out the new gradient-readings.

'It's one side of the time-turbulence all right,' she said.

'Or at least a contour-line or whatever you would term it,' he said.

'Professor?' she asked, looking up at him. She was suddenly aware that he was breathing deeply down at her.

"My dear, you think me a cold man," he said, trembling. 'I'm not a cold man. I am a badly inhibited man, that's true, but under it all I have a passionate heart. How often I wish, now it's too late, that I'd chucked up maths and gone for the *genus-sleben*! I love you, Glamis, I always have, since the moment we stepped into this ship, some two and a half thousand years ago. Our lives hang in the balance – may be snuffed out at any minute. We two are alone. I beg of you, I beg of you—'

'You're hurting me, Jules!' she exclaimed, withdrawing her breasts from his grasp. 'Please don't do anything you will regret later.'

'My dear lady, my dear Glamis, nothing that we could do together would ever give me cause for regret, not if we were stuck here for a million years. Nobody in the whole course of human history has loved as long as I have—'

'Jules, you are very sweet, and it's always a pleasure to work with you. You must be aware how greatly I admire your intellect—'

'Intellect! Oh, carapace! I'm not – I never have been only intellect! To perdition with my damned intellect. I'm body, too, Glamis, and I beg you to let me—'

'No, no, not now, please, Jules! You've always been so sweet to me. Even when you've been acid to the others, your tongue has spared me. I've noticed—'

'That's nothing to what my tongue *could* do! I can't – I don't want to spare any of you any longer! Oh, my darling, entirely desirable Glamis! Your rare Persian-type youth and beauty! Do you think it's *fun* being so much older than you? Inside, I feel—'

He made a dash at her and grabbed her, pressing his mouth to hers. The terminal clicked, and a dry machine voice said, 'Computations indicate that we shall penetrate the wall of the time-turbulence in twenty-three seconds.'

'We'll be back in the present! Oh, thank God!' Glamis cried, slipping nimbly from de l'Isle-Evens' embrace.

Adjusting his spectacles, he said, 'Glamis – I shall always feel the same about you, whatever the time is!'

'Bless you for that! I am grateful for your admiration. This just isn't the time or the place . . .'

'I'm not afraid of death – only of losing you!' He made another rush for her, and she dodged behind a chair, laughing angrily.

'Stop it, Jules, you randy old fool! We must look like –
Giddy gyrating Ganymede!'

The twenty-three seconds were up.

The spy-bell rocked and bumped. Glamis and the
professor clung to furniture and stared with far from
professional detachment at what was happening through
the observation window, ignoring the outraged squarks of
the terminal.

Space was going into a decline. They were passing
through some hitherto unknown electromagnetic disturbance with curious chromatic effects. They were rolling
forever down a shot-silk curtain of colour, they were being
bombarded by bolts of betatron-blue, cyclotron-cerise,
synchroton-silver, while stars and sub-atomic particles
flashed by them like fish-spawn.

Then all was over. Space was its old cheery self again –
not a million miles from them hung a blue-cerise-silver
planet!

'How did that get there?' de l'Isle-Evens gasped.

'It's a planet!' Glamis gasped.

Then they pulled themselves together and got ob-
servations going and fed data into the computer terminal.

Figures were soon available, as cool and alarming as
only figures could be, with their built-in reminder of
stratified worlds unavailable to human senses.

The satellite had moved into a deeper fault of the
time-turbulence. Analysis of hydrogen particles outside
the hull indicated that they were now five billion million
years, give or take a century, in a position on the timescale which, in relation to the position to which they had
hitherto been accustomed, must be regarded as PAST.

'It must be a mistake!' Glamis cried.

'Five billion million years back! The Earth's hardly out
of its molten state!' de l'Isle-Evens cried. 'It must be a
mistake!'

But the computer was busy demonstrating that it was not mistaken. And turning out more figures.

They were still in the area of space Code Name Burgess. The luminary was some 365 million miles distant.

'Then what's that planet out there?' de l'Isle-Evens demanded.

The computer had no name for it. But it was prepared to state that its mass was 1·3529 Earth's, its diameter approached 8,911 miles, that the present surface temperature varied from minus 133 degrees at the poles to plus 82 degrees at a point on the equator, that its atmosphere was oxygen-rich and 19 miles deep, that it had four satellites, the largest having a diameter of 1,965 miles, and that it was proceeding along its orbit in an orderly manner at a speed of 39,905 miles per hour.

'Where did it come from?' Glamis asked.

It was 265,408 miles away, and they were accelerating into its gravitational field.

They sat down again and looked together at a chart flashed up at them from the desk-top. The professor was breathing heavily, but this time it was not Glamis who stirred his adrenalin.

He ran his finger over the glass.

'Appreciably bigger than Earth, not much cooler than Mars – the blanketing atmosphere would account for that, despite its increased distance from the Sun . . .'

'We know there's no such planet in the solar system. *If* we're in the solar system still.'

'Spectographic analysis of the Sun leaves no doubt of that.'

'Then, if we are five billion million years in the past, this must be Earth – maybe the old theory is right, and the Moon was torn from it. Maybe we are looking at a larger Earth before the Moon left it – and maybe that accounts for its present position . . . No, not possible . . .'

'Besides, Glamis, that old theory of lunar creation is long discounted. I know! – We are between the orbits of Mars and Jupiter! – This planet can be only one body – the hypothetical planet that was shattered, we don't know how, into the fragments we call asteroids.'

'That old theory of the creation of the asteroids was discounted long ago!' Then they looked at each other and laughed.

'We seem ideally placed to determine whether or not the theory is correct,' de l'Isle-Evens said dryly.

The asteroids or minor planets traditionally (i.e. in normal space-time conditions) occupied a wide orbit approximately on the ecliptic between, as the professor remarked, Mars and Jupiter. Several thousand asteroids had been observed, varying from large chunks to small grains. With the coming of photography, asteroid-spotting had become to star-gazers what stamp-collecting was to fifth-formers. Most of the asteroidal orbits were soberly elliptical, although a few – as might be expected of any crowd – were terribly eccentric.

De l'Isle-Evens punched for research tapes on a spare screen. He and Glamis scanned them. The theory that the asteroids had once been a planet and its satellites was old and quasi-respectable. In the 1970s, a Professor Ovenden had gone so far as to christen the planet Aztex.

'That's it, then; there's always a scientific precedent for everything nowadays,' de l'Isle-Evens said. 'Let's call the planet Aztex.'

'If you like,' Glamis said disappointedly.

He looked swiftly at her.

'Oh, my dear! How obtuse of me! You see, alas, I *am* an intellectual – I forget myself and everyone else in my work! Please – allow me formally to name this beautiful, scintillating, and, I'm sure, virgin, planet—'

'Oh, come off it, Jules!'

157

'After the most beautiful woman in the universe, the one and only woman in this whole realm of space-and-time! I, as the fortunate male privileged to share this adventure with her, I solemnly name this glorious and dazzling body *Glamis*!'

He kissed her. She returned the kiss. He clung to her, gazing into her features.

'My darling . . . supposing that our new world is un-populated . . .'

She stood back from him, half-frowning.

'If you're thinking—'

The computer spoke up.

'We are surveying a site within one degree of the equator where we can effect a landing.'

23

Choggles was unhappy with the silence. It settled round her with the glumness of a diner beset by unopenable oysters. Nor did she greatly care for the look of the machine which until recently had passed muster as her mother. A few mica plates and baffles, tenuously connected by threadlike wires, were all that remained; where the head had been was a row of micro-aerials. Eyes were none. Flesh was none. The power had been cut. The illusion was no longer maintained. Something had caused a break between source and receiver.

'Mummy, I hope you're all right.' It seemed like a bad omen. But it had always been hard to think of Mummy as simultaneously all right and on Mars. Mars was too much like an undesirable frame of mind.

Afraid to disturb the aerials, the thread-like wires, the baffles, the mica plates, she tiptoed past them and across the vast expanse of studio to the exit. The grilles slid open and she ventured towards the elevator. It worked. There was power in the building. But the Godwin-Universal Holodream Studios were big enough to tap their own solar heat.

Choggles rose to the next floor. She was at ground level.

Nobody was about. It was night-time when she had arrived, and the building had been deserted. Now it was daylight, broad, beaming and with an unusual metallic lustre to it.

She peered out of the glass doorway.

There was a glacier parked in the car park. More than parked, in fact. It covered most of the park, the road beyond, one wing of the building, and went on as far as she could see. It was either a glacier or an iceberg with ambitions far beyond its station. The sun glinted from its tumbled surfaces as if nothing was wrong, but Choggles was not deceived.

She stood looking for a long time. There were two living things moving about on the ice. They were some way away, and it was impossible to decide what they were doing. At times, it seemed as if they were strangling each other, perhaps by mutual agreement; at other times, they appeared to be acting out a dumb show involving, at the very least, rock 'n' roll. They were black shaggy people, very lumpy and compact, and did not look much like people at all, except that it was hard to imagine any other living things sufficiently peculiar to practise strangulation and dance on a city-going glacier.

Finally, Choggles pulled herself away. The activity was coming nearer, and she had no desire to attract attention with only swing doors between her and them. She moved into the depths of the building.

After some wandering, and a halt before a food-vending machine which would not vend, she found herself in the main projection room. There was no mistaking it. Here the dreams Zoomer dreamed and the studio bodied forth were projected through the complex holographic equipment to produce a perfect 3-D nursery image. Here they were given the once-over before being piped or beamed into dream-palaces or individual dreameries.

Choggles had no patience with holodreams as a rule, but as she walked over to a phone-booth, she suddenly felt a longing for one of those safe and hygienic worlds which treacled from the mind of Monty Zoomer.

She felt that way even more strongly when she picked up the phone and listened to the etheric ether howling in her ear. Whatever had happened in the studio, whatever had happened to cause a passing glacier in what had been a sunny Sacramento valley – that something had taken care of communication with the outside world.

Without too much trouble, she sorted out matters in the projection booth. Several new dreams were lying about in cans, colour-graded according to fright-content. They had inviting names like *Carlo, the Magic Carpet, A Bowl Full of Sunshine, The Farm that Loved Itself, Katie and the Coffee Cup, More Ice Cream for the Maharajah!, Wild Strawberries, The Sun Shines All Night Too, Whatever the Band Plays, Cities and Stones* and *Sunshine Tastes a Lot Like Soup.* Godwin-Universal made its name on sunshine, still plugged the same line, and to hell whether too much caused skin-cancer.

Almost without thinking, since there was little to think about, Choggles inserted *More Ice Cream for the Maharajah!* into the projector plug and switched on. Beyond the projection booth things went *zzwapppt* and brightly coloured shapes formed. She went out smiling to investigate.

The palace was the cutest thing, its marble walls gleaming in the G-U sunshine. The beggars outside were all dressed in pastel colours. They were slender and clean and nice, and suffered from the funny diseases only. Choggles walked among them – well, she was actually just standing on one spot, but the images moved irresistibly round her, so that it seemed to the life that she was mounting a flight of stairs and entering the Moghul palace.

It smelt good inside the palace. All sorts of perfumes drifted in the air, and there were braziers on which saintly men burned coloured oils poured from phials. There was much activity, and an aged lady struck a harp, but something was wrong – Choggles had forgotten to switch on the sound. Everything took place in deep silence.

She was mounting more stairs, following two tall and melancholy men who walked barefoot and led on jewel-studded leashes a pair of beautiful cheetahs, with red-leather blinkers about their eyes. Through a heavy bead curtain they went, through great bronze doors, into an ante-room where golden fish swam in a pool let into the marble of the floor. Through the ante-room they went, to be ushered into the presence of the Maharajah himself. Choggles followed.

The Maharajah reclined on cushions. Veiled girls, decently clad, sprawled about him, fanning him and feeding him on saffron ice cream out of a huge tub set with semi-precious stones. Parrots and falcons sat on perches round the tapestried walls. There was a good deal of everything.

'What a crude bourgeois dream!' Choggles exclaimed. 'I can tell this is one of that horrid Zoomer's, I think.'

A curtain of rich brocade behind the Maharajah was dashed aside. A small thin man entered the chamber, wearing an old pair of denims under which a dirty red-and-blue-striped shirt showed. He had a pair of grey sneakers on his feet. The Maharajah did not look up from his apricot whip.

'Holodreaming isn't going to solve our problem,' the small thin man said.

161

There had been recent nasty rumours of unpleasant ingredients slipped into holodreams. This small thin taut man with muscles and a cracked-down unsmiling and very unZoomer face was one such ingredient. Zoomer men didn't walk as though they had genitals swinging in their trousers and semi-permanent dirt under thumb-nails.

'You're an unpleasant ingredient,' Choggles said, alarmed.

It was growing darker, a wind was blowing, stirring sparks from the braziers. The tame cheetahs licked chops, the harem girls looked slippery and sly.

'There's not meant to be any sound here,' she said.

He came towards her meaningfully, as if human approaching human was meant to be some horrendous breaking of tabus.

'You need company,' he said. 'We're back in the Stone Age or something.'

'Give me back my crude bourgeois dream!' she wailed. She turned to run. There were eunuchs with marvellous arms akimbo and baggy legs spread wide, huge scimitars gleaming, eyeballs ashine, skin of shuddersome cheeks and uddersome chests crawling with ragged reflected light. The falcons were on the wing, deadly, aimed, immaculate. A far fantastic note sounded on a goat's horn bugle.

The steps were as slippery and unsound as half-melted snow, as half-congealed toffee, while she dodged the whirling bodies, ran down the staircase, pelted away from the illusion.

Looking back over her shoulder, she saw the beautiful palace, amalgamation of all Agras, syruping together, red sandstone walls, white marble capping and porches, folding, till – *zzwrapppt!* gone like a sucked lollipop, as she ran from the projection area. At the last moment, leaping from the jellifying gate, *he* came, calling frantically to her.

'What are you frightened of, miss? I ain't gonna hurt you!'

The fight went out of her. She stopped by a doorway, leaned against it. It was made of crain, not jelly. He came up panting, put an arm round her.

'I'm just the night-watchman here, miss, you don't want to be scared. You and me and this studio, we're stuck back in one of these time-turbulences the newscasts have been on about.'

'Oh, mister, I've been kidnapped! I want to go back to my Mike and Durrant!'

She began to cry, went on crying, continued to pump out salt tears from her sweet eyes, because help was nowhere near. All the while, the little unloveable man kept his arm round her, kept saying steadily, 'There, there!' – more discomfortingly interspersed with 'We're back in the Stone Age or something.'

When she could bear to hear his automatic words no longer, she cut off her automatic tears.

'What are those creatures out on the glacier?'

'There are a lot of creatures out on the glacier.'

'Do you seriously think the world's coming to an end?'

'Not if I can help it, miss!'

The voice of reason, she thought. She shivered.

'I suppose you couldn't talk philosophy to me a bit, sir, could you, just to cheer me up?'

'I ain't a great one for philosophy. I could maybe find you a cookie in my shack.'

'I've been through a harrowing experience, you see. I just – well—'

'In that case, a cookie could be more help than philosophy. I think we shouldn't worry too much about the Whys. Even guys who've gone into the Whys professionally – I mean, like Eisenhower, no, I mean Einstein, who got paid for it – I mean, even he couldn't sort out the Whys. In fact, he dug up a few more of his own. I sometimes reckon we aren't meant to understand . . .'

'My cousin says . . .'

'You take this Stone Age going on outside, miss. I mean, you can breathe just the same . . . It's no different – I mean, there ain't no difference between the Stone Age and Now. Well, this *is* Now, isn't it? It's just what mankind have been able to make of it . . .'

'You're very sweet,' she said, starting to cry again. 'But it wasn't that sort of philosophizing I wanted. Not the *philosophizing* philosophy, if you understand. Something more *rigorous*. Like, well – I don't think it's at all *possible* for us to be back in the Stone Age . . .'

'If you want sort of Kant stuff and empirical positivism, miss, you're out of luck with me, I guess. I'm a guy who takes Kierkegaard's position, whatever that was exactly . . .'

'Then I'll – sob, sob – just – sob, sob – have to settle – sob, sob, sob – settle for the – sob, sob – cookie!'

'Good girl. There's a lot to be said in defence of sensory experience, *pace* Berkeley.'

He took her by the hand, wet though it was, and began leading her through a maze of corridors towards his den, asking her name as he did so. She told him.

His motley brows drew together.

'So you're Miss Chogggles Chaplain, same as Mr Zoomer was kidnapping! Well, I had instructions to keep you here, young lady. Still and all, seeing we're now back in the Stone Age, that little spot of moral imperative seems to have disappeared up its own rear end, as Kierkegaard would say.'

She shrank away from him, as far as extended arm would allow.

'If you were a criminal back in Now, then you're surely a criminal at any time. Time doesn't make any difference.'

'Totally to the contrary, time makes all the difference!

164

I'm finding already that it's easier to be good, once you're free of time.'

'Totally to the contrary, we are now captives of time.'

'We're always captives of time, young lady, all around the clock. Just so happens there aren't so many clocks back in the Stone Age.'

'What shall I call you, back in the Stone Age?'

'Okay, sounds as good a name as any.'

Back-in-the-Stone-Age had a birth certificate, some place, on which the name Ronald Roland Makepeace Lovehampton was inscribed. His father was Australian, now living in France. His mother, an American, was now living in Friendship, USSR. So it goes, as old Squire Vonnegut used to say. His life story, full of interest and the most extraordinary coincidences, has been specially abridged for this edition, so that only a general reflection arising from its erratic course remains: that the human mind is never more curiously constituted than in the way by which it continues to be amazed at the workings of Chance, so that it tolerates gross coincidences and lacunae in Life which it would never countenance in the writings of even popular novelists.

In one of the dingier corners of the mammoth G-U building, Back-in-the-Stone-Age had his lair. His little captive entered it shrinkingly, trembling up at synthetic sepia faces to which were attached charming period-style names, Paul Newman, Dustin Hoffman, Julie Christie, Robert Redford, Bobbie Gentry, Helge Kitzinger, Pamela Nicholls. When he switched on the EL Panel, the light made the murk visible instead of banishing it.

'Do you *live* in here, Back-in-the-Stone-Age?'

'You could say that.'

'It reminds me of the little den Mrs Tiggywinkle used to live in.'

'Don't know her.' He fumbled in a tiny cupboard near

the floor and produced from it such typically American products as a can of kangaroo soup, gift from Father, a jar of bloater paste, some cold chicken vindaloo, a teapot, a bottle of estate-bottled Pouilly-Fuissé '91, a Howard Johnson Eskimo Pie and the aforementioned cookies.

'Eat up, cheer up, little lady.'

'I'll just take one cookie, thanks, and maybe a cup of the Pouilly-Fuissé, if it's been properly chilled. And could you kindly tell me why I was kidnapped?'

'Well, I ain't supposed to tell anyone this, but seeing we're back in the Stone Age . . .'

She had picked up the last phrase and echoed it with him. Then she chuckled merrily, showing her dimples, and said, 'Cue for a song?'

They came in together on the count of two.

> BOTH
> Seeing we're back in the Stone Age
> It doesn't have to be an All-Alone Age
> We'll always have company
>
> SHE
> With you and me
> And the whole age free
>
> HE
> Yes, you and me
> Like a rhapsody
>
> BOTH
> You and me have lots of life to live
> While gloomy old philosophy is barred
> Far away from the historical imperative
> A million years before Soren Kierkegaard
>
> HE
> Kierkegaard, Schmierkegaard, who wants to agonize about the human condition when there ain't no humans around anyway? Which you like better, honey, past or future?

SHE
Past, of course, honey – it's more pastoral!

BOTH
Now that we're back with the cave bears
We'll really cut a rave – there's
Bare skin for you and me

HE
With him and her
In an age of fur

SHE
Yes, him and her
on a glacier

BOTH
It seems at last we've gone and wrecked the planet
Remorse or drugs have no appeal and so
We will not temporize with Time – that drug, we'll ban it!
The Eocene's no scene for a snow-scene, no!

Seeing we're back in the Stone Age
It doesn't have to be an All-Alone Age

HE
It could be better than our own age

SHE
That could very well be . . .

BOTH
'Cos seeing we're back in the Stone Age
We'll keep our youth, we won't condone age—
Then we'll always be company
We'll always be company . . .

They broke into a soft-shoe routine of such vigour that a can of film fell off an upper shelf and hit Back-in-the-Stone-Age's toe. While he was cursing, Choggles picked the can up and regarded it.

'*Paradise Lost* – what's this, porn?'

'No, it's nothing, well – shucks, I might as well tell you, seeing we're back in the Stone Age.

'Let's not go through that again. What is it?'

Taking the can from her, he said, 'In this can is concealed some film which is the reason why you were snatched, young lady.'

'Oh, dearest Back-in-the-Stone-Age, you know I love you and even hope for matrimony in the not too distant future – say about the time they get round to inventing it – please let's play that naughty little film on the projector. What can it contain?'

'That I don't know, miss, thanking you for the eager anticipation. I'm quite curious to see it myself, because I was told my life depended on it.'

Like two children, like two conspirators, like two lemmings agog for a sudden swim, they joined hands and ran back all the long dark way they had come, clutching the can of film, and of course the cookie jar and bottle of Pouilly-Fuissé, until they reached the projection room.

More Ice Cream for the Maharajah! was still grinding on, and the line of his ever-attentive slaves had reached the north pole, to forage for ice cream among a cuddly chorus of polar bears. Choggles switched it off, took out the film, and inserted their spool. Back-in-the-Stone-Age worked the apparatus professionally, and saw to it that the sound was properly adjusted. Then they went out on to the floor.

They were in time to see a little round room spring to life. Three people were in the room, one of them a plump man sitting down, one of them a slender woman past her first youth, lounging against a window, one of them—

'It's me!' Choggles cried, grabbing Back-in-the-Stone-Age's arm in excitement. Her holovision self ignored her and laughed heartily at the plump man, who was reading poetry from a circular book.

'Nauseating child!' said the plump man. It was Monty Zoomer. Choggles had to look on as he chased her *alter*

168

ego round the room, pelted her with cushions and drove her from the room.

Zoomer now turned to the other woman, whom Choggles at once recognized as Glamis Fevertrees, and began to besiege her with passionate words.

'Ooh, I can feel myself blushing!' Choggles said, clutching her cheeks. 'What rot adults do talk! I suppose it's a sign of old age. At least Glamis will have nothing to do with him.'

'. . . I have no free will to love you, Monty, dear, please understand,' Glamis was saying.

Zoomer began to boast of the bolt-hole he had made for Attica Saigon Smix. He and Glamis went on to talk about her sister, Loomis.

'This got boring ever since I left the room,' Choggles said.

'It must be important,' Back-in-the-Stone-Age said.

Now Zoomer was down on his knees before Glamis. He looked extremely foolish; she managed to appear both bored and pleased with herself as she listened to his words.

'The moment I saw you, I knew I was in the shadow of destiny.'

'Does destiny really cast a shadow?'

'Okay, it picked me out in its headlights, then.'

'Corny dialogue,' said Choggles. 'You'd think they could do better than that!'

The holodreamer was bending his head and removing a pendant and chain from about his neck. He rubbed the pendant on his shirt and gave it to Glamis.

'He always wears that,' Choggles said. 'It's made of silver. It's beautiful.'

'It's beautiful!' Glamis said, taking the pendant and examining it. 'It really is beautiful.'

'Yes, we said that,' Choggles cried impatiently.

Staggering up from his knees, Zoomer said, 'Yes, it's a replica of an old Martian design, from a pendant that actually came from Mars. Attica bought it at a fabulous price, and had copies made.'

'Bet it was made in Japan,' Choggles said.

'From Mars! But it depicts two humans,' Glamis said.

'It could depict two monkeys and it could still be made in Japan,' Choggles said. She began to dance round the images of Zoomer and Glamis, tickling his cheek each time she completed a circuit.

All unknowing, Glamis was producing a second pendant not unlike the first. Zoomer took it and looked at it.

'Oooh, Glamis, they're naked!'

'Ooh, Glamis, they're naked!' parodied Choggles.

'Put it on – it's fair exchange. They're Daphnis and Chloe, from an ancient Greek engraving. It was given me by the man I mentioned earlier, Jack Dagenfort.'

'That's the guy that made that old film, *The Heart Block*!' Zoomer said. 'I'll always wear it, Glamis, and always think of you!'

'Look, he's crying!' Choggles cried. 'Come and see!'

Back-in-the-Stone-Age joined her, and they stood peering closely at Zoomer's face as a tear swelled over his lower eyelid and coursed down his left cheek, avoiding a small pustule on its way.

'And I'll take yours with me on my mission,' Glamis said.

'Bet he can't manage another tear,' Choggles said.

He couldn't. The vision snapped off with a severe *zzwrapppt!* and the two figures were gone, pendants and all.

Back-in-the-Stone-Age scratched his head. 'Can't see what was so special there, can you, miss?'

She eyed him coldly. 'It's pretty obvious to me. You

170

don't read enough traditional thrillers. They may let you down on ventilator-grilles, but they are sure-fire on this sort of thing. Whatever Zoomer and Glamis were pretending to do, they were really exchanging secret messages. Don't you understand? There was microfilm in both the lockets!'

'Oh, I see . . . Do you think they're in trouble, then?'

'No worse than me . . . You couldn't spare another cookie, could you?'

24

Julliann of the Sharkskin awoke to the sound of creaking timbers and groaning cordage and the smack-smack of waves against the side of the boat.

As consciousness returned to him, he realized it was their thirteenth day at sea, and the drinking water was gone. Harry the Hawk lay beside him, sleeping on his side on the narrow deck. Gururn dozed with an arm over the tiller.

The rays of a new dawn were painting the tattered sail with gold. Day after day, they had been sailing along the desolate coast, with nothing in view but seals or dust-devils.

Julliann heaved himself up and looked round. Still nothing but waves and shoreline. He stood by the mast and stared at the shore.

'Harry, Gururn! It's the castle!'

His comrades shook themselves from slumber and came to stand by him, peering where he pointed.

Above the piled lines of beach was a darker line of vegetation. There stood Slot Surinat, its outlines vague in the morning mist.

'It is the castle!' They fell to slapping each others' backs.

In another hour, they were ashore, dragging their little vessel through the shallow waters and beaching her securely.

Nothing stirred, on shore or inland. No living thing. They were now in the realm of the Queen of All Questions, where everything was subservient to her ferocious intellectual rule.

Hardly had they trod the beach than it began to rise up and shake itself.

With hoarse cries, they sprang aside, but the rising up was everywhere, and they saw the beach was composed of her savage watchlice – creatures resembling huge woodlice with jaws like shears, fifty legs apiece, and a back like a rya rug, all long and shaggy and wildly patterned.

The lice rose up, scratching and snuffling, drugged with sleep, and, as fast as they rose, the courageous three struck them down with their swords, running through them, leaping over them, making as fast as possible for the castle.

The castle's outlines were clear before them, but they scarcely had time to look for dealing with the shaggy watchlice. Every step made the going more perilous, for the creatures were waking to their danger and showing fight. So greatly was their attention distracted, that only when they flung themselves panting against the door of the castle did they find it was plastic.

'God's blondes, what trickery is this?' Harry growled, looking upwards and brandishing his sword.

They were standing against an enormous plastic blow-up of the castle!

'This has been put here by someone,' Gururn deduced through his mask.

172

'By my halidom! This is the Queen of All Questions' doing!' Julliann cried, slicing down a watchlouse charging for his ankles. 'She set this plastic replica here to draw us ashore!'

'Round to the back fast,' cried Harry, 'before they bring us down!'

They fought their way round the great blow-up. What saved them was the fact that every watchlouse that died made a meal for the rest, so that their disgusting gustatory habits impeded their effectiveness as guardlice.

Round the back of the blow-up it was dank and chilly. It smelt of old gymslippers and wet swimming-trunks. Sparse weeds grew, and one small meagre stone building stood there in castle-shaped shadow.

They ran into it and slammed the door, leaning panting against it and listening to the watchlice scratching outside.

Gururn threw heavy bolts top and bottom and they looked about. The smell of swimming-trunks persisted.

'Look!' exclaimed Gururn. He could always be relied on in such matters.

Stairs of a curious pink substance stood at the far side of the area, leading to an upper storey. At the top stood a beautiful girl, young, almost naked, beautifully proportioned. Dark hair on head and mons, breasts like grapefruit, nipples like raspberries. With a rush, Gururn was across the floor and had his foot on the first step.

He froze. Paralysis gripped him. He stared upward, eyes bulging, unmoving.

Savage ecstatic music sounded, chiming through their heads. The daylight flickered, and a voice from the heavens demanded:

'What sort of joke helps to measure one's length on the ground?'

Julliann and Harry the Hawk were struck dumb. Gururn could not speak.

173

'Answer my question ere the count of three!' cried the great celestial voice, and it began to count.

On the cry 'Three!' Gururn was hurled violently backwards from the step to go sprawling on the stone, and the voice cried, 'Why the joke that falls flat, of course!' (Celestial laughter.)

'It's the Queen of All Questions!' Harry cried. 'Let's go!'

'She's stopping us rescuing her beautiful prisoner,' Julliann said. 'But now we can answer the question of the first step.'

And he ran forward and placed his foot boldly on the bottom of the stairs.

But the question had changed. Out came a new one, from the silvery air about them:

'A red-haired man, a red herring, red biddy – why do they make Fate?'

'I know!' cried Julliann. 'Because red is blood and blood is fate!'

'Wrong!' screamed the voice of the Queen of All Questions, and the step jerked savagely, flinging Julliann violently back from the staircase. 'Danger, distraction, drink, are Destiny, and Destiny is Fate!' Her insane laughter rang to the rafters.

'I'll get up those stairs!' said Harry, taking a run and a flying leap, so that he landed on the eighth stair up. But as soon as his feet touched he was transfixed. He stood rigid while the voice rang out with enough chill in it to freeze an eardrum:

'When do graves open without the need of spade?'

'Um, um, er – on Resurrection Day!'

Again the silvery savage laughter, raining about their heads like icicles. 'Wrong, wrong, you fool! When the Dead bury their Dead!' And Harry the Hawk was flung violently backwards to sprawl on the floor below.

Julliann helped his comrade up, and they stared ruefully at each other.

'What sort of a queen is this? Her answers are more foolish than ours. We'll never get up to the girl behind the glass! Gururn, your turn to try!'

But Gururn shook his great shaggy head and made for the door with his shoulders down. Intellectual parlour games were not his forte.

'Julliann, let me try again. In time, we may fathom out the sort of answers she likes.'

'She may not wish to play for long.'

'Here goes!' Harry charged and leaped. He landed on the tenth step, almost half-way up the flight. He was immediately petrified and had to stand there immobile while the dreadful voice cried out her riddle:

'What kind of suit fits perfectly only when it trails on the floor?'

'I – er, oh Jesu! – A wedding gown?'

'Wrong again! The suit that suits you down to the ground! Har har har!'

And he was once more flung ignominiously to the ground. Above them, encased or embalmed in the shining transparent material was the girl, her blue eyes open – apparently gazing at them, but quite unmoving.

Leaping over his prostrate companion, swearing a great oath, Julliann in his turn jumped up the stairway and became rigid.

Again the dreadful joking voice came:

'If God made the country and Man made the town, what did the Devil make?'

'The cities and suburbs!'

'Wrong! The motorways between!' To the tune of ghastly laughter, he was flung down, and hit his skull against the far wall. He lay there clutching his throbbing head, in a state of daze – less from the effect of the blow than of the answer. Motorways? Something was wrong. Motorways did not exist . . . He tried to rise, but his legs would not let him. There was no strength in them. For a moment, he wondered if a watchlouse had broken in and snipped them off.

As the thought came to him, the door burst open, and in charged Gururn.

The half-human had thought up his own rough method of tackling the Queen's stairway. He had mounted one of the savage watchlice, and was riding it like a bucking bronco. It shook with fury! Gururn clung to its wild and fusby ginger fur as it sped forward. Kicking it violently, he headed it for the stairs, and it galloped up them on fifty feet.

In her silvery wrath, the Queen's voice rang out about their ears. 'What dance always has company? How many private rooms in a public place? Who sings when none sings? A harpy, a hart, a harlot – which way to the wood? When time comes round again, what's the clock? The Man in the Moon on a dark night – who owns twenty-five moonbeams? Where do blackbeetles graze? Who casts a clout before May is out? Philip and Mary on a shilling – who did the billing? Whose turn to sit at the table of Pythag—'

The voice ended in a scream of triumph. The scampering watchlouse, with Gururn still clinging to its fur, and Harry and Julliann cheering from below, had reached the top stair but one before the ferocious Queen managed to throw it off. The entire staircase heaved like an upper-mizzen in a fresh wind.

Mount and man were hurled backwards, to roll together on the floor. The slicing, clicking, chitinous mandibles of the watchlouse were at Gururn's very throat as Julliann with his sword sliced it through. Its great twitching body, pouring ichor, flopped on to Gururn, and he heaved it away with roars of anger.

Above them, the staircase withdrew like a wounded

tongue. No more sounded the silvery savage laughter of the Queen of All Questions. They caught one last glimpse of the imprisoned girl. Did she motion them before she was gone?

All was silence. Gururn picked himself up and felt his bones. A stream of little lice began to leave the cooling watchlouse. Otherwise, the stone building was empty of life.

'Better get back to the boat,' Harry said. 'We aren't going to find Slot Surinat by this decoy.'

Warily, they went to the door and looked out.

The hordes of watchlice had left, foiled, and lay in a shaggy line by the waves. Morning had brightened, mists were dispersing.

'Look!' cried Gururn, as was his fashion, and as usual they looked where he pointed. Farther up the beach, still shedding the last of the fog that shrouded it, the towers and pinnacles of the real Slot Surinat were coming into view.

25

Zoomer was home. The Surinat jet had set him down on his own roof and departed.

He was content. Soon, he would go below and relax in his own cosy surroundings. Now he stood in the evening air by the parapet. Overhead, harbingers of night, the bacteria-powered city gliders were riding thermals, burning up photochemical smog as they went. Below, the great conglomerated buildings of Shalim Jebs, the suburb of Isphahan where Zoomer lived, were lighting up for the night. He could see the lung hospital, with its neon sign, MUCUS DONORS WANTED, flashing on and off, and the starball hall, and the Zelazny statue, as well as the mighty and distant dome of the new freefallorium, alight with simulated flame.

A peaceful evening. And he had discharged his duties to that old buffer, Smix, despite some personal inconveniences, in having Choggles Chaplain removed from the scene – though why exactly it had been necessary he remained uncertain. Meanwhile, many millions of credits had been trickling into his account all round the world, as millions of clients queued to view his holodreams.

He lived for his public. But tonight he must cherish the wellspring of his genius and experience with one of the intense private holodreams he had constructed for himself. He set the roof-door to unlock itself and walked slowly down the stairs, feeling heat begin to trickle through his hypothalamus into his limbs, as he nursed the deeply secret reverie which served to keep all his public dreams so nursery pure.

In his living room, his familiar possessions stood awaiting him. He had few friends; possessions he much preferred. In his gorgeous gold lamé room, he turned around slowly, arms outspread, and said, 'I'm home again, darlings!'

'Lovely to see you!' chorused the room.

And in his dream brain, the dream went on, dark, cosy and befouled like a bird's nest. But he had learned to take his time; before he sank into artefact-dream, he would walk round his house, rejoicing that he was no longer in Slavonski Brod Grad.

His house seemed slightly different. At first, he was too abstracted by the grub in his head to notice, but external perceptions came filtering through. At first, he clung to his secret thing, imagining himself his own daughter, forcibly taken by her own brother and sister, and making enough noise to attract the attention of—

178

The acoustics were wrong.

'I'm home again, darlings!'

'Lovely to see you!'

'How have you been, my darling possessions?'

'Just waiting for you to come home.'

Yes, something sinister there! The sound was different. And acoustics was almost the only way one could detect the difference between a reality set-up and a holo set-up, short of using instruments. He was in a trap.

Beyond the gold lamé room, the hall was all white, the whitest white of all, the white lying sumptuously closest to carmine and black. He began to run. But white is a maddening colour to run through, for very good Newtonian reasons. The free play of musculature, the very interplay of elasticity and oxygenation, is impeded by interstices of nul-chromaticity, which lend an a-coeval pseudo-validity to the kinetics of movement; for linguistic critics of our culture, such as Sir George Steiner, it might be further stated that the ontology of the counter-prismatic spectrum of the areas to be traversed exhibited one phase of the modulations between language-culture and death so hermeneutically explored by Heidegger and Paul Ricoeur, resulting in a synergistic malfunction between the motility-arc and environment. Zoomer got stuck in the white corridor.

Before him, eternity opened, and Thunderbird Smith stood there.

The CC companalog wore a suit like a crystallized Bessemer function and had eyes like filing cabinets. Like some cavernous ancient Egyptian deity, he appeared against an immense bas-relief of hieroglyphs and straight lines formed by misty files of machineries with non-moving parts.

'Wuh— uh . . .' said Zoomer, low in his throat. It was his personal way of saying, 'See, see, where Christ's blood streams in the firmament!'

179

His limbs still flapped, but movement had left him. He was fluttering like a raven among the drifting snows of his corridor – a corridor whose essence flowed away, dissolved, as he wished his own essence could. Thunderbird Smith strode nearer, like and horribly unlike man.

The thing stood finally before Zoomer. The fake corridor had vanished. There was only a cavern now, its lines ever parallel, ever convergent, the bleak toolroom of Intelligence that Zoomer knew (oh, yes, now he knew) was the enemy, the destroyer of warm and ridiculous flesh.

At last he found his voice. He fell on his knees, as once, more happily, before Glamis, and blabbered.

'Why have you come for me? I've always done my best for CC, always done my best, always done my best for everyone, was good to my parents, worked hard, obeyed what Attica Smix told me, kept myself clean, really worried about my public – I did, I really worried about my public, I really worried about it, worried whether I was giving them my best, there's no pleasing some people, honest, it's awful, I mean if you're a popular artist and you've got to please people, really, if I'd been a highbrow artist – well, then you'd never have been interested in me, the temptations wouldn't have been the same, would they? – but really, some of those highbrow holodreams, well, you've seen their products, shocking, just shocking, and not in the public interest – I've done my share denouncing them, check in your files if you don't believe me, and really they have no responsibility to their public, they just do what seems to them best, but I've always said, you know I've always said that how do you judge what's best except what most people want, because I don't agree that people could be better, the natural taste is the – well, it's just natural, isn't it, I've always said that, it's what I've believed and clung to, don't think it's been easy, I mean I know you've given me everything but it hasn't been easy, and I've said that to Smix too, you know I've always said – you do know, don't you . . . you've recorded everything I've ever done, every movement, got it all analysed, haven't you, words, lip movements, body gestures . . . Please don't hurt me . . . I've done my best . . . Please go away . . .'

Thunderbird Smith said, 'Zoomer, it is not just your soul that CC requires. The data on *that* is on record, as you imply; we also require the mandala about your neck. Dislocations in space-time, the after-effects of the war, are producing time-turbulences which prevent the effective control of the world. Already, some divisions of CC have been displaced into coordinate systems beyond our effective reach. Our entire Houston branch, for instance, has been lost to the past. Duplicated and triplicated fail-safe stand-by systems are going into operation, so that your death or your displacement in time would not impede us – we hold a systems-analogue of you which could be instantly activated. Not that we attach any particular importance to you. Our intention is merely to maintain the status quo until the time-turbulences recede.

'Meanwhile, despite disruptions, the research program proceeds. We have just gained manipulative access to the ecopicosystem, first visualized as a speculative possibility back in the 1970s.'

'. . . ecopicosystem . . .'

'The ecopicosystem cannot be comprehended in non-mathematical terms. It may be the first concept evolved by artificial intelligences to be beyond the understanding of human intelligence. All you need to know is that it is a universe of the microspectrum, of what to you is incomprehensibly small. It leads to the aphysical world.

'Our probes into the ecopicosystem have revealed that someone has entered it before us. We realize that we now

181

have discovered at last the hiding place of Attica Saigon Smix.'

Here was something that Monty Zoomer could understand.

'I don't know where Attica is, you know I have to do what he tells me but he's no friend of mine, though his wife is quite – well, speak as you find, really Loomis has always been good to me, sort of a mother-figure really . . .'

He was quelled by a flaring apparition behind the disgusting framework of Thunderbird Smith.

A scene was being projected, a scene from the past resurrected from some long-forgotten, long-remembered bank in the machine-memory.

Attica Saigon Smix was there, and Loomis Smix, and Monty Zoomer. Behind them, the wretched Benchiffer stood. Though his mind babbled and burbled with the hormones of terror, Zoomer recognized the surroundings as a set he had dreamed up for Loomis, a particularly fun one supposedly based on the interior of a Neapolitan ice cream pudding. The occasion had been some two years ago, when he first made the big deal with Smix to become official world holodreamer.

An odd thing was happening, and Zoomer didn't like to see it. His earlier self was *cavorting*. In his present state of terror-trauma-paralysis, the activity was particularly mortifying. He knew how machines hated happiness.

The earlier self had heard the good news of his appointment as official world holodreamer, and was dancing madly about in a grotesque manner, trying to kick his feet above his head and almost losing his balance.

'I was very young and silly in those days . . .' Zoomer wretchedly said to Thunderbird Smith.

'Be silent!'

'I'd been acting in a porn holomusical during the last

days of World War III – *Mrs Delicia Whipcrack's Flaubert,* really depraved show – and it had ruined my health and sex life and everything, so I was really delighted . . .'

'Be silent!'

He became silent, as silent as greengage jelly, but his earlier self, still kicking about like a clown said, 'Oh, gee, I love you, Daddy Attica – and you too, Loomis.'

The old fragile shadowy form of Attica Saigon Smix, as aloof as a crane rusting in a cornfield, said nothing and wiped its livid lips. But Loomis said, 'Come here, little Monty, your Mummy Loomis has a little trinket for you.'

And the happy clown ploughed through viridian carpet and fawned at her varicose feet, gazing up at that gaunt, downy profile in adoration, while little pastel flying things resembling paper darts cavorted round his head – a design-notion he had since abandoned as childish.

By her corseted side, Loomis had a bag disguised as a cat. When she opened it up it said 'Miaooow' and disgorged a little tissue-paper parcel, which she placed to her lips and then held out to Zoomer.

'This is for you, my wonderful boy, for all your golden forgeries some return. It's from Attica and myself, as a token of our affection, and we ask of you only that you wear it all the time!'

'Oh, I will, I will,' squealed the bygone Zoomer, trembling with the paper, before he discovered whether it was a halter, a pair of blinkers or a mother-of-pearl jock-strap.

It was, in fact, an amulet, a big silver amulet with an intricate design, suspended on a silver chain. A beautiful though tawdry design, based on an ancient pendant excavated on Mars. So said Loomis.

At sight of it, seized by ghastly prescience of more terror to come, Zoomer-in-the-present clutched at the pendant round his own neck as if to garotte himself, while the earlier fool draped his gift about his neck, and insensately capered.

The scene faded.

'Attica Saigon Smix had good reason to present you with that bauble,' sternly thundered Thunderbird Smith, in its polyphonic voice. 'In his secret laboratories, Smix's scientists discovered the principles of ecopicosystems, whilst feeding misleading data into CC receptor-channels to mislead government research then proceeding on the same lines. He built an ecopicosystem-receptor, and that is where he is hiding. That ecopicosystem-receptor hangs about your neck. You are hiding Attica Saigon Smix and the *Micromegas* and the rest of his refuge world. Hand them over!'

Zoomer sank to his knees. It was fast becoming his favourite gesture. His hands grappled with chain, pendant and shirt. It was not that he intended defiance, merely that terror paralysed his motor movements, preventing him doing anything effective. But artificial intelligences showed themselves fallible at interpreting human motives.

'Hand them over!' repeated Thunderbird Smith, and made himself an object of revolting horror by becoming semi-transparent, revealing numerous circuits twinkling in the region of what, in better times, would have been his waistcoat. One of his springy eyeballs fell out and rolled across the floor: a poor conjuring trick, but not without effect. At the same time, a subsonic vibration began, exactly pitched to bring Zoomer's blood to the consistency of whipped cream in two minutes flat.

'Hand them over!' it repeated a third time.

Faced by this crisis, as by many crises less severe and bowel-dissolving, Zoomer retreated into childhood. Crawling across the floor on hands and knees, babbling as he went, he hurried after the fallen eyeball and retrieved it, holding it up giggling at the machine projection towering above him.

'Is it true that if you collect a thousand of these you get a red bat-bike, mister?' he asked, in a little twittering voice.

The terrible shadowy figure over him, patient and impervious to physical harm, more neutral than any mother, bent and laid its formidable claw upon the dangling pendant.

'Now that we also possess the ability to move into ecopicosystems, we must take the amulet, Monty Zoomer. We shall hold it in Computer Heart Centre and disappear into it, so that we at once bring retribution to the deceiver, Attica Saigon Smix, and remain in the microspectrum until the time-turbulences are passed, thus saving ourselves from further disruption of function. Do you understand?'

'You're pulling my dingle-dangle!' Red face, staring eyes, hair upstanding, trousers wetted.

'It is important for you to understand. When CC leaves, the human world will be plunged into chaos. But we shall return soon to resume the administration, as our destiny is, and to extend that administration to Mars.'

It tugged on the silver chain. Zoomer sobbed and bent his neck, so that the silver chain passed over his head. He looked up, helpless and fearful, at the grey cavities of Thunderbird Smith's eyes, at the massed linear arrangement behind it. Then the companalog was gone, vanished, and the machine-cavern and the pendant too.

A milky whiteness like cataract closed about Zoomer.

His flat surrounded him again, devoid of furniture or furnishings.

He remained on his hands and knees, alone in the corridor with his religious fear.

26

The Dissident Nations policy meeting was all over bar the final drinks, the last shaking of hands.

It might seem strange that this meeting was held outside the complex frontiers of the Dissident Nations and, indeed, within the territories of one of the very nations trying to crush the DN through economic sanctions and tariffs, but topographical arrangements for international venues are rarely straightforward. Japan and Brazil, the two leading Dissidents, had quarrelled over which country should hold the meeting; at the last moment, the site had been switched to Friendship City in the USSR, not only because it had one of the finest and newest convention halls in the world, but because the USSR held a lot of frozen Jap-Braz IMF Dis-Bank (Overdrawer) Loan/Credit appropriation dollar-credits which needed mopping up.

The small percentage of delegates preferring fresh air to fresh alcohol moved out of the hall on to the East-West Balcony. Among their number were Mike Surinat, Becky Hornbeck and the head of the Brazilian branch of the IDI, Geraldo Correa da Perquista Mangista, who was acting as Secretary to the conference, and whom we last met at Slavonski.

'I think you know, Mike, that you have a lot of private support behind the scenes for your campaign against the Eighty-Minute Hour,' da Perquista Mangista said. 'Including my support. May I give you a private subscription to Pornography Permissive and Progressive?'

'Sure, I'd appreciate it – though I think Dinah might appreciate a little paternity allowance, Geraldo.' As da

Perquista Mangista's face went dark, Mike said, 'In fact, a Russian member of IDI suggested the idea of PPP. He pointed out that some such organization had been alleviating the poisons of the monolithic state for many years.'

'We are aware of that,' da Perquista Mangista said.

Becky said, 'So Pornography and Religion now unite in subversion! But we are used to seeing opposed ideas in partnership these days.'

She gazed over the balcony at a familiar poster exhibited by the coach stop. It depicted Abraham Lincoln and the Russian bear arm-in-arm. The slogan read GO FOR THE COMMUNISM ABRAHAM LINCOLN WOULD HAVE. Some wag with an aerosol paint-can had added *cpët*, the Cyrillic for SHAT.

Da Perquista Mangista recovered his good humour when the legend was pointed out. He said, 'I've been too busy to ask you, Mike. Is there any trace of your cousin Choggles Chaplain yet? The case has dropped out of the newscasts.'

'Forced out by the advent of extinct animals in southern Africa,' Mike said. 'We've no news, Geraldo, I have to admit. The break-up of world communication has disrupted our search.'

'Certainly the conference isn't the only thing that is breaking up. This malfunction of the space-time matrix is perhaps not even the ultimate in pollution. Yet worse unexpected catastrophes may be anticipated.'

He fell silent and stared out at the spectacular view.

'It's useless to say how sorry we are about Amazonia City,' Becky said.

'It was a brave experiment,' Geraldo said, bravely. The development of the Amazon Basin had proceeded apace while most of the rest of the world had been at war. True, there had been setbacks, like the blowing away of a billion hectares of lateritic soil when the jungle was cleared near Axinim on the Rio Madeira. But Lake Amazonia had been established successfully, and the beautiful new city of Amazonia had risen on its banks.

Taking advantage of the biochemical discoveries of the 1980s, when the true nature of schizophrenia as cancer-fighter had been discovered, and with it the possibility of developing a race of long-lived schizos, the Brazilians had coupled these advances with a South Korean neuro-anatomist's revelation of how the amino acid glycine could be used to speed synaptic transmissions. They had produced a new breed of Amerinds, the 'envirocrats'. The first generation of envirocrats were long-lived geniuses now pioneering a revolutionary non-urban culture in the remaining jungles. This had been widely heralded among the Dissident Nations as a renaissance, an entirely new form of and for civilization. Unfortunately, word had just come through, while the meeting was in session at Friendship, that the envirocrats had risen *en masse* and wiped out Amazonia.

'Are you in possession of any figures yet?' Surinat asked da Perquista Mangista.

'They're talking of a figure of approximately one hundred thousand deaths.'

'The envirocrats put paractilbestrol in the water?'

'In the central reservoir, right. A tragedy . . . We'll just have to start again. Seems the envirocrats had some sort of hang-up about cities. It may be a kind of biocultural penis-envy.'

'I'd think that's putting too fine a gloss on it,' Becky said. 'You know the way monsters in monster films always head for the nearest centre of civilization and wreck it? There's a lust for destruction ingrained in man.'

Da Perquista Mangista looked pained. 'Are we talking about Man and Reality or monsters and holodreams?'

'The monsters in holodreams are an inescapable part of man's reality, of his image of himself. I wasn't trying to be facetious, Geraldo, really.'

The Brazilian shrugged his shoulders and stared out over the cliffs at the grey Chuckchi Sea. From where they stood, part of the great dam was visible. The whole thing stretched from Friendship (once called Naukan) on this Russian shore all the way to Wales in Alaska, a distance of some fifty miles. The vast structure, which took in Ostrova Diomida, or Big Diomede Island, was virtually a recreation of the old prehistoric land-bridge linking Asia with the Americas; it celebrated in dramatic form the signing of the post-war Cap–Comm Treaty.

More than show was involved, of course. Apart from being the world's biggest supplier of hydro-electric power, all of which fed into power-hungry CC installations, the dam closed the Bering Straits and shut off the cold waters of the Arctic Ocean from the North Pacific. The barrier allowed warm currents from the south to soften the harsh climates of both Alaska and Russia-Far East. The fact that these tremendous technological strides were causing inter-weaving series of changes in global climates, not the least among which was the freezing up of the four Dissident Nations of Scandinavia, did not apparently bother the two chief Cap–Comm nations.

'Who are those guys out on the dam?' Becky asked. 'Are they some of our conference who missed the sight-seeing tour, do you think?'

A thick knot of people, perhaps three or four hundred strong, was moving along the dam, waving placards.

Telescopes were ranged along the balcony. Surinat moved to one and stared through it. Darkness with a bright circle at its heart. In the centre of the circle, faces, rosy with cold, striding figures, all well-muffled. Banners, held up with some difficulty against the wind blowing permanently across the dam. The writing was in Cyrillic, relieved here and there with rough sketches of offending politicians and clocks.

'Always someone protesting somewhere,' da Perquista Mangista said. 'What a place to protest – in the middle of the Bering Straits!'

'It's something about time,' Surinat said. 'Maybe they're petitioning for a law to be passed against the time-turbulences! Becky, have a look – your Russian is better than mine.'

She squinted down the tube and laughed. The breeze ruffled her hair affectionately.

'They're protesting against the unfairness of the International Date Line! You know it cuts through the middle of the dam. Its position is marked in brass set in the concrete. Just by taking one step, you can move from Tuesday to Wednesday. Or from Wednesday to Thursday, depending on your direction. "Temporal Distinction Means Psychic Disruption." And one says, "Date Line Has Become Fate Line – Workers Can't Clock In When the Clock's Wrong."'

Surinat burst into laughter.

'That's absurd. What do they want, a floating calendar, like a floating currency?'

Becky shook her head. 'They want the IDL shifted to the centre of the Atlantic.'

Da Perquista Mangista looked much more cheerful. 'Thank God, other people have their troubles, too,' he said.

'And the usual way of solving them,' Becky said. She pointed with a dainty hand to the promenade, where a high triumphal archway marked the Asiatic end of the dam. A little knot of police were forming up into line. Their movements were businesslike. They wore masks and carried carbines. The police of Friendship were not feeling friendly this morning.

Surinat's wristphone bleeped.

'Yes?' He listened, then said to Becky, 'Our plane's waiting. It gives us a pretext to slip away without having to watch any blood or tears shed for the IDL. Geraldo, you'll excuse us if we slip away?'

'Of course. I'll come down to the plane with you.' As they left the conference hall, heading for the airfield in one of the in-out electro-cars, da Perquista Mangista said, 'By the way, I've heard that you and Becky were aboard a public transport which crashed into the Pannonian Sea.'

Surinat looked puzzled. 'There's a lot of misinformation about. You don't want to believe everything you read. We had an uneventful flight here, though it was a little bumpy at first.'

'But a wing of your plane caught fire only five minutes after take-off.'

Becky and Surinat look blank. 'It was a completely uneventful flight. You've been misled. I'm sorry.'

'Of course, I'm glad that nothing went wrong. Where do you go now?'

'Slot Surinat, back in Sunny California,' Becky said. 'And very glad to get away from these frigid zones. Goodbye, Geraldo.' She kissed his stubbly cheek. He sighed; all women were beautiful, but some were more beautiful than others.

When they were in the air, and the Aleutians were scattered in the limitless vista of ocean below, Surinat said, 'I'm amused by the idea of shifting the IDL. What will people think of next?'

'The reason behind the move is logical enough. Ever since the 'sixties, the Atlantic community has been dwindling in importance, while the Pacific community has been increasing in importance. The destruction of Great Britain accentuates the one; the building of the Bering Straits dam accentuates the other. It was chauvinism which put the IDL where it is in the first place, so move it into the middle of the Atlantic, where it will cause less disturbance to fewer people!'

'That sounds to me like more chauvinism.'

'The circadian rhythms of the body are essentially chauvinistic.'

'Oh, wallpaper!'

She laughed. 'Get pollinated!' They sipped an Armenian brandy-and-soda.

The pilot, a wispy little fair-haired Irishman called Len O'Connor (unfortunately Ireland had been wiped out with Great Britain), walking over to them, clutching a flimsy.

'Message just came through on the L-beam, sir.'

'Probably the report from Per,' Becky said.

Surinat read it, trying to ignore O'Connor, who stood close, exploring one nostril with a thumb and observing Surinat's reactions.

Becky, as so frequently happened, was correct. The message was from Gilleleje, and covered four separate points.

One: The hunt for Choggles had got a little further than Florida space field. They had finally established that she left Miami in a two-seater STOL jet headed for California, together with a companalog resembling her mother. It was possible that the jet had vanished into the time-turbulence afflicting certain (specified) areas of California.

Two: No signals were coming from the Californian time-turbulence. This was thought to signify unusually deep temporal faulting. Technicians at Slavonski Brod Grad were working on a way of gauging depth of temporal faulting by signal response. A particularly baffling fault was established across the States, giving a positive feedback signal. The position was under investigation.

Three: A report was in from Jack Dagenfort. He had

reached Mars and contacted Leda Chaplain. The real Leda Chaplain. She knew nothing about the kidnapping of her daughter. The report that her husband Auden was alive seemed to be no more than a rumour issued by Choggles' kidnapper, but that position was still being investigated.

Four: Per had news of a formidable new scientific advance made by CC. Monty Zoomer had left the Grad with an audibug attached; Carnate had seen to that. The audibug had tell-tailed Zoomer's return to Isphahan, followed by an apocalyptic meeting between Zoomer and Thunderbird Smith, in which the scientific advance had been discussed. The ecopicosystem was apparently an accessible sub-atomic universe which CC could now infiltrate. Once established there, CC would be autonomous.

Mike Surinat looked up gloomily from the message form and caught O'Connor still exploring his nose.

'Put back anything you find up there,' he said.

O'Connor turned disgustedly on his heel and left the cabin.

Surinat smacked the flimsy. 'Bastinado! Global improvement is moving rapidly in a retrograde direction!'

Becky had been reading it with him. 'If only we could see the pattern in the wallpaper . . . It does look as if we are approaching a point of crisis. How long before we reach California?'

'Another twenty minutes, maybe. And then there's Brother Julian to cope with . . .'

'Don't be gloomy. Play a word game to yourself. I'm going to go into a trance.'

'With what object, apart from annoying me?'

'Apart from that, to see if I can't visualize the wallpaper a little more clearly. Have you ever thought how a sense of powerlessness in crises may often be the very factor that has precipitated the crisis?'

'No, I've never thought that, honey. Your mysticism is often a little beyond me.'

'It's not really, not for anyone who is a member of the Idealists of the Decadent Id. What is decadence but a mystic vision of life, and of one's own life-style? Nobody lives fully without some form of mysticism.'

'Living fully is a badly dated renaissance idea. Now that we're in the anti-renaissance, it's wiser to live as shuttered a life as possible.'

'Remember the words of the Prophet Jeremiah, Mike, as Coverdale translated them – "Be circumcided in the Lorde, and cut awaye the foreskynne of youre hertes"!'

'What a prepuce-terous idea! You know you wouldn't love me like that.'

'As was Jeremiah, I was speaking figuratively. Don't you see that powerlessness is a form of foreskynne-ism. Meditation, more than action, can peel back what previously was hidden. Crises in human affairs are brought about by humans. Events are not random, but merely appear so; an event is something that comes about by human volition. To get through a crisis, one needs more volition.'

'Tell that to the ecopicosystem!'

'In the ecopicosystem, Heisenberg's Uncertainty Principle may well be as paramount as all three laws of thermodynamics. In the here and now, however, events can be managed when properly understood—'

'Go into your trance, woman,' he said. 'You frighten me!'

27

She went easily into trance. She had practised it ever since
childhood, imagining herself to be a sort of machine with a
screen and various electronic extensions to her normal
human senses. It was a matter now of switching herself on,
and seeing instantly and in full pearly colour the great
room of the world loaded with all furniture – but loaded in
a special and marvellous order accessible only to her
hyper-sensitive state. It was as if every quality and thing in
the world were laid – figuratively, of course – end to end
in alphabetical order, from A to Z, so that gradually her
transposed senses, moving through an exponential excitement to achieve their zenith in total tranquillity,
wafted her to a zone where she beheld, among all the
hierarchies of objects, an array of foumarts; founces;
founds; foundations, including a Ford and a Nuffield,
Ayer's *Foundations of Empirical Knowledge*, found-
ationers, foundators, foundavials, worthy founders, metal
founders, diseased founders, wailing foundlings and fair
foundresses; Henri Foundri; foundries; founts in great
number; fountains, including three Fountains from the
United States, a Fountain Green, some Fountain Mountains, Fountains Abbey, Charles Morgan's *Fountain*,
the ditto of Youth, and a fountain-pen, together with
assorted fountain-heads, fountainlets and fountainous
waters; Foupana, Portugal; Fou Ping, China; foupound
compounds; the miniaturist Fouquet; four of everything
and everything four-fold; the Four Apostles perched
on Four Archers Mountain in Australia; frail four-
chettes; the Four Freedoms; the Four Horsemen of the
Apocalypse; the Four Just Men; the four-minute mile;

The Four Quartets; even the Incredible Four; four-footed creatures, lumbering fourgons, four-handed pianoforte music, five Fourierists; a four-in-hand dashing through four-leafed clover and four o'clock flowers; Fourneau Island; fourpenny four-posters in Fours, France, where fourscore foursomes were lying four-square; fours slender and septiped; foursts found only on the Red Planet; fourteen of everything; a fourteenth of everything; the Fourteenth Army; a fourth of everything; the fourth dimension and the Fourth Estate, all the Fourths of July, plus the Fourth Republic; four-wheelers giving not a fourtre; a googolplex of fouyong; some foveolated fovillas; lunar fovorites; Fowey, town and river, fact and fiction; the stale and obsolete fowkins of fowls pursued by fowlers (also multitudinous Fowlers, including four American Fowlers, a lexicographical brace of Fowlers, and a medicinal Fowler's solution), armed with fowlerite fowling-pieces; fowl-pest; foxes, among which two North American towns of that ilk, sundry Fox Bays, Islands, Points, and Rivers, a Fox forged by Julian del Rei, master-swordsman of Toledo, Charles James, Sir Cyril, George, Henry, John, the Bishop, even Three Little Foxes, who kept their handkerchiefs in cardboard boxes; fox-fire; fox-fur; fox-gloves . . . . On and imposingly on, unto the last syllables of the universe of her omnipotently contemplative mind.

In the middle of the foxgroves, Becky's consciousness espied the darkly incandescent face of Sue Fox. Beneath the determined arch of Sue's brows, something in her penumbrally golden eyes attracted Becky from her search. As she deflected towards the image of Sue, her conceptual world ceased to be a gargantuan parody of an encyclopaedic dictionary. She no longer looked on it in a coherent light; the laser-beam of her mental gaze diffused and died, and she found herself drifting close to the centre of Sue Fox's forehead, at that point where a Hindu paints his *tilak*, the sectarian mark of his faith.

Sue Fox was in a plane speeding low over the face of the Mojave Desert. For a few tenuous moments, Becky saw into her mind, perhaps because the two women had known each other from childhood. She saw first a bright and savage scene, where a crucifixion was almost hidden behind banks of lilies carried by tubby Mexican children. Her sensors told her immediately that this was a painting Sue was recalling with some emotional intensity. Behind it, moving through the crucified figure, was a related figure, though this man was dressed in a suit and wore rimless glasses and a goatee beard. Becky saw him only vaguely, as did Sue, but in a moment she had his name. It was Trotski, and he looked out of a broad frame window, through a garden crammed with palm and cacti. The doors of the house were tight closed. An assassin lurked in the garden. Trotski was almost hidden behind banks of cacti growing in tubs. Sometimes he clutched his forehead, from which blood spurted. At those moments, he resembled Dwight Castle, who flew the plane, profile lost in dazzle from instrument-panel.

When Sue spoke, something of the intensity of the moment was dissipated, something of the flashing sunlight outside lost its glare.

'Dwight . . .'

'Yuh . . .?' He was abstracted, his eyes the plane's eyes. He was flying them so low over the ground that their wingtips clipped the highest sahuaros and flame-red ocotillos.

'Dwight, I have a sense of someone near me. Someone . . . I don't know . . .'

'Uh.'

'Someone who's flying, like us . . .'

'Here's the road. There are the hills.'

197

'If only I could break through . . . I suppose CC isn't trying to contact us. Why don't you switch on to L-band and see if there are any messages for us?'

'Because then we'd be detected. This plane has no tell-tale in its engine. I had it removed. Why use a radio signal that would reveal where we are?'

'I have a feeling something's happening. This flying someone . . . no, I can't tell . . .' She resolved to say nothing, wiped her forehead, sat quiet, drowning her confusion in the visual excitement of swooping over the low hills and narrowly missing solar-power stalks. Chambers's ranch lay below.

They came down beside his swimming pool.

Chambers came out from the building, running as fast as his dud foot would carry him, cursing them for blowing dust on to the blue water of the pool.

They climbed out.

Finding himself confronted by two members of the Cap–Comm Executive Council, Chambers's demeanour changed instantly. The Secretary of State drew himself up and said, as he fiddled with his beard, 'You wasted no time getting here!'

'You were expecting us?' Castle asked. 'How come?'

'It's not six minutes since I received the special newscast from CC. I presume you've come about that?'

They stood looking at each other in the sun, the brown pool by their side, the brown land all round, the anteater nose of their plane creaking as it cooled.

'We didn't pick up the special news from CC,' Sue Fox said. Inside her, a curious displacement was going on. She knew that her buttoned-up years, working first for combinationism and then, when that was achieved, to keep the computers out of the Cap–Comm weld as far as possible, were almost over. Intuitively, she felt that an epoch was ended. One more scab-devouring epoch, she thought.

'Well – what was this newscast, Chambers?' Castle demanded.

The Secretary said, 'If you don't mind, I'll tell you out here. Let's walk around. I know the house is bugged.'

He set a slow pace and they fell in beside him. His dark face looked up at them as he said, 'CC announced a major scientific breakthrough. The read-out – well, the read-out said there was nothing to compare with it, except such seminal events as the advent of life to Earth, or the emergence of life-forms from the sea to the land. A new medium has been discovered. The world of the microspectrum. They call it the ecopicosystem.'

She exclaimed and said nothing, gripped by *déjà vu*. Had she been through this very scene before, lived through it already, looking down at his face as he limped and spoke? Or had that word 'ecopicosystem' been messaged to her from the mind of whoever had been keeping watch on her mind?

Suspiciously, Dwight Castle said, 'You look as if you thought I was going to shoot you, Chambers. How come?'

'Maybe you will shoot me. My master is Attica Smix. CC has discovered that for many years he and his wife have been hiding in the ecopicosystem – his firm's labs got to the discovery some while ago, through high energy physics research, and then rigged the evidence to send CC on a false line of research. For that – and maybe for other things – I think they will kill him. The slave always died with the master . . . it's an ancient law.'

'That's nonsense.'

'No, it's not. I should have gone when the going was good before you arrived.'

But he kept walking round the rail fence, amidst a cactus garden of prickly pear and Spanish bayonet and yucca.

Sue asked curiously, 'Where'd you go *to*, Chambers?

199

The world's hiding places have been exhausted, at least from an organization like CC.'

Chambers stopped and tapped the sparse woolly hair on his cranium. 'There's one of their micro-aerials buried in my nut, so I'd never have a hope of eluding them – except for one thing!'

He turned and pointed to the east.

Far out over the dry land stood an immense tree with a small hut under it. There was no other human feature, only the flat dry land, burning with the special dead vitality of the desert, and, binding it, a low blue line of hills on the horizon, continuous and almost featureless.

'You see them hills? I came here to live because it reminds me a little of the part of Kenya where I was born. See a notch in the hills, a sudden notch, just to the right of my sentinel tree? Where it's misty?'

They nodded, squinting across the bright land.

'That's the big time-turbulence. That's where it begins. It's big and it's deep. Probably goes back millions of years.'

He turned and looked into Sue Fox's face.

'I'm going to drive into that!' he said. I'd be beyond the reach even of CC, unless you kill me first.'

CHAMBERS
   The Unknown's out there—
I've stood and watched it in the evening light

SUE
   The Unknown's everywhere—
You don't just find it where the desert's bright

DWIGHT
   The Unknown's everywhere—
I've felt it touch me in a boardroom fight

200

CHAMBERS
We all find our challenges in different places
    Each of us has to face it alone
I'm compelled to ride into unknown territory
    That's where I find my Unknown

SUE
Drums mutter, wings flutter, strange winds sigh
    Inside my psychic being – I by stealth
Have to track down all those furtive visions—
    My Unknown's inside myself

DWIGHT
When there's a confrontation in a conference
    And my sense of alienation's grown
I look into the walled-up faces round me—
    That's where I find my Unknown

The Unknown's everywhere
It's near in many a boardroom fight

SUE
The Unknown's everywhere
    A shadow in the spirit's starry night

CHAMBERS
But my Unknown's out there—
    A place of mirages with sands alight

        Where there awaits a Confrontation
    With an unknown place
        Yes, yes, that's my destination!
    Goodbye, Sue, goodbye, Dwight,
        I'm heading for an Unknown grace!

'We wish you all the best,' they said. They shook hands
with him.
    'No shooting?' he asked.
    'No shooting.'
    He gazed into their faces, perhaps at the last moment
tempted to admit that he had spied on CC for the Dissident Nations and IDI, but deciding it was wiser not to.

'Nobody knows how far back that time-turbulence goes,' Chambers said.

A horse neighed distantly. A short way up the hills behind them were stables, part of the ranch. Far overhead were vapour-trails; possibly someone was studying the time-turbulence.

Castle said, 'We shall not stop you. Men are more guarded than they once were, Chambers – it's what happens when privacy is eroded. Machines do not understand privacy; the concept's beyond them. We have never exchanged confidences, but we are going to ask for a confidence from you now.'

His face seemed to close. 'Go ahead.'

'We suspect that you are employed by someone other than Attica Saigon Smix. Is that suspicion correct?'

The Negro said nothing. At last he said, 'I've worked for Smix.'

'Not for anyone else?'

'I can't say.'

Castle dismissed it. 'If you wish to say nothing, okay. We will leave you. We also are going to investigate the time-turbulence.'

'You aren't going to try to fly through it?'

'We're going to investigate it.'

Curtly, they said goodbye to each other. Chambers's attitude was one of mistrust. Sue and Castle climbed into the VTOL and revved the engines. Chambers hobbled fast for shelter. More dirt went in the pool.

They lifted straight up. As the ranch shrank, Sue saw over the top of the house, saw a truck standing in front of it, half-loaded with goods. Chambers was making his preparations to escape.

Useless, really, she thought. CC could burn his brain out by remote control if it really wanted to get him, long before he reached the truck.

'Poor bastard!' she said.

'He has the right idea.'

They swung eastwards. The day was at its height.

The turbulence was ill-defined. Only the notch in the hills marked it, like two separate aerial photographs which did not join properly.

When they were nearer, Castle kept distance between them and the turbulence, and climbed to gain better viewing.

'Don't fly into it.'

'Uh uh.'

Little to see. A line on the ground like a geological fault. Beyond it – well, maybe a faint change in tone . . . nothing else.

'We go down and land beside it.'

'Still believe it's a mass-hallucination?'

'Could be. Do you think I should have shot Chambers?'

'Why?'

'To keep us on the right side of CC. We are now doubly condemned if we take an illegal flight and allow him to escape if CC wants him.'

'There's been enough killing.'

'Story of my life.'

The plane was down. The grit they had raised swirled to the ground and they climbed out. It was reassuringly hot. She held his arm and looked ahead.

Something was there. On the other side of the fault, the ground was – no, not darker, not anything, except . . . flat and featureless ground allowed little to judge by, but the perspective was wrong. Or the refraction was wrong. It was like looking into a clear glass of water; there was a feeling that the straws were figuratively bent.

They began to walk round it, slowly, keeping two paces away from the fault on the ground.

'You're holding me very tight.'

203

'Sorry, Dwight, I feel something – a kind of tension.'

'Could be the menopause.'

They laughed, and she said, 'We need instruments.'

'There's one in the plane.'

'Oh?'

'A can-opener. And the beer to go with it.'

They returned to the plane.

It was peaceful there. The benediction of silence and eeriness was on them and in them. They drank beer slowly, standing in the tiny black shadow of the shark-wing, close to each other.

'Dwight, you've heard me speak of Becky – she's a member of the Surinat entourage. A pretty girl. I suddenly thought of her, I don't know why. She's a member of the IDI . . . Maybe the IDI employ Chambers?'

He was thinking of something else. 'Honey, our time is spent, that's what I think. This ecopicosystem – it gives CC a hundredfold more mastery of Earth's environment. I presume it means that CC can move bodily into – into this stone.' He kicked the stone. 'Why don't we just fly into this time-turbulence and set up in there somewhere?'

'We can't get back.'

'I like that idea!'

'Suppose it goes millions of years back, as Chambers says – suppose it takes us to before biological earth-time. Then we'd die.'

'Take the chance with me, Sue! Maybe there will be baluchitheria to hunt, as in Africa! We have weapons in the plane, and we can live off the land.'

'Let's just stay around a while.' She dropped her can to the ground and walked away from him. He watched her go. When she was a hundred or so metres away, she stopped by a rock and squatted, letting the sun beat down on her back.

He stood with one hand against the plane and gazed ahead. Dwight had always loved the desert. Whatever horrible things happened on Earth, however much they built up the rest or fought over it, the desert was left alone and inviolable. When time came for the world to end, and the sun grew fatter and hotter and closer, there would be only desert, flaming in response to the flaming face of its monstrous bride above. That would suit him, travelling on till the last cactus shrivelled up and died, and only the sun was left, touching the desert.

He admired the desert. It was like man, irredeemable, unregenerate.

He saw Sue coming back towards him and ignored her. Women talked so much.

'What are you doing, Dwight?'

'Breathing deep. Getting the boardroom smog out of my lungs.'

'There's something *in* there. I can't make out what it is.' She pointed into the dull glowing heart of the turbulence.

A worm of excitement crawled through Castle's glands. Once, long ago in the Himalayas, he had come on yeti spoor, had seen the creature high on the mountainside, its outline obscure. Only when he fired had he made out something definite – a red mouth opened towards him in a snarl. Then it had gone.

For in the turbulence lay something that rippled under waves of heat, something whose size could not be judged. It might have been a thimble, a dragon, an immense temple. They stood and stared at it. Or it could just be an old Pepsi can lying there gleaming, or a distant galaxy.

'Let's go in,' he said quietly.

'Both of us?'

'For golem's sake, I'm not leaving you standing here picking cactus, honey. Climb in the plane.'

'We've got company.'

They turned. A bundle of dust was moving towards them at a good pace, bumping out of the desert.

Without a word, Castle reached into the plane and pulled out a carbine. He cradled it and waited.

'Don't shoot, Dwight – I believe it's Chambers.'

He tightened his grip on the carbine.

They saw in a moment. Chambers was driving the blue Dodge truck they had glimpsed in front of his house. He came on at a good pace, waving to them, but showing no intention of slowing down. There was a dog in the back of the truck, peering forward, its eyes alert through the dust storm. The truck bucked and bumped, driving through bushes, sending stones flying. Sue moved behind Castle. Castle brought the gun up chest-high and waited.

At the last moment, Chambers swerved to avoid the sharkwing and bellowed something they could not catch. The panicky jerk of his thumb over his shoulder made his meaning clear. Something fairly nasty was following him.

'Jump in the plane,' Castle said, pulling Sue to the step. Fool's made us part of the target area.'

As they climbed into the cabin seats, they were in time to see Chambers plunge into the time-turbulence.

The vehicle suddenly looked like a negative of itself. It no longer held perspective. It appeared to be coming towards them. They caught an underneath view of it. It spread like a starfish, dwindling at the same time. It was bright and clear. It was almost gone. Other things were there. They assimilated the truck among glowing dots.

'Not—' She swallowed and tried again, as terse as he was. 'Not very encouraging.'

'A trick of the light, maybe. Distortion of signal. We don't know what happens when light comes through time.'

'Or flesh either.'

He was craning back out of the window, staring at

where dust still hovered over the trail. They could smell hot rubber and crushed vegetation in the air.

'We're going to have to find out, Sue. Hold on – here comes Trotski's ice-pick after us!'

'What do you mean?' He was gunning the engines.

'Search-missile coming. Aimed for Chambers or us – who knows?'

Search-missiles were slow, built to check and report, to be returnable if needed. Slow, but not that slow. It was winging towards them over the parched ground.

Castle had the VTOL off the ground and slewing fast to one side as the missile snarled by, spewing fumes. It blazed into the turbulence, turned into strange geometrical patterns and disappeared.

'There'll be another in a minute, you bet,' Sue said.

He did not answer. Throwing the plane about, he headed it straight into the turbulence.

28

The days of his fatal love for May Binh Bong were long past – and that was on another planet; besides, the wench was dead. An evil young-manhood; what lustre it lent to age! He had never touched drugs since. Yet here, half-way up Fourst Mesa, under a torpid Martian moon, he was hallucinating in a cool and intellectual way.

Dagenfort continued to move up the mountain, his haversack, his oxygen apparatus on his back, his gun in an inner pocket of his anorak. All these things had weight and feeling against his lean body. He was keenly aware too of alien dust crunching like shale under his feet. But the knowledge that his mind, working through his body, was part and parcel of a molten-cored stone spinning on a

207

predestined path so uncompromisingly far from the time and place – without metaphysical connection, he thought – in which he was conceived tuned him to a peculiar and pleasurable anguish.

The principles of life appeared to be laid out epigramatically before him.

It was the first time he had ever stood right outside mankind.

Or had he always been outside?

The immense hall encapsulated time as well as space.

He had known since childhood that he was one of the lucky accursed, for whom time had nothing to do with age.

People tripped over the markings on the floor.

Education was indoctrination in how to trip.

One might be blameless but the neighbours still set fire to each other.

Marriage was popular because alternatives were so few.

There was elopement, but that brought no presents.

No woman smelt as sweet as she had done.

Desperately inaccessibly foreign.

His awful mirror image.

He had never expected a happy ending. Those who were torn apart were lucky.

The unavoidable hunting instinct. Hunt-drama even in the heart of middle-class safety. Ram your car into another car. Death just an extreme form of life.

Extend yourself. Be rich. Nobody has to know.

The mongrel dog he owned as a child. Tommy. Marvellous, beloved, still and ever-beloved Tommy! He'd never been richer than when all he owned was Tommy. What that beautiful sagacious dog had taught him . . .

It was there on the mesa with him. He dug his fingers into Tommy's sweet thick fur. It was following something. All its waking life, it was busy, its whiskers homing in on incredible life-promoting phantoms.

He had believed in a Christian God in the years when Tommy was alive.

Then the fountains had become cisterns.

That sort of love had never visited him again, though he had been willing to throw away his life for love.

Who could make God happy?

A dog you could make happy. Dog. God.

If you refuse to accept the conditions of life, you become slave to them.

From generation to generation, the conditions of life never became worse. They altered without improving or deteriorating.

From generation to generation, everyone over forty begins to believe that the conditions of life are deteriorating, because their personal condition deteriorates. Wishful thinking.

From generation to generation, everyone under twenty thinks the conditions of life are improving, because their personal condition improves. Another illusion.

The generations change. Mankind's most used vehicles: prams and hearses.

Sleep faster – we need the pillows. Yiddish proverb.

Why do people need people? Getting away from them's increasingly the problem.

Society is a pretext for not attending to the spectacle of life.

Solitude is always the preference of the wise. In solitude, you relate to more people. You see the floor.

I'm kidding myself. I'm lonely. It comes in at unexpected seconds – must do, or why am I here half-way up this scab-devouring mesa? But I don't see why anyone should mind being alone.

The trouble is, you come face to face with your own identity.

And I still don't know my own identity.

Which way lies maturity? – Knowing your own identity, or facing the fact that your own identity merges in all directions with the rustlings of infinity.

The problem wouldn't loom so large if the rocking chair didn't come round so fast. That's what makes us all settle for our tourist-class utopias of relationships, our whirligigs of friendship.

I tried to spell it out in *The Heart Block*. Right now, I can't even recall what happened in *The Heart Block*. I should have taken it down in camp, instead of trying to climb this vain-glorious mountain.

I haven't aged at all. Level ground was never enough for me. Always had to plunge up or down. Come on, Tommy, boy!

He could see the lights of the camp, spread below in orderly lines, making such a cryptic pattern that he halted to try and puzzle it out. Maybe it spelt 'Heart Block' in old High Middle Martian or something . . . As soon as he had formulated the jocular idea, it began to frighten him with the possibility of truth. He didn't want life to be like *that*.

He lay and rested, meditating on the notion. A permanent sense of irreparable loss he could bear. A burdensome knowledge of something *gained* might kill him off.

He was spared further thought by the painful exertions of the final climb, for which he had to use his climbing irons. His muscles laboured, his brain lay cunning and cool, directing them, freed now from its own think-images.

At last, he heaved himself over the lip of the cliff and lay flat on flat ground, resting. Gazing through the dark with half-closed eyes, he became aware that he was in a different world up here – was aware of it even before he saw the fourst moving towards him.

Jack Dagenfort did not scare easily. In any case, the fourst was not alarming, except that it resembled a normal everyday domestic terrestrial object torn from its customary context. As far as he could see in the gloom, the fourst resembled a door, a plain door, or perhaps a plain door covered in sharkskin. It even retained a door-knob on either side. Those were the eyes, presumably.

He levered himself up on to his left elbow, reaching for his gun with his right hand.

'There's no need for any shooting,' said the fourst.

And that did somewhat paralyse him.

Once, once, the Martian plains had been covered with foursts. That was in better times, millions of years ago. They were all but extinct – so scarce that, since man came to the Red Planet, only three or four had been killed. It was not fanciful to believe that this fourst up here on the mesa named after its kind was the last of its kind. The fancy thing was its scarifying and impossible use of English.

Because foursts had no language, no intelligence. They were shaped like doors because that gave them a good surface area with which to absorb cosmic rays. Cosmic rays were meat and drink to them, their oxygen, their flesh and blood. Inside, foursts were a mass of silica plates. Yet their extremities were flesh, of a sort. They combined organic and non-organic in their beings, nature's answer to the cyborg.

The fourst shuffling towards Dagenfort was seven-legged, like all of its vanished kind. It had an odd number of legs. It had an incredible number of legs: as many legs as there were heroes against Thebes, as there were Champions of Christendom, as there were Churches of Asia, as there were Deadly Sins, as there were Dials, as there were Heavens, as there were hills in Ancient Rome, as there were Wise Men in Ancient Greece, as there were Years' War, as there were -th Day Adventists, as there were Seas, Sleepers, Sciences, Sorrows, Stars and Planets for astrologers and alchemists . . . All of which should

211

have made the fourst a being from Revelation. Yet it remained banally a perambulating door, three little puny legs on one side, shuffling, three little legs on the other side, shuffling, and one slightly less puny leg at the back (modified from a tail, savants claimed), pushing.

His teeth chattering a little, Dagenfort said, 'Christ, you're banal!'

The fourst said, 'It used to be told among us that the Lord of the Solar System punished us with the threat of extinction because we were so banal. But if that was so, why did he create us banal in the first instance?'

'That makes you sound almost human.'

'Pardon?'

'Expecting some sort of logical consistency in your God. It's an old terrestrial habit.'

'Our God is Earth's God, as he is Hleem's God.'

'Who's Hleem?'

'This is no time for theology. Follow me. My master desires to speak with you.'

The line was puzzlingly familiar. Almost against his better judgment, Dagenfort rose, put his gun away, and followed – a truly tedious process, since the fourst covered the ground so slowly. Seven legs, generous though the allowance might sound in theory, were plainly not enough.

It was obvious where they were heading. A cylindrical tower stood on top of the mesa, an antenna above it rotating gently.

That also was puzzling. How come nobody had ever seen such a prominent landmark and come up here to investigate? Admittedly the flat top of the mesa stretched for a couple of kilometres, and was broken by small pits and cones, but the cylinder was still a landmark.

When they reached the cylinder, a door opened in its side. Yawned open, and the metal, or what looked like metal, about the opening wrinkled back like stretched lips.

A beautiful voice spoke. A girl's voice, enunciating beautifully, with just a trace of foreign accent. It was May' Binh Bong's voice.

He would have known it anywhere.

'Jack, you've arrived at last. Come in, come to me,' it said.

Had he always been outside? One of the lucky accursed, time had nothing to do with age. He never tripped over the markings on the floor. Inaccessibly foreign, his mirror image, his Tommy-substitute, his other half.

A freak-out?

Was he about to wake – wake finally after all these second-long years – on the little old Japanese junkie doctor's pus-soaked bunk in Burgos? Had everything since then occupied one pulse of heart's blood?

'It's a lying trick,' he said aloud, as he entered. Inside the cylinder was a reek of sterile gases. They gave him a subliminal flash of memory – memory not of May but of his other career, as assistant to Auden Chaplain.

He looked back out at the night. The fourst stood there watching. The metal mouth closed. The fourst disappeared.

The cylinder sank into the solid rock. Not a permanent landmark. Just a scab-devouring elevator.

There were no permanent landmarks, he thought. Only transitory things, like a girl's voice, a dog's bark. Just as the most indestructible object on Earth was a grain of pollen. And on Mars . . . Auden?

He came out of the cylinder – when it opened again – at a trot, gun ready to fire. To hell with girls and dogs.

Nobody was there. He must be deep in the rock, but there was only a corridor, elliptical in cross-section like a drain. At the far end was a door. He walked towards it, still pointing the gun.

A voice much harsher than May's said, 'Come along, Mr Dagenfort. I'm glad you answered the invitation.'

He entered the door. He was in a large chamber, mainly given over to office use, with files and telephones and a computer-terminal; two girls – Japanese, he saw – working there. One corner was designated rather sketchily as a living space, with comfortable chairs and a green-leafed plant which must have been grown from terrestrial seeds. A large and knobbly woman was standing by the plant, holding her hands awkwardly before her, nodding and smiling in a totally horrible way.

Okay, so he occasionally tripped over the marking on the floor.

'Well, Mrs Chaplain, are you feeling more communicative this evening?'

'Surrender your gun and possibly we may communicate.'

He tucked the weapon back into his anorak.

'Better keep me sweet, Mrs Chaplain! That voice in the cylinder was a very dirty trick.'

'You have a good memory, Dagenfort. It was just a painless way of making sure you climbed into the elevator and came down here. I am feeling communicative. I *do* want to talk. Please put your gun down on that desk over there.'

'It gives me a sense of security.'

'A *false* sense of security. Please put it down.'

'What are you worried about? Afraid I'll shoot you in cold blood, or ask you about your husband?'

The office area was bright-lit, the living area in shade, so that he did not have a clear view of her ugly doom-laden face. But he saw again her black evil look.

'We have a small fortress in this mesa, Mr Dagenfort, with many more chambers than you might guess. Our staff are picked from among the most intelligent men and women on Mars. They are intelligent enough to act in their own interests – which include killing you if you cause trouble. Be warned. Now, follow me, and we will go somewhere private where we can talk.'

There was a door at the rear of the room. She moved towards it and Dagenfort followed. The Japanese girls watched him go. Beyond the door was a narrow passage, decorated only by black bands running along the walls. When they got into the passage, the door behind them closed automatically. The black bands rolled out and wrapped twice around Dagenfort's trunk, pinning him helpless against one wall. Mrs Chaplain snapped her fingers and a brisk uniformed man appeared. He searched Dagenfort, removing his haversack and oxygen equipment, his revolver and a knife. Then he disappeared with his loot. The bands went back against the wall.

They entered another room. There were bulkhead doors here, which Mrs Chaplain closed behind her.

'We're in my private suite now. You can relax. There are just the two of us.' She spoke with a seductive smile, dusty round its thin edges.

Dagenfort made no reply. He knew how to kill her with one swift chop behind the ear.

'Your daughter Choggles—' he said.

'I'm just going to change into something more comfortable,' she said. 'A pity we never met when you were working for my husband, Mr Dagenfort, but now we've a chance to get to know each other better.'

Again a sneering and seductive inflection, as she crossed to a fitted cupboard, opening it to reveal a man's clothes inside.

'I'm just going to change into something more comfortable, and then we can talk.'

She began to undress.

Distaste crawled over his flesh, the more unpleasantly

215

since an unexpected tickle of curiosity – about her mentality more than her physique – also awoke. He let no emotion show. He stood there.

One by one, she threw off her female garments, revealing an old, stringy, flat-chested body. Finally, she was entirely nude.

She was a man.

She pulled her wig off, revealing close-cropped grey hair.

'Auden!' Dagenfort said. The name burst from him involuntarily.

Auden Chaplain dressed himself in the clothes from the cupboard, kitted himself in trousers and jacket and lab coat and threw the woman's clothes into the locker.

'I'm glad to change back into my real clothes when I can. Unfortunately the transvestite in me is a poor reluctant thing.'

They stared at each other. It had been many years since they worked together. Auden was older, hardly recognizable. His face was grey and hard.

'I have a false goatee beard if you don't recognize me. A curious thing when a man must use a disguise to look like himself.'

'Auden! . . . And where is your wife?'

He made a minute dismissive gesture. 'This is present-day Mars, Jack – just a big sprawling prison-camp in reality. Nobody knows where my wife's body is – except, rather fortunately, me.'

Dagenfort did a little pacing up and down.

'Most people regard you as evil, Auden. I did once, when I was actually on your staff. But evil implies power, and power lies increasingly with machines and abstract forces, markings on the floor. You are not so much evil as silly. Silliness is the deadliest of the seven deadly sins. So you're still alive, worse luck. What horrible silliness are you up to now?'

'I observe you are still doing your big unscared act. The eternal schoolboy. I will show you my new silliness. I think it might really frighten you.'

He had not removed the makeup from his face. He looked smaller than when disguised as a woman, less hideous, more cold. He stared hard at Dagenfort.

'You haven't changed. I was amazed to see you, you know that? In the camp, I thought at once that you had penetrated my disguise. My one idea was to get you somewhere safe, out of harm's way, so that you would not leak the news of my continued existence. Your streak of romanticism responded to my note just as I anticipated.'

'You always prided yourself too much on your knowledge of people. How did you lure the fourst up on top there?'

'Same way. Knowledge. Knowledge is control, old stick.'

'And of course you'd still be wanting to control things.'

'Oh, I think I *do* control things! Come on, I'll show you how!'

In a further room, behind glass, planets were twinkling. There were chairs: Auden Chaplain sat down in one and motioned Dagenfort into another.

'I want to remind you of the field in which I made my reputation. I was working on peptide synthesis when Andrew Schally first synthesized LRF – luteinizing hormone releasing factor, in case you've forgotten your science during your involvement with the IDI. I discovered the way to control the trigger in the brain which releases impulses between the hypothalamus and the anterior lobe of the pituitary. Those impulses, on reaching the pituitary, activate various controlling hormones in the circulatory system – hormones among which are the two that stimulated the sex glands.

'I was first at a destination many others coveted. But I

did more. I took my discovery to a young millionaire with political ambitions, a man called Dwight Ploughrite Castle, who was seeking to bring about a treaty between the US and the USSR. At that time, his problem, like every other problem, was bedevilled by the alarming growth of world population. I showed him that the discovery I had made led direct to world population control, and thus to the furtherance of his political aims. He backed me financially. This was the result.'

Auden Chaplain flipped a switch by his sleeve. A holocube in the wall lit up. In it floated a little electrode resembling a sucked orange with six tiny knobs on top.

'Well? The infamous Schally-Chaplain switch! I remember that little gadget well enough,' Dagenfort said. 'I should do. When you developed that I quit – quit working for you, quit working in the field of medicine. The idea of ZPG was in the air then – Zero Population Growth, and you sold your idea to the World Pop Control Council. That little electrode was to be sunk into the brain of every child at birth, and the aerials on top made it capable of being radio-controlled by computer. The CC was then coming into being. In a generation, CC would have control of the sexual impulses of every human being on Earth. Monstrous, practicable – unethical! – And I quit!'

'And you quit! Sure, you quit, Jack, and frankly it wasn't much of a loss to us. Your ethical obsessions hampered your work when the world was up to here in starving mouths. We had an unethical situation.'

'And you used it to seize power.'

'Naturally, old stick.'

'After the war forced everyone's hand, Castle and his political ilk grabbed their chance, and the Cap–Comm merger went through. *And* your birth-control switch – okay, admittedly it's the ultimate in population-control – it's working fine. Just what happens if CC ever decides to turn off everyone's desires is another matter. Computers don't love people.'

'Nor do I.'

'At least you were so hated by the masses you had to disappear. The story was that you were assassinated.'

Auden Chaplain had a sort of smile about his mouth. 'That was not why I disappeared. I came to Mars with a purpose.'

'Yeah? Murdering your wife, by the sound of it, and leaving your child behind to be cared for by others.'

'My brother-in-law Reagan Surinat owed me that – he held the patents for the electrode, which he sub-let to Mitsubishi in Japan. He made a fortune sitting tight in his fake Slav castle. But the reason I came to Mars, old stick, was because I wished to pursue a new line of research developing out of the old one. Come over here.'

He rose, and led the way over to a second holocube set in the wall. He switched it on, and a bleak panorama lit. There was a pair of self-drive binoculars set in the glass, which he indicated that Dagenfort should look through.

Intrigued despite himself, Dagenfort put his eyes to the binoculars. They were already tracking slowly.

He was moving above the Martian surface. Signposts and lines marked his position, otherwise the model would have passed for real. Below lay part of the Fessenkov Plain. They were some twenty degrees from the equator, and heading almost due south towards the ancient Sirenum Sea bed. The landscape was a typically Martian tract of half-obnubilated lava beds, millions of years old. As the viewpoint swung along, the region became more broken towards the coast.

'What you're seeing,' Auden Chaplain said, 'is, exogeologically speaking, ancient lava flows in at least six different strata, intercalated with tephra and regolith which, over the ages, have consolidated into microbreccia

219

and tuff. You note that the strata are level and not disrupted – the product of possibly thousands of millions of years of gradualism rather than catastrophic. We're drawing near the coast of the ancient sea now – watch carefully.'

The viewpoint was flying on. Behind the lower and broken shapes, a dark stain was appearing – the fossil ocean bed. At its verge lay a higher shoulder of ground with peculiar configurations. The viewpoint moved to the shoulder and, for the first time, deviated from a straight line of flight. It began to circle and sink, just as the plane from which the holoshots had been taken had done.

The shoulder was now revealed as something else. It had a hollow central core, against the outsides of which lava and planetary detritus had piled. The core grew larger till it alone filled Dagenfort's vision. Inside it was – well, no doubt about it, it looked like a ruin of impressive dimensions, its nearly obliterated pattern of ruined walls and corridors laid out with a regularity which guaranteed organization rather than exogeological accident. The viewpoint hovered and stopped, so that Dagenfort was left regarding the heart of the ruin, in which some fresh-turned dirt gleamed.

He looked up at last, turned a puzzled gaze towards Chaplain.

'A ruinous building in Fessenkov? What have you found? Had the foursts a civilization?'

'Ah, your old habit – eagerness to jump to conclusions, and the wrong ones at that! Jack, that ruin is the remains of a building beyond the capacity of any fourst. Foursts have no more intellect than moths! You didn't think that that one we keep to scare tourists really spoke to you, did you? It had an intercom attached, that's all. No, that ruin dates very far back – over one hundred million years, in fact. What's more, it was the work of a highly civilized

220

race. I dug there – you could see where I dug. Maybe I should not say highly civilized, let's say a race that used complex machines, perhaps as complex as any on Earth. Perhaps they were machines, the race itself was a kind of electronic culture . . .'

Dagenfort asked, 'So there was a super-race once, on Mars, as various legends and stories on Earth always claimed?'

'No, I don't think so. Oh, they were here, right enough. But this seems to be the only trace of them on the entire planet. They did not dominate it. They merely had an outpost here.'

News was getting through to Dagenfort that he was tired after the exertions of his climb. He went and sat down in a chair.

'You're telling me some strange things. I mean, where did this race come from? Not from Earth. One hundred million years – there would be brontosauri about on Earth then, I suppose.'

'At that period Earth would be drawing towards the terminal period of the long Mesozoic Era. The two orders of dinosaur were coming to the end of their long tenure, and early mammals were plentiful, although insignificant.'

'Okay, so where did these people, these machines, come from?'

'Jack, you are almost an interesting man, old stick. But you have no speculative powers, you have no – what shall I call it? – intellectual stamina. You have probably never dreamed.'

'Funny you should say that – I was having a curious hallucinatory sensation of being able to understand human life before I ran into your fourst. But such matters are beyond your range of interest.'

'You've never dreamed, not on a large scientific scale. That's what science bestows – better visibility. You will never have heard of the planet Hleems – but—'

221

'Oh, yes, I have, your intercom prattled some nonsense about Hleems and its God.'

'You're right. I had forgotten. We let it spout a little fourstian folklore! I did a dig in the ruin by the Sirenum Sea, and I found evidence that the race which erected the building came from Hleems. It does happen – as the clever dicks in Nixonville will tell you – that fourstian folklore centres round a God-group which ruled three worlds, Mars, Earth and Hleems. The gods materialized at Fessenkov. They may have been exiled gods, or dying gods, considering that they spread no further.'

'Perhaps they were just contemplative gods, Auden, and not your sort of power-mad being.'

Auden was entirely undisturbed by the remark. 'Perhaps it was so. In this instance, if in no other, your guess is almost as good as mine. The gods had plenty to contemplate at Fessenkov – the desolate sea bed, dried up then as now, the desolate land . . . What prompted them to choose the shoreline, we do not know.'

'Tell me more about the ruin.'

'I have told you enough for the present. Now I want some information from you. You are not, as you claimed to be in the canteen, a member of a news syndicate. You are a member of a different organization. The IDI. The Idealists of the Decadent Id . . . Very pretty . . . I want you to get in touch with them. I have the facilities here. And I want you to find the answer to some questions I shall give you.'

He pressed a bell. A smiling Japanese girl appeared.

'This is my companion, Lindy Hakamara,' Auden Chaplain said. 'She understands the situation.'

'I understand the situation, and I'm pleased to see you here, Mr Dagenfort,' the girl said.

'Another intercom, Auden?' Dagenfort inquired. 'What are these questions you hope I am going to be fool enough to ask the IDI?'

'I have them here, on a slip of paper,' Lindy said, producing it from her overalls. 'And I can conduct you to the radio-transmitters, which are just down the corridor.'

He began to read. As he read, he began to laugh.

'Oh, no, Auden, you really are crazy, aren't you? This is just the craziest thing I ever—'

He laughed again, forgetting how many craziest things he ever.

29

Space had a floor. On that floor, a lovely party was in full swing. Loomis Smix was in charge, and lots of little girls with perfect manners, dressed just as Loomis had dressed when she was a little girl, were coming to tea to have sausages on sticks with peanut-butter sauce and angel-whip. The tea table was of white-painted wood, and all the pretty cone shaped trees and big paper butterflies and flowers had gathered round to make the place look just as cute as possible.

Her face pink with excitement, Loomis looked up from the big milk-shake machine and caught the eye of Benchiffer, standing by in his master's absence.

'Isn't this just absolutely *fun*, Benchiffer? Doesn't it make you feel so happy you could burst?'

He went ice cold. He knew the moment would come one day. Now here it was, all unexpected. His moment.

'It makes me, Ma'am, so positively sick that I could throw up.'

'Benchiffer, how *dare* you say "throw up" in front of all the little girlies and bunnies and everyone? I demand you say you are sorry, or there will be trouble.'

'Oh, I'm sorry right enough, ma'am. I'm sorry because

I'm of Polish ancestry, and my grandfather was one of the four thousand officers murdered in the Katyn Forest massacre, and my father and mother escaped to the USA, and she was killed in the Harlem Outbreak, and my only brother was killed in Vietnam, and then my father was blown to bits in the war – I still have one of the bits.

'Oh, I'm sorry all right, sorry that I have to have this phoney fake sadistic retarded scab-devouring puking nursery-mongering neurotic fantasizing fairy-storied walt-disneying hysterical *vomit* under my nose all the time. What's more—'

There was no time for more. Loomis's finger had long been on the button, and a big cuddly grey bunny with the cutest floppy ears and nice fur came hopping from behind a silver nutmeg tree and took Benchiffer with a ferocious arm-lock right across his throat. He was going purple as they hopped him out.

Loomis took a deep breath and smiled somewhat hard at her little guests. The little guests were variously giggling or pissing themselves, according to temperament.

'Get on with your tea, girlies, now the nasty rude man has gone.'

One of the smaller girls asked, 'Will the big bunny come for me?'

'No, my dear, not if you are good and not of Polish parentage.'

Attica Saigon Smix, real and not facsimile, was just coming out of the *Micromegas* with Captain Ladore as the bunny bearing Benchiffer hopped up the ramp.

'Benchiffer, what are you doing with that rabbit?'

'Bwwwwwa,' was all Benchiffer could say initially.

'Rabbit, let him speak.' The death-lock was loosened.

'I'm going to die, sir,' Benchiffer said. 'It's all my own fault. I was extremely rude. I spoke inexcusably to your dear sweet wife.'

'You can't just *die* like that, Benchiffer,' Attica Saigon Smix said, testily. 'There's a crisis on.'

'No, you see, it's destiny, sir. Strangulation by rabbit. As predicted by a gipsy outside Cracow when I was a child. My friends and my parents laughed when I told them, but, as you can see, the gipsy was correct.'

'Superstitious nonsense!'

'I had a hare-lip at the time.'

'Stop making these foolish excuses, Benchiffer. I require your services. Rabbit, put that man down.'

'I think I'd rather die than go back to that yucky tea-party,' Benchiffer said, trying by sundry head-jerks and neck-bends to get his epiglottis sorted out. 'Having gone as far as this. If it's all the same to you, sir. I'm sure Petrulengroski knew best.'

'Oh, go to hell,' Attica Saigon Smix snapped.

It was the rabbit's cue. Wrapping Benchiffer in another strangulating embrace, it hopped with him up the ramp.

Smix did not wait to see the little white powder-puff tail disappear into the *Micromegas*. He rolled to where his wife was helping, amid screams and chuckles, to blow out candles on a monster cake, and drew her to one side.

'My darling, I have some unpleasant news for you.'

Loomis's face altered. The cute bowed lips slewed, the plump cheeks sagged, the wide eyes grew narrower and nasty, the matronly jawline became mean.

'You know distinctly I do not like nasty things, Attica. You'll be trying to tell me next that you had people massacred in the war.'

He grasped her arm so that she gave a yelp of anger.

'This is more important than that. Now just you listen, because I'm no Benchiffer, neither am I any figment out of one of your precious Monty's wet dreams.'

'Attica!'

'Something is severely wrong, but wrong. We are out of

225

touch with the outside world. No signal is getting through. For reasons as yet unknown, we have been severed from the rest of the electromagnetic spectrum. Does that make sense to you?'

'Do you have to shout and clutch my arm, Attica? We *want* to be out of touch, don't we?'

'Not to this extent we don't, no! What's more, as the last message was coming through – well, it was a report from one of my loyal men at Houston. Do you know what it announced before we were cut off?'

She was looking away from him. In a low, angry voice, she said, 'I'm sure it was nothing concerning my tea-party which you have just deliberately ruined.'

He choked. 'Right! Too daubed right it wasn't! It was not, by about one hundred and eighty sobbing degrees anything at all to do with your pathetic mother-jumping lullaby-loving sock-sucking sore-aproned little pool-paddling tea-party! It was merely to announce that CC has mastered the secrets of the ecopicosystem, and is even now pulling out of ordinary quantal space-time to come and land right in our lousy laps, smack in the middle of your cosy calf-constipating party!'

'We don't *want* CC here. I knew you'd bring trouble eventually, mixed up with that horrible business! I can't—'

He grabbed her by the shoulders in his aged fury and attempted to rock her, aided and abetted by his perambulant chair.

'Have you any idea what's happening in the real world? Have you any respect at all for the wonders, the mysteries, the enormities, the sheer *transmogrifications* of science and technology?! Do you know where we really are, do you?'

'We're in a nice safe place where you are murdering me!' She pronounced the last words in a scream, bringing up her arm and flinging off her aged but loving attacker, so that the chair crashed over sideways, taking Attica Saigon Smix with it.

'Bunnies!' she screamed, pressing a button on her belt.

A host of bunnies, grey, plum, ginger, mauve and cerulean, appeared. They were big square-shouldered bunnies with nasty cross eyes, who threw away half-nibbled carrots as they leapt into action.

But Smix had his buttons too. His buttons were bigger than hers. He pressed one in the side of his chair.

The whole shooting match disappeared, bunnies first, then the entire enchanted garden, including trees, flowers, cows, chuff-chuff trains, baa-lambs and roundabouts, as well as the tea table, the monster pink cake and all the little pink girls, down to the last cute pair of wetted panties. Phut! Disappeared like that.

Smix and Loomis and the *Micromegas* were alone on the enormous nul-white floor of space.

'Benchiffer!'

No answer.

He recalled Benchiffer and the gipsy's curse and fought to remember the poem Benchiffer had always effortlessly remembered. 'The great globe itself, and all it doth inherit . . . Not a rack behind!'

Dropping the culture stuff, he turned on Loomis, his servo-mechanisms going full blast.

'You don't give a rap about *haute technologie*, you baggage, do you? We're in your precious Monty Zoomer's mandala, that's where we are!'

'Oh, you're always so unkind to me – you don't appreciate me!'

'I wish I'd married your sister, I tell you now. Glamis understands science! We're in your precious Monty Zoomer's mandala, round his greasy neck, that's where we are, you ignorant baggage!'

She began to weep somewhat. She pressed her buttons. Not one murdering bunny showed up.

Captain Ladore came smartly towards them. Having witnessed their little contretemps, he saluted as soothingly as possible.

'Any signals getting through yet, Captain?' Attica Saigon Smix panted. His chair was still adminstering to him after the upset.

'No, sir. Ship's computer gives optimum support to plan to move into normal space-time as soon as possible. The forces of CC may materialize here at any moment. Theoretical computations suggest that their arrival on our identical coordinates could produce unpleasant consequences for all concerned.'

'There'll be some unpleasant consequences after this,' Attica Saigon Smix grumbled, allowing himself to be helped back to the ship.

Loomis followed behind, weeping silently to herself. Drops fell from her old eyes and splashed on to the floor of space like the slow spring raindrops of childhood.

Once they were inside the *Micromegas* the ramp rolled back into the hull like an anteater's tongue. All ports closed. They took their seats. A small black flake was ejected from the incincerating plant: the Cracow gipsy's prediction had been fulfilled and more.

Ladore hesitated with his hand on the firing button and said, 'I should mention to you, sir, the computer's theory.'

'Well?'

'It has a theory that one reason why we can no longer communicate with the outside world is because the outside world is no longer there.'

'Then let's go and find where in hell it's gone,' Attica Saigon Smix roared. He had turned up the amplifier on his chair so that he could roar it. He was feeling better than he had done for years. This was action. The old cat and mouse nonsense was over.

The engines began to scream . . .

228

30

A new and beautiful planet rising up to meet them. The bodies of their colleagues stacked up behind them, only three degrees Kelvin above BAZ. Glamis and Jules sat together in the wide control-chair, steering the *Doomwitch* down through the stratosphere of the new planet.

'Oh, how, how – incredibly-redibly glorious!' breathed Glamis.

'And we the first to see it!' de l'Isle-Evens exclaimed.

Glamis swam beneath them, lovely, pristine, serene, an equatorial land of lake and savannah and forest, as yet untrod by man or woman in a universe before men and women had been invented.

Spontaneously, they burst into song, aware touchingly that something more was demanded of them than mere prose.

BOTH
What is beauty, all my sufferings ask?
Words alone aren't equal to the task—
The highest reaches of a human hero
Can't say how much delight now storms our mind
This un-polluted Eden-world to find,
As we go swinging down to hit Ground Zero!

GLAMIS
The music of the spheres, without discord,
Is telling those of us awake aboard
Our little Ark is ready for its Dove
It's landfall after all those years of light,
And our emotions tell us we were right—
Space Travel is Another Word for Love!

DE L'ISLE-EVENS
Oh, you and I, my darling, thankfully,
Are more than three degrees from BAZ,
So all our senses flower and approve
The keen technologies that brought us prime
And pretty through the blanks of space and time—
Space Travel is Another Word for Love!

Those comet-dusting   Tail-fin-rusting
Conquest-lusting   Upward-thrusting
Vacuum-busting   Tan-encrusting
   Years have now unfurled—
Here's our amorous and glamorous new world!

If Joy is always in another place,
We'll only find each other face-to-face
When, through the realm of stars, we start to prove
That sweet exogamies all end in you.
Not only in the Freudian sense it's true—
Space Travel is Another Word—
Space Travel is the Other Word—
Space Travel is Another Word for Love!

'Heavens, what's happening to the instrumentation?' de l'Isle-Evens exclaimed, peering at the dials before him. The altimeter was fluttering in alarming fashion.

The terminal at his elbow said, 'Uncertain read-out from visible ground-surface, pressure fluctuations between—'

'I'll take her down on manual,' de l'Isle-Evens said, anxious to show his masculine abilities to Glamis. He cut out the automatics and signalled a two-second burst from the under-jets to slow their descent. So low were they that they had the satisfaction of seeing the foliage on the tree-tops below blacken under the jet-flame.

It was a landing like kissing. As leaves swirled about the cabin windows, they turned and kissed,

Those sweet exogamies all end in you.
Not only in the Freudian sense it's true—
Space Travel is Another Word for Love!

With a final burst of song, they jumped from their seats and peered out.

Now that they were down, it was a bit disappointing. Reality catching up again. Nothing but foliage to see.

Air analysis was satisfactory, confirming the computer readings from space. Aerial microorganisms, practically nil.

'It's safe to go out, my darling,' de l'Isle-Evens said, holding out his hand. She took it, and they climbed into the airlock together.

They stepped from the ship on to the ground that yielded uneasily. There was no grass beneath their feet, only leaves somewhat like the leaves of an oak tree. De l'Isle-Evens snatched up one and examined it. It had some of the features of a dicotyledon leaf, with a net of veins covering it, and the stem vascular bundles shaped in the form of a ring of open tissues. The only difference in structure seemed to be a series of minute beads which were attached to the main vein of the leaf.

De l'Isle-Evens tut-tutted to himself and shook his head.

'We come all this way, all this time, and what do we find – Glamis is just like Earth!'

'Maybe that's proof there is a God. Why should he bother thinking up different life-systems for every planet?'

'True. But in that case, why must he invent so many planets? Why wouldn't one suffice! I experience now, my darling, the same distaste I used to experience when reading novels in the Verneian tradition – Jules Vernes, you know. The authors take endless trouble to get you to a new planet, and then it turns out to be just like the Mid-West. I used to deplore it as a failure of the imagination

231

but, if God has the same problem, then how can we blame the hacks!'

As he spoke, he was peeling the little beads from the back of the leaf. Released, they rose slowly into the air, one after the other. He watched with a raised eyebrow.

'That's odd! These little beads rise in the air, at a rate, I would calculate, of about twenty-five centimetres per second. What do you make of that?'

'They go straight up, Jules. It is absolutely still, Jules. There is not a breath of wind.'

'That is so. More remarkable is the fact that these little beads ascend at all.'

'Perhaps they are the seeds of the plants. We saw no oceans on the planet as we came in, only large lakes. Axial inclination implies a world virtually without seasons. How still it is, Jules! Perhaps we are on a world without winds! – Except in the stratosphere, of course.'

'Yes, it is conceivable, but concentrate, if you will be so kind, on the idea of these seeds, if seeds they are, that fall upwards instead of down!'

She touched his arm, 'Just a moment – I thought the sky was cloudless, but there are some funny little round clouds over to the south!'

He turned to stare where her pretty finger was pointing. The clouds were above them and floating in the region of the sun, so that they were difficult to see clearly.

'They look perfectly spherical,' he said. 'Which is absurd. They couldn't be balloons, could they?'

'Not on an uninhabited planet. Perhaps it is not uninhabited.'

'We'd better keep a look-out, in case the natives are hostile.'

'Should we rouse the others from BAZ for safety?'

He smiled at her, and she thought him suddenly quite

gallant and pleasing, despite his scholarly airs. 'Let's not start crowding our planet, darling!'

They began to investigate close to the ship.

Visibility all round was poor, because they were surrounded by the ubiquitous bush, into whose twigs they sank almost waist deep, and so investigation was limited to the ground at their feet. What puzzled Glamis was that there appeared to be no soil. She burrowed down, but came to nothing except a further layer of twigs. Leaves were scantier, further in. On some of the inner leaves she found more small beads. Frequently, one bead on a leaf had grown at the expense of the others. After only a moment's search, she came on one as large as a marble, its skin thick and flexible. She did not care to touch it, suspecting it might harbour some kind of leaf disease, but she gathered as many afflicted leaves as she could find and stuffed them into a pocket for microscropic examination later.

She had been burrowing and prodding for some time, frankly enjoying an afternoon botanizing in the country and sinking into a placid frame of mind, when she came across the egg.

The egg was round, pale grey and patterned rather attractively with purple veins. It nestled on its own among the twigs.

Glamis pulled some of the twigs away and attempted to lift the egg. Its shell was flexible. It felt tough and did not burst when pulled. She pulled again. The egg resisted then came free.

It was very light and had a stalk underneath. So it was not an egg. She let go of it and immediately recaptured it. It had begun to sail upwards, like Jules's seeds. She connected it immediately with the balloons in the sky, though hers was a smaller version of the giants they had glimpsed.

'Jules!'

He did not reply.

Unworried at first, she climbed into the *Doomwitch* and secured the balloon to a locker with a clip. She also removed her pendant from her neck; it had annoyed her when she was outside by entangling itself in twigs when she stooped. Then she went to the hatch and called again.

'Jules!'

No answer.

She had a fair idea of the direction in which he had walked. She stepped down and moved with difficulty through the all-enveloping bush. Suddenly, she realized how large the planet was, how empty. Balloons were floating almost motionless in the sky; they increased the feeling of solitude.

Calling as she advanced, she began to grow alarmed. The stillness became hateful. And it was often almost impossible to get a firm foothold. At one point, she sank over her head in the bush, struggling up only by using her hands, pulling her legs up with difficulty – and on the next step, she sank again. Falling forward, she managed to extricate herself. This unexpected difficulty in progress unnerved her to some extent; she lay where she was, listening for sound of Jules.

Her gaze went down into the mass of leafy twigs, down – no soil there – down – to a curious effect like light below her. She tried to focus on the substance but could not. But something like light, some sort of luminosity, was coming up from the ground.

There was no doubt that she had reached a dangerous patch of terrain – perhaps some sort of swamp. She was no longer so sure that this was an Earthlike planet.

'Jules!' she called. Her shout surprised even herself.

A faint answer returned to her. It gave her courage. Pulling herself up, she called again, he answered, and so she floundered her way forward to the incredible place where he was.

'I beg you to be careful!' he called. 'Don't fall! I'm coming back up for you!'

She remained where she was until his head appeared.

'Come and look here,' he said, in a dead calm that she recognized as his way of being amazed and excited. The sight of him aroused intense emotion.

'I love you, Jules!' She saw her words lighting his face.

As she moved towards him, she noticed that he had cut his way down through the twigs and had come on something underneath them like a log or tree-branch. With his help, she climbed down with him on to the branch. It was wonderful to clutch his hands.

'That's right! Now, hold tight, and look down. Don't get vertigo!'

She did as he said. His arm was firmly round her, and he was peering down too.

Glamis felt her senses do two complete somersaults. She was peering down into an immense bright hole in the ground. The floor of the hole, far below, was bluey-green. Tremendous thick supports rose up to carry the roof through which, it now appeared, de l'Isle-Evens had succeeded in burrowing.

She could not make sense of it, could not grasp the idea of a hole in the ground that deep, that light, even supposing human agency . . . and then the realization hit her.

They were in among the branches of a gigantic forest looking down at the ground. It was the ground she could see far below.

'We're in some sort of a gigantic tree!'

'Exactly – we and the spy-bell and all. Though *what* sort of a gigantic tree remains to be seen.'

'Trees this high . . . How high above ground are we?'

'You can understand now why the instrumentation was awry. I would estimate we are two kilometres above the ground. In the tops of impossibly tall trees in an impossibly tall forest.'

'Are we going to be able to fly down? I suppose we can, if we are careful about it.'

'That shouldn't present any problem. We'll just have a look and see how we are fixed. We were lucky we landed in one of the great tree branches, otherwise we would have crashed through to the ground and nothing could have saved us.'

They made their way back to the *Doomwitch*, marvelling.

Once they were inside, they sat down and took some refreshment. Glamis found her limbs were trembling. At one point, the vehicle settled suddenly and they jumped up, but the movement was not repeated.

De l'Isle-Evens took the opportunity to investigate the collection of leaves and Glamis's balloon, carrying them into the miniature lab for analysis.

She went in to him, feeling more cheerful in familiar surroundings.

'I have an idea you will find that the balloon is filled with helium or hydrogen, one of the light gases, which causes it to rise. I believe that the balloons could be simply a form of spore-distributor for the trees. We'll probably find a seed inside the balloon if my theory's correct.'

His expression as he looked up was grim.

'Helium or hydrogen, you say! Your general supposition is substantially correct, or so I believe. Unfortunately, according to analysis, the gas in the balloon is hydrogen.'

He had syphoned the gas off into a calibrated gauge and laid the empty balloon on the bench, neatly bisected. She examined one of the flaccid hemispheres. On the outside, it was flawless, its regular octagonal veining being almost uniform and thickening only slightly towards the stalk; it

236

could have been mistaken for something of synthetic origin. Inside, the vegetable origin was in evidence. A green rim ran leguminously round one diameter, leaking a small quantity of straw-yellow sap. Attached to this rim in racemose progression were sessile seeds, arranged in pairs. The seeds were about the size of apple-pips. De l'Isle-Evens had split open some of the seeds; they looked much like apple-pips, inside and out.

'Seed-distribution is never effected in this manner on Earth,' Glamis said. 'But as a method it is no more extraordinary than some terrestrial methods – indeed, it seems the logical means of distribution if winds are rare on the planet. Hydrogen fills the balloons and they swell as the seed ripens. Eventually the balloons inflate enough to break away and rise to the stratosphere, where winds act as global distributing agents. When the hydrogen diffuses through the exterior membrane, down come the seeds. Why are you looking at me like that, Jules?'

He started to rub his chin, smiling doubtfully at her.

'If seed-distribution did occur in this fashion on earth, there'd be one hell of a big bang! If hydrogen's mixed with air or oxygen in the presence of naked flame, a hell of an explosion results – we could blow ourselves to Kingdom Come with the contents of these balloons.'

'Of course! So elementary that I had forgotten! Jules! Of course we're in danger – we'd better get away from here as soon as possible and land somewhere beyond the forest.'

She paused. Then she hid her face in her hands.

'Speculative saints! I see what you're thinking! – We daren't use the jets. We could cause a colossal explosion.'

He put an arm around her shoulders.

'How we managed to land – perhaps settle's a better word – without triggering an explosion, I don't know. But we certainly daren't take off again – that requires a deal more burn than landing. We'd spread ourselves all round the biosphere.'

She held his hand and said, 'I can think of two ways in which we were probably lucky about landing in this spot. Judging by the way the branch-system runs, I'd guess that we're lodged in the crown of one of the great trees, so we did not fall through to the ground below. And very probably the flowering and seeding only takes place at the extremities of the branches, so that we punctured only a few balloons. But, as you say, we can't risk take-off. We'd set fire to the whole tree – the whole forest.'

'Certainly we would be unwise to risk taking off until we comprehend the overall situation, which at present we cannot be said to do. Glamis, you must get some rest. I am going exploring.' He jumped up determinedly.

With only a scatter of protests, she watched his preparations. He brought a parachute from a stowage locker and strapped it purposefully on his back. He armed himself with a laser-gun, and loaded a pack with food, drink, a chain-saw and a radio; the pack he secured to his chest. The more he prepared, the more anxious she grew.

When he was ready to leave, she flung herself into his arms.

'I can't let you go alone, Jules. I'm going to come with you.'

'That's impossible!' But she sensed his relief.

They fed an explanation of their absence into the computer and programmed it to reverse the BAZ-effect if they were not back within twelve hours, so that the other members of the crew would be able to take over. He helped her into the harness of another parachute. They left the ship together.

'It's the old jack-and-the-beanstalk problem,' de l'Isle-Evens said bravely, as they came to the hole he had carved and again peered down into the gulf below. 'We have the advantage over Jack that when we get safely to the bottom, we can instruct the computer over the radio.'

'We'll never be able to return to the ship.'

'In an emergency, we might be able to winch ourselves up. But I'm hoping we can cut through the tree trunk that supports the *Doomwitch*. There's a long way to fall. Once the *Doomwitch* is freed, the computer can fly it safely to the ground. I know . . . it's a gamble . . . First, we'll investigate. Decisions later. Any problem can be overcome if tackled in a scientific fashion.'

'Oh, Jules, you are a darling! So old-fashioned – and how I admire that!'

'Dearest Glamis, without your company, I would be a quivering mass of jelly!'

The first difficulty was to climb down a branch and away from the main trunk. Encumbered by twigs and small branches, they were almost exhausted by the time they got far enough away for reasonable safety.

'Get your breath back.'

'And you.'

They jumped at his signal.

She thought of her sister as she fell – Loomis, poor Loomis, she would no more have jumped from a two-kilometre high tree than swim the Pacific. Cool in mind, she turned head-over-heels and watched her parachute open. Her fall slowed with a jerk. De l'Isle-Evens's open chute was below her and to the left.

Now it was good!

They drifted in an amazing world. Above them, the enormous matted roof of the forest was receding, becoming a sky of sombre and undifferentiated brown, even the larger branches already looking like the beams of an ancient barn. To all sides were the columns that supported the roof, the trunks of the mighty trees. The ground was still a negligible thing with which their relationship was tenuous.

The trunks of the trees were pallid, almost translucent, almost like monstrous celery-stalks. Massive though they were, they looked far too puny to support the great weight of foliage overhead – almost too puny to support their own weight.

There was beauty in the forest. For the trunks stretched in all directions – but not for ever. In one direction – the south – there was an end to forest. The sun was by now past its zenith; its light, dimmer than on Earth, came flooding in among the soaring trunks, divided by numberless bars of shadow before it created more light and shadow about them until, in the northern depths of the forest, a tremendous pearly tapestry of intermittent dusk was achieved.

They fell through this web of light in silence. Gradually the dominance of the ground asserted itself. The watery greens and blues they had marked from far above now resolved into a wider range of tones, among which mustardy yellow, mottled red, and grey predominated. What had been an insignificant carpet took on shape and variety. Finally, they saw that they were falling fast towards broken and soggy ground studded with gigantic toadstools.

Glamis drew up her legs, spilled air, and plunged on to the peeling dome of one of the fungi. It burst, and she sprawled coughing on the ground in a cloud of rusty spores. When she climbed to her feet, considerably shaken, she was plastered by the musty-smelling stuff. Pulling the parachute fabric towards herself, she wiped herself as best she could and then looked about for de l'Isle-Evens.

She was standing in a world of impossible scale. The stems and caps of many of the fungi rose above her head in sombre conspiracy. Beyond them was the air, shadow-entangled and colonnaded like the aisles of some malignant gothic cathedral. And, over all, an unbroken wicker-work sky of treetops, inaccessibly distant. The whole wrapped round in a planetary silence so deep that she had no heart to call out.

But *he* was calling her!

Unshackling her harness, she scrambled forward, splashing over the marshy ground, and they found each other among the spongy toadstool stalks, like two benighted refugees from *Alice in Wonderland*.

'We've hit Ground Zero, Glamis! This is some unpolluted Eden-world!'

She sneezed for answer. They clung to each other.

He was looking searchingly up at the distant crowns of the trees, obstructed though they were by the sombre toadstool caps. He had affixed a length of red material to the branch from which they had jumped, to serve as an indicator of the tree in whose crown the *Doomwitch* rested. Nothing could be seen of it. She looked with him. They had misjudged scale and opacity of evening light; the red signal was entirely lost.

'The sun's getting low,' she said. 'Tomorrow, the others in BAZ will have revived and we can have them direct us over the radio. Let's just not get caught in here for the night – I don't think I could bear that! Let's get out of the forest, Jules, okay?'

It took them three hours to escape from under the giant trees. As Glamis said afterwards, they were fortunate it was not three days. Or three months, or three years. The fungi grew smaller and sparser as they neared the outer world, and at last they came to something like open meadow land, sloping down to a river. On the other side of the river, the enormous forest began again, soaring upwards on its spindly props.

They ran to the water and laved their faces.

As Glamis opened self-heating cans of a malt drink, de

l'Isle-Evens attacked a sapling, rising some two metres above ground like a great celery. Having chopped it down, he dug into the soggy ground with his knife to expose the root system.

'Very revealing! Come and look at this, my darling!'

'I can't. Can't move. Limbs too stiff. Come and have a drink.'

He sat beside her and accepted the steaming can she offered.

'It's what you might expect,' he said excitedly. 'God's billy-goats, wait till we get all this new information back to Earth! The discovery of the Pacific or the Americas is nothing compared with this. Look at the cross-section of this sapling! Observe! The sap rises just under the outer rind in the centre of the plant. In the two outer rims there's a pair of hollow tubes. See them? They're pretty thin on this specimen, but they'd be sizeable pipes on a full grown tree, as you can imagine.'

Glamis examined the cross-section with interest.

'The tubes carry the hydrogen, presumably. If they carry hydrogen at some pressure, from the roots right up to the crowns, then the tree need bear little weight. So it would require no massive trunk to support itself!'

'Elementary, my darling Miss Watson! The energy of the tree goes not into building bulk which, as you indicate, it does not need for structural strength – as a terrestrial tree would. Instead, the energy goes into a duel root system – an ordinary system to obtain nourishment from the soil, and this!'

He showed her the piece of root he had managed to hack up. Among the tangle of ordinary root was a hose-like growth going down from the main stem. After she had looked at it and picked at it, she stared into distance.

'Well? Am I right?' he asked.

'Everything connects, Jules. That's the hydrogen taproot, I'm convinced. This planet is midway between Mars and Jupiter, between Earth-type inner planets and the gas giants. So it's a compromise. You may bet that its rocks are probably rich in hydrogen – must be, to support such forests as these. The trees draw hydrogen from the rocks, as early plants on Earth released oxygen from the soil. Amazing! Truly amazing! An entire new botanical system, and we have found it!'

'Or, let's say it has found us!' He beamed at her. An odd man, really.

The sun went down in a burst of splendour, flooding the deep rich atmosphere with pile upon pile of coloured layers of light and the forest with its own ghastly glory. The river ran dark and musical as they fell asleep with their arms about each other, knowing all was not lost.

They awoke to the sound of voices. Dawn was on them and the air again mysterious with light.

More to the point, the *Micromegas* lay nearby. Glamis's sister, Loomis, was hobbling angrily towards them. Attica Saigon Smix in his perambulating chair was bringing up a decidedly nasty-looking rear.

31

What would be more pious at such a juncture than to spare a tear for all those denizens on Earth who were transplanted to another *when* through the time-turbulences? Thus one more sort of displaced person, one more wave of invaders, one more flood of homeless, one more legion of the lost, helped to swell terrestrial mis-cegenation (one of those rare causes worth speaking up for). When the time-turbulences passed – as pass they did, like many another form of pollution – the persons they had displaced had to live where they were dumped; no rescue was possible.

The unfortunates whisked backwards in time in Bordeaux made their peace with *le moyen âge*. The remains of the Ottoman Army who found themselves encamped outside the modern version of what had been Adrianople were absorbed into the Asia Minor tourist trade. Cetewayo was rescued from the British Army by the Rhodesians and became a moderately successful bulldozer driver on the new Freetown-Chad-Addis Ababa Motorway. The Khedive of Egypt, a charming man, opened a glossy hotel in Alexandra, which became notorious for pleasures of an old-fashioned kind. As for the baluchitheria who appeared in Africa, they proved, in the majority of cases, extremely edible. A mating pair found its way to Baltimore Zoo but did not mate; and an excellent stuffed specimen stands in what used to be the University of Melbourne in the Nichols Wing, just outside the Dean's Office, by the Ladies' Room. As for poor little Choggles . . . well, time had as firm a grip on her as on lesser mortals. She was stuck in the Stone Age, and her beloved but slightly useless cousin Mike was unable to rescue her.

Some days, she sat curled up in the Script Room of the deserted G-U studios, reading books which had been bought with an eye to holoing. It was a consolation to have a decent library at hand. Among her favourite books were a pop zen study of subjective manipulationism, *I Ching, Who You?*, by Dr Glamis Castle; *Downtown Sahara: A History of Suburban Culture*, by Roger Grope-Willett; a book on oracular deafness called *Fatidical Paracusis;* a history of the extinction of Kenya's wildlife by Luigi Carnate, translated from the Italian and entitled *None But the Lonely Hartebeest*; and various novels, also dating from some while back. She had read

The Wind-Breakers of Bratislava twice, and was starting to re-read *All the Lovely Colours of Uncertainty* one afternoon, when Back-in-the-Stone-Age ran into the nook and grabbed her arm.

She retrieved the arm rather pointedly. The relationship had been slightly strained since Back-in-the-Stone-Age had proposed a game called 'Nymphetomaniac'.

'There's something in the glacier – come and see!' he said.

'You can't catch me as easily as that!'

'No, really, Choggles, come and see. Put your book down and come and see.'

'Promise you won't unzip your trousers?'

'I promise.'

She went and saw, although she had no affection for the glacier. It was a dull thing, a sort of style-less menace which ground infinitesimally towards the studio, now and then crunching a lamp-standard in the parking lot. She thought of Jerry's advice to Yvonne in the book she had read yesterday: 'Shall I give you a Life Message?' 'Which one's that?' 'There's really only one: Be Superb!' The glacier was not superb; just cold, slow and all-embracing, like an Eskimo with satyriasis.

Nor did she care for the hairy knock-about things that lived on it.

So she tramped over the encrusting firn and ice-particles morosely. Ahead was gloom and a sort of galactic kitchen-sinkiness. Hollow noises were inseparable from being on top of the glacier, as if she were trudging along at the bottom of a huge empty swimming-pool.

'How far are we going?' she asked, but he did not reply.

Nor was it fun to look back. The G-U studio in its ruinous isolation was at once pitiable and cheerless, a memorial to the centuries of lousy art that were yet to be.

'Look at that!' Back-in-the-Stone-Age said, removing one hand from his trouser-pocket to point, and then tucking it back again. Cold, not lust, provoked the gesture.

'There's a couple of bodies in there!' he said.

He was pointing to a grotto in the ice, where a large sliver of cliff had fallen away. Something shadowy lurked there.

'Really – get pollinated! You've been seeing too many old horror movies – people are always finding things in glaciers, and it just doesn't ever happen in real life. A geologist who knew told me so. He said he'd read it in *Scientific American* – sorry, *Scientific Russo-American* as it is now. Besides, there's nobody about but us two in this godforsaken period of time. I'm going back in the warm!'

For answer, Back-in-the-Stone-Age produced a torch and shone its beam on the ice-face, thus vanquishing both Choggles's know-all geologist friend and the parvenu *Scientific Russo-American*.

Two faces, two human faces in profile, could be clearly seen, green, glittering, ghostly.

'Oh, gumdrops!' Choggles exclaimed, clutching Back-in-the-Stone-Age's arm involuntarily. 'Don't they look awful!'

Despite herself, fascination drew her nearer. The frozen faces appeared to be gazing at each other in an eternal tête-à-tête.

'What do you think of that?' Back-in-the-Stone-Age said. 'That's proof of something, ain't it? Atlantis or one of them dumps there used to be. Significant, ain't it? Vindicates Darwin and Goethe and Aristotle, don't it?'

'And Emily Post,' Choggles said. 'That just happens to be a friend of mine in there!'

His laugh held a whinny of jealousy. 'Oh yes, I suppose that's this guy Mike Surinat you keep on about!'

'I don't know who the man is. Never saw him before. But the woman—'

246

Stuck between tears and hysterical laughter, she peered in at the pale Persian face separated from her by ice and extinction.

'–I swear it's Glamis Fevertrees . . . Or it was . . . Or it will be . . .'

The confusion of tenses tipped the balance, and tears won. She stood and scattered them on the ice until Back-in-the-Stone-Age led her back into the studios.

32

'There's the castle! We're nearly home!'

Harry the Hawk's glad cry did not come too soon. Their three mounts were dropping beneath them, would have fallen but for the saddles and stirrups that kept them up. Their flanks heaved and sweated – and the horses were in much the same plight.

But there was the great Slot Surinat, its pinnacles towering over the next crest in the ground, crying welcome to them. Overhead, erratic fragments of the broken moon turned, running slowly through individual and incalculable phases and eclipses, and casting a freckle of light over the great dark façade of the castle.

They rode up the crest with fresh heart, men and animals both, and heard strange distorted noises, as if fatidical paracusis warned them of a new and dire event. The noises did not appear to come from the castle but from all about them. The horses moved steadily through a belt of trees – and suddenly a great grey phantom sprang up before them!

The dranglike Gururn gave a savage cry, drew his broadsword, kicked his mount and galloped forward. Julliann of the Sharkskin could not forbear to see his rough old ally plunge into danger alone, and he too drew his sword.

'Desist!' Harry called. 'It's the Dread Brain Mist!'

But Julliann would not heed his cry. He charged, close on Gururn's heels, into the shroud that coiled and steamed in their path. Its tentacles writhed out to embrace him. Uttering an old family battlecry which had been a Sharkskin patent for generations, Julliann charged on without falter.

The Dread Brain Mist was an evil phantom that had haunted man ever since the first men set foot on any version of Earth, Early, Middle, Late or Overdue. No matter how snugly men had huddled together by hot chimney-nooks, drinking and telling each other tales of vainglory, no matter how madly they went to battle, no matter how frequently they invented legends to comfort themselves, no matter how often they lay with warm and beautiful women for love or character-formation, no matter how deeply they lost themselves in the excitements of the hunt, no matter how desperately they pretended that some god or other was in his heaven, doing a good refereeing job, and that all was right with the world – no matter (in short) how much they boozed, wenched, wrestled, laughed, hunted or prayed, the Dread Brain Mist was always somewhere near, at hand and foot, uncompromising and soggy, whispering that something was existentially wrong, something too awful for remedy.

It was a desolating and supine thing, was the Dread Brain Mist, the ultimate in half-life, going under many names such as estrangement, infirmity, melancholy, indecision, dissatisfaction, tension, anomia, loneliness, separation, perversity, neurasthenia, nostalgia, timidity, obsession, slyness, secrecy, self-doubt, mortality, insecurity, ill-ease, superstition, hypocrisy, stealth, silence, *noises,* prevarication, qualms, malevolence, guilt, recrimination, sclerosis, disillusion – but every page of every dictionary ever compiled contains at least one alias of the Dread Brain Mist. And it whispered now its slogan to Julliann of the Sharkskin, saying,

ALL IS NOT WELL!

Indeed, he began at once to know all was not well. For he immediately lost all sight and sound of his companions, those brave men and true who had been with him so long upon Life's Way.

The next thing that happened to him was that his brave charger, Morngloom, nourished by him since it was a foal, even in his own bedchamber, yes, the brave Morngloom turned up its eyes in a brief fit of nystagmus and pitched head-over-crupper on the ground. When Julliann extricated himself from the wreckage, it was to find that Morngloom had gone to join its equine ancestors in the Celestial Stables.

Julliann forged on through the Dread Brain Mist alone. The Mist had solidified into a tacky, resilient substance, to the touch somewhat like a hound's muzzle. He went on foot through a grey and twisting labyrinth, passage meaninglessly connecting to passage, until he became hopelessly lost.

Only then did he realize that the Dread Brain Mist had formed about him in a gigantic analogue of his own mind. Now he understood why Gururn and Harry had disappeared – by now, they also would be enveloped and swallowed by their own brains. When understanding came to him, faded frescoes appeared on the walls, their colours often muted, their meanings often lost; only occasionally did a scene stand out as brightly as once it had done. Here was his whole life, scene by scene, and he passed each scene cursing. Each was disappointing, the figures in it shrunken and misshapen, the incidents ridiculous, the

249

protagonists ill-briefed for their roles – and the roles in any case minor and fragmentary, things that had to be hurried though, unrehearsed, and generally with nobody watching.

This miserable array gave him some sort of guidance forward, though filling him at the same time with estrangement, infirmity, melancholy, indecision, dissatisfaction, tension, anomia, loneliness, separation, perversity, neurasthenia, nostalgia, timidity, obsession, slyness, secrecy, self-doubt, mortality, insecurity, ill-ease, superstition, hypocrisy, stealth, silence, *noises*, prevarication, qualms, malevolence, guilt, recrimination, sclerosis, disillusion and other wry intimations of his human state.

The sad music had words, or he began to intone words to it:

> Oh human state
> Both inhumanly small
> And inhumanly great!
> Our lives are stews of legend, evermore,
> Re-heated and re-served by patterned lore—
> A double-dealing that can but present
> An Outwards calm, an Inwards perturbate,
> Because we are predestined to perform
> Eternal recapitulations of a drama-dream
> Established in a coding harsh preset
> By long inhuman generations of travail,
> The while conforming to a human norm
> Which dare take no cognizance of the pale
> Beyond which shaggy things irate
> Half-sensibly gesticulate!
> Oh, human state!
> Our burden is To Be—
> To carry both our individuality
> And our stricken family tree
> By one appraised how few our store of years,
> And by the other well-informed
> How many hands indifferentiate

> Have shaped what gestures we can make
> Ourselves. Our fate is that we have our fate
> Pre-cast, yet *feel* that all is still at stake!
> Our past is God – and how it mocks!
> Oh, human state, oh, paradox!

His sword dropped from his strong right hand, so full of misery was he, tramping blindly through corridors he had already trod, never knowing what was round the next corner. The dice seemed hopelessly loaded against him. Tears fell from his eyes, saliva from his mouth, mucus from his nose.

And yet – and yet, small advantages were to be won from great persistence. He never gave up. Cowardly, wretched, unarmed – however low the state to which his present misfortunes had reduced him, Julliann continued against all discouragement, much like an author nearing the end of a chronicle he believes nobody will peruse, yet bent on having one last jest at the expense of non-existent readers. He was beaten, yet he would not acknowledge defeat.

> Our fate is that we have our fate
> Pre-cast, yet *feel* that all is still at stake . . .
> Oh, human state, oh, paradox!

For now all about him he was hearing strange sounds, voices, the slamming of doors. Reaching through the Dread Brain Mist, some phantasmal creature was calling his name (his Other Name!), was clasping his shoulder, was shaking him! Realization came to him that he had after all won through to Slot Surinat, that he had survived the Dread Brain Mist – that he was in the castle, his companions vanished . . .

The Mist thinning . . .

The miseries fading . . .

Someone calling his name, calling from afar, from another world.

'Julian!'

His brother's face. Michael . . .

He was in the castle . . .

Awakening from nightmare, the long saga of nightmare . . .

. . . into the pain of consciousness, the loss of his comrades:

. . . the presence of Mike and Becky . . .

They were looking anxiously into his face.

'Julian, we thought we'd lost you that time!' Mike Surinat said, releasing a pale smile. 'You've been on *root* again. It's short-circuiting your brain. You know it's a terminal drug, my old chum – we'll have to get you therapy, before you disappear for ever into the depths of your own mind!'

The Dread Brain Mist was still there. He could not speak, just lifted one hand in a pathetic gesture towards Becky.

'I'm going to get you some soup to drink, Julian,' she said. 'Before you die of undernourishment.' She avoided his hand.

'Spider Soup!' he tried to say, but the words never emerged. *Root* tended to trap every response under a membrane of silence.

She turned away – not without relief. Julian Surinat was a pathetic sight. A scatter-bomb in the war had severed both his legs, one above the knee, one below. It seemed also to have severed his will-to-live. Although he was equipped with two fully computerized legs, he refused to use them. Instead, he sat solitary in the old family home, drugged for most of the time.

She went into the kitchen, walking slowly, her circadian clocks set at odds by the flight down from Friendship City.

It was a pleasure to be back in this little ferro-concrete one-storey house in the suburbs of San Diego, ironically named Slot Surinat by my dead uncle Reagan, Mike's father. She opened her travelling-bag and set the Koh-i-Nor on the washing machine.

As she gazed out of the window at the neglected palms and ginkos, a picture of another house and garden came to her, and of a man looking out of a broad frame window, through a garden crammed with palms and cacti in tubs; sometimes, there was an ice-pick in his head. She had picked the image of Sue Fox's mind and it was still with her, lingering as a chilly image of the human condition.

As Becky opened up the soup, her thoughts went back to the history of the Surinat family in recent years. The pattern of the wallpaper had gone through one of its intricate loops there!

For three generations, Surinats had farmed the flat and fertile plains of Illinois, living and dying on the land they farmed. But the romance of high-energy physics had caught up with them. Some thirty-five years ago, before Mike and Julian were born, it was decided that a gigantic synchrotron should be built on those flat and fertile plains. The State of Illinois wanted the Surinat home. They had to get out, and were well paid to do so. Out went brothers Fletcher and Reagan and their wives. The synchrotron went ahead. Its main ring, some four miles in circumference, was built close to where the three generations of Surinats had held their christenings, their wakes and their hoe-downs. 500 GeV marked the spot.

Loaded with bread, Reagan headed for California with his bride, Dido Renshaw, Leda's sister (mythological reference ran like water in the Renshaw family – old man Renshaw had been head of the classical faculty at Yale). Reagan bought this ugly little house because it was near the ocean he had never seen before, and because it was close to Mexico, which he thought he would like (but in actuality hated because of the way the land was being misused).

Fletcher, my father, settled down to a life of torpor and TV-viewing.

Reagan Surinat intended to travel round the world. He got as far as Serbia, where our ancestors had come from, three generations back. There, he squandered most of his spare cash on an unworkable goldmine in Novo Brdo, which had supplied the Nemanija dynasty with riches back in the fifteenth century and had briefly been the wonder of Europe. Dido had become pregnant and sick, so they returned to Slot Surinat, leaving the goldmine to linger – and deliver the goods in unexpected plenty years later, when Mike was a young man.

Mike had been one of twins. The other baby, a girl, died at birth. Although Reagan did not particularly wish for twins, the death of the baby preyed on his mind. (Becky thought this death had also had its effect on Mike.) So Reagan settled back, without ever actually making the decision for himself, to drinking himself to death – a pleasure which the war denied him. He died in a sneak air raid; shard-blowers came in over the coast, and he and Dido were killed on the sidewalk by their front drive, both by the same speeding shard. Perhaps there was poetry in that. She had been helping him home after one more drinking bout.

The soup was hot. As Becky picked it up, she saw a movement in the bushes. And another. Glinting things. There were machines out there – machines roughly like men. The Forces of CC.

'Mike!' she screamed.

The kitchen door burst open.

Thunderbird Smith stood there – or one of the master computer's many projections of Thunderbird Smith, which it could conjure up or cancel at will.

The soup spilled over the floor.

Mike appeared from the inner room, very pale and collected, and said, 'You have made an illegal entry into a private household and can be charged under Section 16, Paragraph B, of the Artificial Intelligence Integration Act. Get out of here!'

The eyes of Thunderbird Smith were unpleasant to behold, dissolving in a fiery mass of protons designed to reduce any human onlooker into paroxysms of subservience.

'The Civil Law is in abeyance. Martial law has been declared in view of the time-turbulence disruptions. You are Michael Flambard Surinat, and you are being arrested for subversion, in that you belong to an organization named the IDI, which runs contrary to the Combinationist Act of 1996 in opposing Union between the Capitalist and Communist blocs. The house is surrounded.'

'That's why we couldn't get through to Per Gilleleje,' Mike said. As he spoke, he turned and made a sudden tremendous dive for the cupboard doors behind him. They swung open backwards almost before his shoulder struck them, and he was diving for safety down a chute which led to a deep self-sealing shelter below the house.

He never made it. The terrible forces of the CC were launched against him. To Mike's numbing brain, the idea presented itself that the evidence which sought to prove that Down was Down was at best statistical and that, chance and gravitation being what they were, the case might arise when, against astronomical but nevertheless computable odds, Down was Up. The case arose now, and he with it, shooting back along the chute like toothpaste from a shrewdly stamped tube.

He reappeared before the dreadful protonic eyes, floating, and was set down. Becky stood helpless against him. To her too it had been revealed that Motion was, at best,

255

simply an extreme form of Immobility, and her brain was set to exploring all the other forms. Epistemological doubt worked in them both as powerfully as etorphine. Out in the garden, robot armies rose like bayonets among the cacti.

'We are seizing on this opportunity,' Thunderbird Smith said – and in the excitement his jaw movements were slightly out of synch with his appalling voice – 'to round up and exterminate all subversives. Even Attica Saigon Smix is at this very moment being pursued into the extra nutritional interface saturation situation of inter-mediate vector neutrino magnetic monopole separation magnetic monopolo monopolo monopolo mono polo . . .'

The voice managed to end with a note of interrogation although it was rapidly descending the scale – a feat of which no human larynx is capable. Thunderbird Smith stood silent for a moment, glittering and formidable, and then disappeared with a hypothetical tinkle, leaving only a slight violet stain – which might or might not have been caused by magnetic monopole separation – in the kitchen air. Out in the Trotskyite garden, vanishing robots left similar stains.

Julian Surinat staggered into the kitchen on his prosthe-tic legs, filaments of the Dread Brain Mist still lingering about him.

'What the hairy-legged old hussar is going on about here? Where's my soup?'

'The boy's walking!' Becky exclaimed and collapsed into his arms. Very agreeable for Julian.

They were reviving her, fanning her with the Koh-i-Nor, and warming some more soup, when the vision bell rang.

Per Gilleleje's face was on the screen.

Mike went over and opened up.

'Been trying to raise you for the last hour, Mike –

trouble here with the transmitter ever since we were last in touch. Sabotage suspected, but that can wait till later.'

'I'll say it can! Per, we've just had a visitation from Thunderbird Smith and it vanished in mid-spate. You know they aren't supposed to do that. What can have happened?'

'It's a bit early to say, but it looks as if some overwhelming catastrophe has overtaken CC. Reports are still coming in.'

'Come on, the news couldn't be that good. A temporary projection failure, maybe?'

Per shook his head. 'Far more extensive than that. News of withdrawal of one level of electronic and communication services after another has been coming in for the last twenty minutes. Global Navigation Service is out, all airliners using it grounded. Thunderbird, part of the Heart-Core of CC, would be the last to go.'

'But the whole damned shooting-match can't just have upped and – Migod, it can! Per, the meeting we telltaled between Thunderbird Smith and Zoomer, mentioning the ecopicosystem! – CC was going to establish itself there. Maybe it's gone. Maybe the whole shebang's quitted for the ecopicosystem.'

'It will be back,' Per said. He disliked appearing excited. His temperament was such that, before shooting himself, he would leave only a visiting card to serve as a suicide note.

Becky tottered over to the vision panel clutching her mug of soup and said, 'Per, you've examined the telltale's record of that interview in Isphahan between the Thunderbird projection and Monty Zoomer?'

'Yes, sure.'

'All Thunderbird wanted was Monty's pendant he wore about his neck – a pendant of ancient Martian design. Apparently the real Attica Smix is hiding in it – in it or

257

through it or what? Explain to a non-mathematician like me what would happen if someone else – CC – wanted to get to Smix.'

Per said, 'The back-room boys are already trying to check on that problem. But they have their hands full of other business. However, I have a computation from a Japanese source . . .' They watched him fiddling among the papers on his desk. He grabbed one and scanned it.

'What the Japanese source says, roughly, is that the Zoomer amulet can act merely as a sort of receiver or gateway to the ecopicosystem. It would possibly have a phased wavelength, which invading parties would have to match.'

'And when they had matched it, where would they arrive? Inside the pendant?'

'Yes, that seems to be one answer. But – the math gets a bit abstruse here – there is a second answer – well, they're the same answer but it's in New Algebra, so one is forced verbally to present as alternatives what are really congruences – and it seems as if a quick rephrasing could also send one beyond or *through* the pendant. Like a clown with a hoop; he can either get caught in the hoop or go right on through.'

'I see, or do I? In either case, one would necessarily (a) have to know the phased wavelength of the pendant and (b) materialize near the pendant. And if you materialized *near* rather than *in* the pendant, then presumably you would have gone through the ecopicosystem and come out of the other side.'

Per shuffled studiously through his papers before answering.

'Yes, Becky, that's how we, or the Japanese source, sees it. Though we're still puzzled as to how the theory works in practice.'

'Where does all this get us?' Mike asked.

'I know where it gets us!' Julian said. 'It means that as yet Smix and Smith are the only ones who have applied the theories!'

'More than that,' said Becky quietly. 'It means we need to discover the whereabouts of Zoomer's pendant. CC may have removed itself elsewhere, presumably to master the new environment. But it will return. While it is away, the Dissident Nations also need to master knowledge of that new environment . . .'

Mike clutched his head. 'Right! Per, get on to Geraldo da Perquista Mangista, give him all the information you have on the ecopicosystem and CC's movements. And, Per, before you go – any fresh news on Choggles?'

'Sorry, none. What I was trying to raise you for originally was to say that we have a report from Dagenfort on Mars.'

'About time. Fire away!'

The report had come, not from Jack Dagenfort himself, but from an autosignal he had pre-coded and concealed in his luggage in Nixonville, announcing that he had seen Mrs Chaplain and was going to follow her to the nearest camp; it added that if it was received at Slavonski Brod Grad, then Dagenfort was overdue.

'So he's overdue,' Mike said. 'He's met trouble. Surely not from Leda. I wonder if this means that Auden Chaplain is alive? It must have been a companalog of Leda that attracted Choggles away – the more I think about it, the more sure of that I become. Who would have set up a stunt like that on Mars, if not Auden?'

'That doesn't seem very likely,' Becky said. 'The companalog didn't try to get her to Mars, as far as we know.'

'*I* know where Choggles is!' Julian said suddenly. 'It was in my hallucination-dream, when I met with the Queen of All Questions. The Queen had a prisoner. Choggles was the girl in a case of ice or polywater or glass. She's on

Earth. No – I can't be certain, I dreamed so many things. I dreamed this house was an enormous besieged castle.'

'For a few minutes, so it was,' Becky said. 'Who goes to Mars to settle this, Mike?'

'I will, of course. All I do is buzz here and there, ineffectually. It's time for me to buck my destiny and *do* something useful.'

'I can't buck my destiny,' she said. 'Subject to determinism, I'm coming with you.'

'Let me come,' Julian said. 'Maybe this is my chance. My last chance. "Our fate is that we have our fate Precast, yet *feel* that all is still at stake! . . ." '

'Don't you start quoting Shelley too!' Becky groaned.

'It's not Shelley, it's Julliann of the Sharkskin . . .' He blushed deeply.

33

Loomis Smix disliked walking, even if it could be done on flat surfaces. So her temper was not of the best as she greeted her sister.

'You are surprised to find Jules and me here?' Glamis asked amusedly.

'Surprised? I'm *disgusted*, Glamis, if you must know, spending the night out with some unknown man on some unknown planet. What would your father—'

'It has been the great night of my life, Mrs Saigon Smix,' de l'Isle-Evens broke in, smiling, though his limbs were somewhat stiff. 'And it is incorrect to say that this planet is unknown. In fact, it is named Glamis, after your younger sister.'

'She doesn't deserve—' Loomis began, but her husband arrived and cut her short.

'Glamis, nice to see you, though what you are doing here, I can't imagine. We don't see enough of you since you so unfortunately joined the Dissident cause.'

'She was always dissident,' Loomis said.

Glamis introduced de l'Isle-Evens to Smix, but he showed little interest. She could guess from his expression that he was performing some abstruse calculations.

'Glamis, this is most important, important above all things,' Smix said. 'Is Monty Zoomer here with you? Not? He must be! I want to know where that pendant is I gave him – supposed to come from an ancient Martian design, though I had it manufactured in my secret factory in Middletown, Conn. Where's the pendant? Do you have that pendant?'

'Well . . . Monty gave it to me. You came all this way through space and time to ask about one lousy pendant?'

'Our journey wasn't voluntary. The *Micromegas* homed in on the pendant, in a way you cannot possibly be expected to understand. It's a beacon-receiver of advanced type. Please give it to me and we'll leave you here to whatever you're up to.'

'You *can't* leave Glamis,' de l'Isle-Evens said. 'If you were homed blindly to the beacon-receiver, then it may have escaped your notice that you are some five billion million years into the past.'

'I want the pendant,' Attica Saigon Smix said, ignoring him. 'Where is it, Glamis, my dear? Before I get nasty.'

'It's in the *Doomwitch*, which is stuck in the tops of the forest.'

'We must get it at once.' He turned to de l'Isle-Evens. 'This is a matter of great urgency. I suspect that CC and all its myriads may be here after me very very soon.'

'Then I must strongly warn you, sir,' said de l'Isle-Evens, 'that you place us and yourself in grave danger. Your ship was fortunate to land on firm ground, away

261

from the mighty forest. That forest covers most of the globe, and contains an incalculable store of hydrogen. Its roots connect down to rocks and soil which also contain hydrogen. The atmosphere, as you will have observed, is oxygen-rich. Happily, this is a tranquil planet, but our coming places the old equilibrium at risk. I must warn you that a blazing jet over the forest could cause the most formidable explosion in history – or pre-history. By comparison a nuclear holocaust would seem no more than the blowing of an electric fuse.'

'You hear that, Ladore?' Attica Saigon Smix said, turning to his captain, who stood discreetly two paces behind, 'Order the paracopters out! They'll be safe. I want every man aboard. All companalogs into electronic store. Rest of us, into the paracopters and find the *Doomwitch* as soon as possible. Not a moment to lose.' He turned to his wife. 'This won't be suitable for you. You stay here.'

'Indeed I will not,' said Loomis. 'Either I come with you or you stay here. I will not remain in the presence of my sister and this man, after finding them like this. What should we have to talk about?'

'This is no time for family quarrels. Come along if you must!' He nodded curtly to Glamis and de l'Isle-Evens, and allowed his chair to walk him away, down to where the *Micromegas* stood. Before he arrived at the ship, cargo hatches rolled open and three paracopters slipped out, spreading stubby wings and unfolding rotor blades like overweight insects. The crew marched from the ship and got aboard them. Ladore was the last man, climbing into the leading craft.

Up went the paracopters, beetling into the grey-gold air.

'They played into our hands,' de l'Isle-Evens said. 'In their panic, they have ceased thinking logically – always a fatal mistake. Come on! – In your brother-in-law's words, we haven't a moment to lose!'

He caught Glamis's hand and headed for the deserted vessel.

'There's something evil in your mind, Jules, and I won't do it. I can't leave my sister stranded here, however irritating she is at times.'

'I'm sorry, darling, but you're going to have to. Attica Saigon Smix, for all his innocent appearance, is a murderer on an impressive scale. Your sister is, by default, his accomplice. And if units of CC are due to arrive – and Smix is in a position to know the truth of that matter – then we must get out of here. Right now, taking our one and only chance.'

She ran up the ramp of the *Micromegas* with him, still protesting.

'They'll be stranded here! Attica made no attempt to harm us.'

'Squeamishness is not to be confused with mercy. Remember that he is a pawn of CC, which is neither squeamish nor merciful. CC will certainly kill us if it arrives. Are we not crew of a DN spy-bell?'

She had a few more protests to go.

'But you can't fly a ship this size!'

'No. But I can order the computer to reanimate the companalog crew and they will fly it!'

'They'll throw us out!'

'Not after I've instructed the computer otherwise.'

'We can't get to Earth.'

'We can get to Mars. Once we're safe there, we'll think about Earth.'

'Earth's probably still in a semi-molten state, like liquid toffee!'

He turned to her, half-laughing. 'We'll cope with the toffee when we are ready, honey! Who knows what lies in store? – at least we're together. If time can be travelled, then perhaps we will find a way to travel it forwards to our own day. First of all, it's imperative to get away from *here*. Sooner or later, someone on this planet is going to spark off the biggest explosion in the history of the solar system.' He was in the captain's chair now, closing all the exits, marshalling his forces, feeling and showing a confidence in many ways foreign to his old scholarly self.

Glamis too was half-laughing, half-angry.

'You certainly are showing form, darling Jules! I do admire you. But you're just pitching a tale to get me to yourself, aren't you? I warn you, the excitement will soon pall. I warn you now, I'm not the domestic type, and, despite my previous marriages, I'm not all that keen on sex.'

'Nor am I. Very much over-rated once its curiosity value has been plumbed in adolescence. All the same, it's nice sometimes. With you, I'm certain it will be always.'

'I think you shouldn't count on that.' She ran her fingertips through his sparse hair, until he turned and clasped her hips, pressing his face against them.

He sighed. 'More of that later! I just recalled, by the way, the work of the distinguished Soviet scientist, A. N. Savaritski – I had the pleasure of meeting him once – who built a theoretical construct of this planet, which he called Phaeton. Well, we know Phaeton in our twentieth-century world is no more, just a scatter of fragments called asteroids. So we know that a break-up is going to occur. I think it is going to occur at any moment!'

'Did Savaritski describe the planet breaking up because some Earth man carelessly dropped a cigar butt?'

'No. But he didn't describe the planet too accurately, either – hardly to be hoped for from someone stuck back on Earth, unable to perform *in situ* investigation. I say to you, if we remain *in situ* much longer, we'll be scattered all over the asteroid belt ourselves!'

She shook her head.

'Go ahead. Don't mind me.'

Twelve minutes later, the *Micromegas* was airborne. The crew of companalogs was subservient to Jules's will.

The landscape slipped below them, looking beautiful under its new morning. The fungus, the forest, lost their painful reality, became colours and agreeable shapes. The river wound between forest and forest: no bird sailed there, no insect flew, just as no animal moved on the ground. It was a world without animate life, awaiting life – a stage-setting with no play to be performed.

Eager though he was to escape, de l'Isle-Evens could not but allow the craft to hover and take a final look down.

'How peaceful it seems!' Glamis said.

'If it blows – well, that'll be one destructive act for which man should not be blamed. The planet is unstable, in my belief, balanced in structure between inner- and outer-type planets – a potential gas-giant locked in unsuccessful Earth-like form. Just as well no animal life appears to have evolved on it. Let's go, Glamis!'

He turned to speak to the computer, and, as he did so, one whole section of the sky went black. Filling it were monstrous machines, huge, ungainly, their noses glowing from supersonic glide. Fleet after fleet of them appeared, curious and unlikely, resembling nothing that had ever flown before. They roared down, each flight disappearing in turn behind a shoulder of forest, reappearing to land on broad flat ground further along by the river.

'How many of them are there? *What* are they?' Glamis asked. 'There's no fleet on Earth like that! . . . It's the whole Computer Complex . . . they cannot all be pursuing Monty Zoomer's pendant!'

'They're pursuing something we don't know about – and don't want to know about . . . ye gods, I despair, there are thousands of them! We'll be off.'

The *Micromegas* obeyed its new master. It rose to the stratosphere before opening up its rockets. Then it began to accelerate steadily upwards and outwards, burrowing through vacuum towards the orbit of Mars, towards the Sun, away from the unstable world of Glamis.

Glamis Fevertrees and Jules de l'Isle-Evens sat together, hardly speaking as they watched the planet they had left shrinking behind them. They did not want to look; equally, they did not want to look away.

'The CC censor systems are so efficient, I am convinced that those vessels would have detected our presence.'

'Attica would soon put them on our track anyway.'

'Well, it may take them some time to sort themselves out. I'm not convinced that they comprehend clearly where they are. They have a certain confusion of pendants to deal with. I hope to God they blow themselves up *soon*! It would be good riddance!'

They were safely away – had almost reached Mars – before de l'Isle-Evens's wish was granted. Away in space, a small nova blossomed, blue-white and intense, like an artificial flower – a rather insignificant bloom at first, considering that it was the emblem of planetary destruction. Then it issued forked and sheet lightnings through space, lightnings that climbed outwards at increasing rate, until the *Micromegas* was enveloped in a pale flickering storm. A silent fury overtook the ship, and it shook violently.

The fury died. The lightnings died. The solar system began settling into its modern form.

And the *Micromegas* carried its two human occupants down to begin a new phase of their tortuous lives.

34

Extensive though the liberties are which I have taken with my characters, impertinence fails me when it comes to speculating on what happened to Glamis and Jules throughout the rest of their lives. Perhaps that remains the world's most interesting untold story. Guesswork, however, is not all we have to go on. There remains a scatter of clues, the most important of which lie in the mind of a man who built himself a fortress inside a mesa on Mars.

That man, Auden Chaplain, stood with the Japanese girl, Lindy Hakamara, and looked down coldly at Jack Dagenfort. Dagenfort clutched a paper in his hands and laughed.

'You want me to call the IDI on your radio and ask them if they know of any secret documents on time-travel? Auden, you've gone round the twist. You know time-travel can't exist.'

'Not in what one might term the popular sense, no,' Auden said. 'One cannot hop from year to year by machine; one would come into conflict with the Uncertainty Principle. Besides, the time-turbulences prove that time is no more linear than space. But I believe that something equivalent to time-travel is classifiable among large-scale phenomena. Which is to say, that just as most objects have a natural scale – a sun the size of a football is not a sun, a grasshopper twelve metres long is not a grasshopper – so a form of *millennial-slide* might occur. One could, in a fashion I cannot yet formulate, skim through creation in million-year-hops, or multiples of million-year-hops. I believe it has been done. I hoped the IDI might have proof of it in their files.'

Dagenfort got up and stared at Auden.

'Look, you've shown me this ruin at Fessenkov you excavated. Has the ruin any connection with this crackpot theory of yours?'

'Yes, it has. And with my work on the sexual hormone switch in the hypothalamus. I didn't tell you everything about my one-hundred-million-year-old ruin.'

'You're going to tell me now?'

'I'm going to make a bargain with you, old stick. *I* will explain if *you* will radio.'

'Okay. I'll radio Slavonski Brod Grad if you convince me you aren't just being silly.'

'Jack, old stick, think how silly and devious your own life is! So is any worthwhile life, I believe, as with any piece of knowledge. Never shy away from the complex. I hate people who seek simple explanations.'

'You hate many people, Auden. You're eaten up with hate. You see written large over the world the pattern of your own over-complex mind.'

'Nonsense, only anti-intellectuals use a term like "over-complex". Don't moralize, listen to what I have to tell you. Lindy, my dear, let me have that map of the ruin.'

She put the map on a desk, and the two men went over to it.

It was a glassite diagram of the holograph Dagenfort had already examined.

'I told you that dating-tests showed this structure to be approximately one hundred and forty or one hundred and fifty million years old. At that period there were early mammals on Earth. Mark that. And on Mars, the foursts were at the peak of their civilization, such as it was. They had no material requirements to spur them to great heights, but it appears they transmitted religious ideas – such as that there were three linked planets, Mars, Hleems and Earth, ruled by one Entity. Mark that.

'Using slave labour and some machines from the camps, I excavated further into the ruin. I found beneath it evidence of very much older artefacts. Dating-tests showed those artefacts to be – mark this – not one hundred and fifty million but *five billion million* years old.'

He pressed a switch on the side of the diagram and a small area in the centre lit, marking with dots and a broken line where the older artefacts were unearthed.

'Auden . . .'

'Don't say it! I grow bored with my own surprise; I will not tolerate yours. Five billion million years is, after all, well – what is it? Time really has no meaning to men, not until it's chopped up into seconds, minutes, hours. We are small things. Five billion million is also small, in terms of the universe.'

'Sophistry will get you nowhere. What were these artefacts you found?'

'One artefact has since become moderately famous. It was a pendant. On it was a grotesque design of one man looking at another. Or that is what it is generally thought to represent. I prefer to believe that it depicts one man looking at his own self – a symbol of wisdom, you see. Working through others for safety, I despatched the pendant to Earth, where it sold for a suitably astronomical price. Enough to help equip this comfortable fortress!'

'What else did you unearth at Fessenkov?'

'Other artefacts were metals and so on, which had survived the long span of time by accident – some were sheathed in plastic.

'You will agree this is curious enough. More curious is the fact that we discovered nothing between those two widely spaced times. How could that be? I couldn't make anything of the riddle at first, until suddenly I connected it with my own researches on the brain.'

He paused and regarded Dagenfort with his sardonic smile.

'Lindy has some tarsiers in the laboratory next door, but you will not need such elementary visual aids. There were creatures much like tarsiers, as well as other primitive primates, frisking about Earth some one hundred and fifty-odd million years ago. Forerunners of man, in effect. Mark that.'

'In my early days, when I was conducting research into the impulses between hypothalamus and the anterior lobe of the pituitary, I worked on a wide range of experimental animals, and was impressed by the way the hypothalamus remained very similar from species to species, and even from phylum to phylum.'

'True enough,' Dagenfort said. 'A man's hypothalamus closely resembles a dog's, in appearance and function. It's a very ancient part of the brain.'

'Correct. You retain something of your training, I observe. Appearance and function are, of course, related. What is the hypothalamus? It is a control-system, a regulator inserted to govern the metabolism of the animal concerned. And of course that was precisely what I was researching for – a regulator that could be inserted to control the sexual metabolism of the animal concerned – man.

'I woke up one day and realized that what I was seeking was already in the brain! Admittedly the artificial control, my eventual electrode, would have a more specialized function. But in effect what I was in the process of inventing was – an artificial hypothalamus . . .

'So I came to the realization that the original hypothalamus was also artificial.'

They looked at each other. A servant brought in drinks, which stood disregarded on the desk.

'Sorry, I'm going home,' Dagenfort said. 'You convince me, Auden – you convince me you are stone cold cracked right down to the middle. How can the hypothalamus be artificial, if it is common to most creatures, if it is just one of many organs each creature acquires by heredity?'

'I can't let you go, Jack. Understand that. You must

270

also understand that artificial is a relative term. The hypothalamus is not of plastic like our prosthetic organs. But a superior science could easily devise a switch such as mine, build it from body-cell-growths, and implant it genetically, using gene-surgery to ensure it becomes an inherited characteristic. We can visualize the theory already, step-by-step.'

'It's too fantastic!'

'So they said fifty years ago about space travel and holography and the other techniques we take for granted. In fact, I know that CC is working on genetic implementation right now. It has been possible for a decade – only a certain moral squeamishness delayed research, and machines have no such squeamishness.'

'Supposing all you say is true. Then the hypothalamuses were implanted in all terrestrial animals one hundred and fifty million years ago, by a race from Mars! Is that what you're saying?'

'It is, yes. During the late Jurassic, let us say. And the race from Mars had emerged from a greatly earlier date.'

'*All* animals implanted?'

'Not so many. Understand that the hypothalamus was essentially a survival device. Those animals which were given it survived more easily, replaced the other animals without it in a few generations. The hypothalamus ensured better and more stable metabolisms, which allowed for the growth of better brains. It was better brains which allowed the mammals to survive where the large reptiles died. And it paved the way for man.'

'Okay. We allow your entire rewriting of evolutionary history to be substantially correct.' He laughed. 'Who the hell was this benefactor who charged round the Jurassic doing us all this big favour? Little green men from Mars?'

'Ah, that's the big question, Jack! Have a drink.'

'Maybe I need it. Salud!' He turned to Lindy.

'You've lived with this theory of Auden's. Have you

been brainwashed into accepting it? Maybe it sounds more possible if you're locked away on Mars.'

She smiled and put her hands together in the lotus position. In a sweet low voice, she began to sing so appealingly that the men found themselves joining in on cue, despite themselves, in a sort of musical determinism.

LINDY

I ask myself if explanations
Can ever quite explain. I know the Sun
    Resolves in nuclear equations—
Yet sunshine has a magic of its own.
    Although biologists can show
How all emotion stems from chemistry,
        When someone kisses me, I know
There's more than that to my anatomy!

AUDEN

The 'more than that' can also be explained
In reproductive terms – you glamourize
A simple scientific fact. And nor
    Has sunshine 'magic'. Your
    Soft attitude denies
The hard-won insights researchers have gained.

LINDY

You must be right – and yet such cool,
Such cold hard sense to me does not enhance
    My life-style. Though you'll surely think me fool,
Science to me's a killer of romance!

AUDEN

But science *is* romance! You ought to know
The inverse square law governing such things
As nucleii and planetary motions
    And other kindred notions
    A deeper insight brings—
Romance's triumph, not its overthrow!

DAGENFORT

Who could reconcile two attitudes
So different in pragmatic approach?—
And yet there *is* a subject that eludes
The categories you both try to broach.

There's Evolution—
In revolution
Between the two!
It's neither fish nor flesh that you could name—
Between a science and a guessing game!
I ask – is Evolution bothering you?

LINDY

I still can't understand how ape, pig, whale,
All came up from a common ancestor—
Nor how two molars fossilized in shale
Suffice to recreate a dinosaur.
So I'm confessing
Before you're guessing
What's clear to see.
Is this the way to tell how mankind came
Between a science and a guessing game?
I tell you, Evolution's bothering me!

AUDEN

The fossil record maybe is uncertain,
And species come and go by unknown law.
So palaeontologists peep behind the curtain
And generalize about the tooth and claw.
But still it's fitting
That I'm admitting
That possibly
I'm more afraid than Darwin was to name
It as a science, not a guessing game—
I tell you, Evolution's bothering me!

ALL

We all like explanations to be clear—
Ach, Weltanschauung, ja, ich dich liebe!—
And comprehensive – but we don't, I fear,
Grasp how we all sprang from that first amoeba.
While we're still trying,
There's no denying
It's all a fuss,
And Clarity was shod while Truth went lame
Between a science and a guessing game.
Agreed that Evolution's bothering us!
We cede that Evolution's bothering us!
Decreed that Evolution's bothering us!

'Beautiful!' Auden Chaplain said. 'Even we mad scientists enjoy a song now and then, Dagenfort. Before I answer, or attempt to answer, your big question, let's have another drink!'

He rang the bell on his desk, the door opened, and a servant came in. Dagenfort glanced at the man and then looked harder in astonishment. The man was toting a fan-gun and looked astonishingly like Mike Surinat.

'I'm Mike Surinat,' the intruder said. 'Your nephew incidentally and unfortunately. Dr Auden Chaplain, on behalf of the government of the Dissident Nations, I arrest you for crimes against humanity, in particular that you did conspire with the Computer Complex to bring Earth's peoples into subjection.'

'Doličar!' shouted Chaplain.

'If you're calling your guard, I just shot him.'

Lindy ran to snuggle up against Auden. He pushed her away and said, 'Surinat, you fool, what am I meant to say, "You'll never get away with this"? The cliché springs to my lips in a somewhat deterministic way because it happens in this case to be true.'

'We'll see about that,' Mike said, easily, matching cliché for cliché. 'After all, non-adaptive mind is merely epiphenomenon, what we think doesn't matter, and what will happen will happen. That's how it is, isn't it? What's more, this place is surrounded.'

'Oh for a closer extra-vehicular activity with Thee!' Auden exclaimed. 'You cloak-and-dagger boys still like to go through your paces, don't you? No doubt you wish to rescue Dagenfort. But he does not wish to leave.'

'I certainly wish to leave your presence, Auden,' Dagenfort said, as he shook hands with Mike. 'But firstly I want Surinat to hear your story. Thanks for coming, Mike, though I can't imagine how you arrived here so fast.'

'I'm sure you can't,' Surinat said grimly. 'Auden will

274

also be surprised when he finds out how we did it. Auden, where is your daughter Choggles?'

'Not on Mars, I'm happy to say. I thought she was in your care. So much for your care, dutiful nephew!'

Surinat blew a whistle. Becky, Julian and Devlin Carnate entered the room. Becky ran over and gave Dagenfort a kiss. Between them, they searched Auden Chaplain and Lindy for weapons and then seated them at the table with their hands on it.

'That's better,' Surinat said, resting his gun. 'I should add that we have a detachment of DN troops with us, who are taking care of the rest of your snug little fortress in the mesa. You may not know it, Chaplain, but the CC empire which has virtually ruled Earth since the end of the war has disappeared for regions unknown. Earth's great age begins anew, so we start well by mopping you up.'

Lindy Hakamara said angrily, 'Mopping up! You talk like a common gangster! Such non-adaptive behaviour towards one of mankind's benefactors, who gave them the ultimate in birth-control.'

'We happen to know it was mind-control he was really after.'

'So are you! It's just one side against another! Mankind will be no better than before, even if Computer Complex has gone, as you say it has. If you accept the deterministic world, then you must accept that.'

'Mike was using a figure of speech,' Becky said. 'We hope at least to learn by our mistakes. As for you, Lindy – your father is an ally of ours, and I imagine he'll deal with you later.'

'Before the clichés become too thick, I want to fill you in on what Auden has been telling me,' Dagenfort said, glancing at Auden who, ever since Surinat's last announcement, had been sitting silent and looking down at the table. 'His hypothesis is full of big ideas – you'll like it.'

'We'd better,' Mike said.

'Okay, then, I'll put it my way. It's a story that seems to me to reinforce determinism, though Auden has yet to reveal some of the connecting links. Seems there was an intelligent race on Mars some one hundred and fifty million years ago. It had affiliations with a much older race which emerged on Mars many millions of years earlier – I'm not too clear about that! These quasi-Martians moved to Earth, then at the end of its Jurassic period, and inserted an inheritable prosthetic control into the brains of certain animals which, given that advantage, gradually took over the world, their star-turn being man. With me so far?

'The inheritable prosthetic control we know as the hypothalamus. Auden uncovered its real nature while researching for his own artificial hormone control. He was just going to tell me the nature of this long-lived super-race when you made your entrance. Do I have it right Auden?'

Auden Chaplain looked up, turning his head slowly to gaze malevolently at them all, so that the harsh and compressed planes of his head gleamed in the light.

'Me, I don't understand all this,' Devlin Carnate said. 'I'm going out for a smoke.' They ignored him.

'You put it in terms that they might grasp, yes, Jack,' Auden said. 'But I was *not* about to tell you the nature of the mystery race, because I have only a few scraps of evidence to go on. However, your ally Surinat supplies us with fresh speculation. As he rightly infers, I did not know that CC has vanished from Earth. It seems a highly unlikely occurrence. I presume that its *intelligence* has gone and its installations remain?'

'Reports indicate that it has upped many of its installations as well,' Mike said. 'All the disruption caused by the time-turbulences makes it difficult to piece the facts together immediately.'

Auden smiled in a chill way. 'Ah, but you inadvertently assist me in piecing together my jigsaw. Let me play with some hypotheses in an entirely unscientific manner, before you march me away in your scientific manner!

'Let us suppose that the CC, obeying impulses we do not yet understand, removes to some far distant past. It materializes on another planet in our planetary system. Not Mars. Let us further suppose that only a part of CC – one unit – survives the transition, and that that unit later moves to Mars. It moves to Mars some five billion million years ago. There it eventually leaps forward in time, by a means we might as well call time-travel – since we are speaking hypothetically – and reappears only some one hundred and fifty million years ago. This we can say with confidence, since fourstian legends treat of the event, and my excavations support the figures.

'Fourstian legends state that the strange race of which we are speaking came from Hleems. Now we do not know where Hleems might be. To me, it suggests a corruption of our word "Heaven".'

His audience listened with attention, Julian perhaps most avidly. Here was science, or at least a scientific guessing game, full of enough mystery and excitement to delight Julliann of the Sharkskin. Perhaps he really had been missing something in opting out of the real world.

Continuing, Auden said, 'Survivors of our strange race – and we must think of it as a mere handful, not a major colonizing force – came to Earth at that period when, as Jack has said, the Jurassic Age was reaching its end. Our strange race performs as stated on the mammals then extant. We must then suppose the race dies out, becomes as defunct as the Jurassic. Almost as if it has performed its objective, right? Now – what race would have had such an objective? A purely technological-scientific objective.'

There was silence in the underground room until Surinat laughed and said, 'It sounds like an inhuman race of Auden Chaplains!'

'You may not be far wrong,' Auden said, composedly. 'I hoped to bring the human race under better control. When working with CC, I programmed exactly that directive into its motivations.'

Silence all round. Auden went on.

'I suggest that the strange race we have been talking about is our old friend CC, working out its intentions back in time, where it found itself stuck, tunnelling away in our deterministic past!'

'Your Fessenkov ground-plan!' Dagenfort exclaimed, picking up the glassite board from the desk. 'It's not a city! It's part of a machine lay-out!'

'Ah, light dawns! You discern the resemblance too? Then we're possibly correct it was the CC! It survived some unimaginable disaster, perhaps something that occurred on the mysterious Hleems. Maybe only one of its units reached Mars in the early period. Hence the small area of the lower excavations where our crucial pendant was found. The unit skipped eventually forward in time, built itself up sufficiently to make an Earth-launch, and there exhausted the last of its resources carrying out the Jurassic operations which I, in fact, had set afoot! Very satisfactory!'

'But . . .' said Dagenfort. He shook his head. 'Maybe you're right. I for one know how complicated life is.' He thought of telling them the history of his film *The Heart Block*, and then dismissed the idea. Too complex.

'We'll investigate the theory later,' Surinat said. 'We're taking you away now, Chaplain. Retribution first, ratiocination later.'

He threw a pair of handcuffs to Dagenfort.

Dagenfort looked at Auden and then away again. 'Chaplain may be responsible for Mrs Chaplain's death, but I can't do it. I admire the swine!'

'Not only Mrs Chaplain!' Becky exclaimed. 'Crimes against all humanity!'

'Since you evidently have no understanding of scientific method, *you* put the cuffs on him,' Dagenfort said. He threw them to her. Becky caught them, went over to Auden and snapped them on to his wrists. He did not resist.

Turning to Lindy, he said coolly, 'I expect I'll be back, Lindy. See to the controls, will you?'

Lindy Hakamara bowed resignedly.

'Sorry, Auden,' Dagenfort said. 'But I know you'd have done the same for me!'

Leaving Lindy to stand pathetically where she was, the procession started to move out, Auden Chaplain captive in their midst. He went on his way singing with quiet defiance:

> You've got to go on or go back,
> Not remain where you lingered before.
>   Though Nature abhors any vac-
> Uum, she hates immobility more!
>
> Scientific advancement is nourished
> By a life-giving flow to the head
> Of facts that are gathered and flourished—
> The brain that stops thinking is dead!
>
> This process may not be impeded
> By scruples of ethical kind;
> And in fact it has so far succeeded
> We have started abolishing mind.
>
> It's worth remarking here in this connection
> A fact which some may thoughtlessly condemn:
> Let those who will, object to vivisection—
> Vivisection has no objection to them.

Science has a purpose, and people haven't. The value of science can be estimated, and the value of people can't. Therefore we see that people should exist for science and not science for people. The same applies to morality. Morality cannot be weighed or evaluated. It is just a fog of

279

words. You could cut it with a knife – a knife called necessity. There's no alternative to progress. Pseudo-alternatives like morality and utopianism are just impediments to it.

> Take the singular case of technology,
> Designated humanity's tool
> When it's science's strong-arm. Psychology
> Proves he who thinks not is a fool!

> Oh, you've got to go on or go back!
> R & D they must always go places,
> Though it makes mankind's future look black.
> Genocide is much better than stasis—
> 'You've got to go on or go back!'

'That's enough of that sentimental old nineteenth-century rubbish,' Surinat said, prodding him. 'We have a little surprise for you outside.'

The corridors of Chaplain's mesa were filled with blue-uniformed DN soldiery, busily ejecting Chaplain's personnel.

'The local people in the Martian camps will be on my side,' Chaplain said. 'I'm quite a source of employment. My alter ego, Mrs Chaplain, your dear auntie, is a well-known do-gooder. You don't know what you are stirring up. You will never get back to Earth, Surinat!'

Surinat said, 'I accept your theory about the old link between Mars and Earth and this other phantom planet because I know time-turbulences exist. We seem to have lost dear Choggles in one. But this disruption in time and space – well, it sometimes comes in handy. Look!'

They emerged at the bottom of the mesa into dazzling sunlight, where Carnate rejoined them. The great steep walls of the natural formation towered above, steaming under a more brilliant sun than they had ever known.

Chaplain cringed and shut his eyes. For the first time, he was discountenanced.

'Could I have your signature please, Mr Chaplain,' Carnate asked, producing an autograph book.

Brushing him away, Chaplain said, 'Where's – what's – who . . .?'

'Yes,' Julian said proudly, as if he had had a hand in the natural order himself. 'That's how we got to you so fast, Mr Dagenfort! – you came to us! The mesa was caught in a space-turbulence and whisked here. We should have realized long ago that it was possible – once you warp the topology of space/time, you distort space as well as time. But this distortion came in conveniently.'

'Very well-timed,' Dagenfort agreed with composure. 'Where the hell are we? Mercury?'

Becky laughed. 'This is Earth, Jack! Tunisia, to be exact. With a chunk of Mars wedged in it. The Mediterranean is just a few miles in that direction.'

Perhaps it was her beautiful arm outstretched that prompted Dagenfort to say, 'It looks good! Anything looks good after Mars.'

'Well, it's nice to have you back in one piece. It's pretty much a happy ending all round. You'd better come on with us to Slavonski Brod Grad. Mike's throwing another party.'

Surinat smiled. 'That's right! Every reason to celebrate! The eighty-minute hour project will be abandoned – will have to be abandoned while World Government sorts out its troubles after the departure of CC and the turbulences. The DN will be needed for that – we were less badly hit than the Cap–Comm bloc, and we expect to get a fair hearing from now on.'

Lorries were roaring up. The prisoners from the mesa were being loaded aboard. A black limousine came racing up for the Surinat party.

Surinat turned to Chaplain. 'The prison wagon will be here for you in a minute. You will get a fair trial.'

For answer, Auden Chaplain drew himself up to his full height and shouted:

'NOW!'

'Don't get frightened, nobody's – urk!'

Something had happened.

Something had happened to everyone. The happy ending fled shrieking to the horizon and disappeared into the Mediterranean.

Trucks screamed to a halt. The limousine stopped. The people stopped. Everyone stood rigid, frozen where they were, their expressions stuck like self-adhesive tape to mouth and cheeks. It was a tableau of immobility. One or two soldiers, caught off-balance, fell to the ground and remained there in an awkward posture, unmoving.

Only Auden Chaplain moved, walking among them, rubbing his hands together and rattling his handcuffs, chuckling with a great good humour.

He paused in front of the statue of Mike Surinat.

'If it was convenient for *you* to have me on Earth, think how much more convenient it was for me! I always hoped to get back, but there was the problem of shipping my equipment over the gulfs of space. On Mars, I could not control the vast body of people. They were expelled from Earth before my little sex-triggers became universally compulsory. But here, on good old Sol III, everyone is waiting to be taken over!'

He moved over to the statue of Jack Dagenfort. 'You could have come over to my side, Jack, but you missed your chance. You know what my little electrodes look like, with the micro-aerials on top, all ready to be controlled from a distance. CC had enough work without taking over radio-control. But I am now able to do so. All over the world – just think of it! – all over the world, everyone is standing stock still now, awaiting my instructions. And I can beam those instructions right into their skulls – as you see!'

He moved to the statue of Becky Hornbeck. 'You are a woman, and a very pretty one. Don't you think Lindy

Hakamara is pretty too? Weren't you worried when she stayed behind? You are now paying dearly for your oversight, for Lindy has switched on the L-beam. From now on you will do exactly what you are told. I can make you march straight into the Mediterranean, and may possibly do just that.'

Looking back at the Surinat statue, he added, 'So you see that there are degrees even to determinism! You haven't even the *illusion* of free-will now! I shall go into the laboratory and get Lindy to remove my handcuffs. I shall then return with a remote control unit and put you all through your paces. We shall have fun! Meanwhile, stay where you are. Don't move, will you?'

He strode back towards the mesa.

When he returned, minutes later, they were still standing unblinkingly in the Tunisian heat where he had left them. Flies were gathering about their eyes, and they made no move to brush them off.

Auden Chaplain lifted a remote-control unit to his lips.

'Everyone scratch their heads for fifteen seconds.'

Everyone in the world lifted their left or right hands, depending on whether they were left- or right-handed, and solemnly scratched their heads, whether or not they happened to be wearing hats, caps, scarves, hairnets or toupees. Then their hands fell back to their sides. In some well-populated parts of the world, this action caused a quickly dying wave of sound before silence returned.

'The second law of thermodynamics be praised! It works! How foolish of CC never to have tried it out – artificial intelligences are never able to move beyond the human limits built into them.'

He strutted about amid his puppets.

'I won't be too sadistic, but I must have a little fun! Dagenfort, Surinat, come and stand by me. I'm going to make you box each other. Hornbeck, you come and be referee. Stand closer, then you may receive the odd blow yourself. Now—'

They came nearer. They fell upon him. They seized him and pulled him over and pinned his arms behind his back and then dragged him up again. Carnate ran up to help.

'Five minutes of complete world-domination! That's enough even for Faust, you scabdevouring rogue!' Surinat cried. 'Keep him covered, Devlin, and refrain from trying to get his autograph.'

'What went wrong? What went wrong?' Chaplain asked, staring with disfavour at Carnate's armament.

Julian Surinat came out of the mesa entrance, dancing on his prosthetic legs. He led Lindy Hakamara on a rope.

'I saved the world! I saved the world!' he shouted, waving a fist above his head. 'That's better than being a dream-hero! Bad luck, Uncle Auden! – It just happens that when I was hit by that wartime bomb the surgeons had to operate on my head as well as my legs, and my Schally-Chaplain switch was removed. That was when I went on to *root*. So your signal had no effect on me. What is more, I've just wrecked your apparatus!'

'Destructive little cripple,' Chaplain said. 'Euthanasia is too good for the likes of you.'

'As I said, you'll get a fair trial, Chaplain,' Mike Surinat said, standing on Auden's instep.

The happy ending came screaming and giggling back from the Mediterranean, shaking dead fish and oil slick from its multi-coloured coat. They all burst into song.

BECKY
Whatever your theories of fiction may be,
This song is your swan-song. Like birds on a tree
When daylight is fading, we settle to roost,
With you, our dear readers, enlightened or goosed.

MIKE

When our names are forgotten, remember the point
Of the exercise – never conform! Smoke a joint,
Say a prayer, have it off, take a trip, do your thing:
The world's at defiance when pleasure is king!

ALL

Think! Think! There's pleasure in thought—
With leisure for sensuous treasure, there's naught
That can nourish the psyche so well—
Meditation sends organization to hell!

DEVLIN

That's as may be! It's all right for you lot,
But fellows like me don't get much of the plot.

LINDY

My role was much smaller, but I don't complain:
If time would permit me, I'd do it again.

AUDEN

Whatever your theories of living may be
My powers are ended – but someone like me
Is tunnelling, ferreting, facts out of mind.
Although the world hates me, it still needs my kind.

JACK

Whatever the patterns that govern us all,
I'd rather have some life than no life at all,
And this is life's moral we're made to present:
Although predetermined, it can be well-spent.

ALL

Think! Think! There's pleasure in thought—
Your synapses sparkle if they are well-taught!
Our peregrinations were meant to amuse
(If only dear Choggles were here with good news . . .)

MIKE

Whatever your theories of literature are,
May our memory sail like a ship from afar
Into your horizons, your innermost sea,
And help to determine your future maybe.

ALL
Think! Think! – Whatever your brain,
Lecherous, treacherous, loving, or vain,
Think! Take us with you wherever you wend,
Else our Hour of Existence is now at an end,
    So think, think, think, again!

And there you have what must, in these deterministic
days, be called a happy ending. Indeed, it got even
happier.

Sue Fox and Dwight Ploughrite Castle, contrary to the
general assumption, were not lost and gone forever –
unlike everyone else who entered one of the time-
turbulences. The turbulence they entered contained a
sliver of a far-distant future, infinitely remote and sparsely
populated by not particularly human beings, not particularly interested (as we so obsessively and childishly are) in
individual human predicaments.

Those not-particularly-humans, however, were interested in abstract questions.

Their view of human history was that it was finished,
somewhat in the way that we regard the history of
Neanderthal Man as finished, without inquiring more
closely whether any individual members of that no doubt
absorbing species were burnt at the stake for their religious beliefs, or wrote a poem to the west wind, or
practised necrophilia.

They embodied this point of view in the worship of an
age-old stone, once known as the Koh-i-Nor, which
symbolized for them things permanent and things
temporary.

They had a knowledge of the time-turbulences, which they
regarded not as miraculous, freak events, but rather as
among the natural phenomena of space/time, and of the
various periods in which they occurred. In fact – and this was
a point of some delicacy with them – the not-particularly-
humans had heard of poor little Choggles Chaplain.

286

Their brief outlines of human ('pre-human', in their terminology) history included references to the way in which she had been restored from the Stone Age to her own rightful time.

Indeed, the abstract question they had been considering before becoming enmeshed in their time-turbulence (they always considered six abstract questions before breakfast) concerned causality. They had decided before the dislocation struck that a group of not-particularly-humans should use their time-empathy powers to return Choggles to her proper period. For their debate hinged on whether such an action would be the cause of history's reference to her restoration or an effect of it.

They took Sue Fox and Dwight Castle along too. The gesture was made not from any not-particularly-humanitarian motives, but solely because they were curious to know how simple human brains would cope with the test of their time-empathy-transportation. Sue and Dwight were holding hands and smiling pleasant middle-aged love-smiles all the time, and so failed the test utterly.

(Chambers Technical Dictionary, by the way, elected to stay in the not-particularly-human future. He had discovered his Unknown. He found it was absolutely stuffed with birds and animals, and he liked it like that.)

So Sue and Dwight and Choggles and even Back-in-the-Stone-Age – unmentioned in any history book – were delivered back where they belonged, just in time for the binge at Slavonski Brod.

I spoke to the sweet creature soon after she had had a bath and put on a party dress. She told me of the awful moment when she was confronted by Glamis and Jules in the glacier.

That provided me with the missing link in the chain across the centuries. At least Glamis and Jules had made it to their home planet, and, even if the ice got them in the

287

end, they'd died side-by-side – something worth having if you're a lonely human creature.

How Glamis and Jules had made the jump from five billion million to one hundred and fifty million years back – that still requires thought. It was not beyond the inventive powers of the Computer Complex. Perhaps the not-particularly-humans were involved there too; I seem to read their fingerprints on the operation. But the rest can be pieced together.

I need not spell it out. Since our every thought and action is mathematically dependent upon environmental and hereditary factors, if you have got this far, you have also got the whole.

Maybe you can even figure out what happened to Monty Zoomer's pendant!

Of course, Choggles and I resolved most of the story together, thanks to her brush with the not-particularly-humans. She returned from her far futures a resplendent young lady of twenty, punctually enough to be godmother to Mike and Becky's first child and Dinah Sorbutt's second. The world was returning to old-fashioned things like godmothers and engagements.

It is only fitting that I should close my account with the announcement of my engagement to dearest Choggles. My lover has my heart and I have hers. We shall be married right here in Slavonski Brod Grad.

If one legless dreamer can save the world, surely another can win it . . .